Riddles

Riddles

The Hunt for Dillinger's Loot
By
Ronald C. Milburn

Dedication

I dedicate this book to Mrs. Madeleine Mannin Herman my eighth grade English teacher at Jefferson Junior High School in Charleston, Illinois. She encouraged me to, "Never stop writing."

Acknowledgement

Thank you to my wife, Susan Milburn, and her sister, Shelley Ryan, for proofreading my manuscript.

Table of Contents

Introduction

John Dillinger was a notorious bank robber of the 1930s. He robbed twenty-four banks along with his gang. The bold criminals secured weapons by robbing four police stations. He helped friends escape from prison, and he broke out of two jails.

His largest score was the Central National Bank in Greencastle, Indiana. It was Parent's Weekend at Depauw College, and business was good. The local merchants deposited their proceeds in the bank, but Dillinger made the withdrawal. He took $75,000 which by today's standards would be almost 1.5 million dollars.

Dillinger was born in Moorseville, Indiana in 1903 and died in a shootout in Chicago in 1934. Betrayed by the woman in red, Dillinger was lured into the Bayou Theatre in Chicago. On the hot summer night, the FBI agents waited outside and gunned him down.

His parents buried him in Crown Hill Cemetery in Indianapolis. Or did they? Conspiracy theorists claim the wrong man was interred.

Though his father first claimed the body wasn't that of his son, he later changed his story. Some people believe Dillinger's father lied so his son could escape to live a quiet life.

This book of fiction tells the way it could have been if Dillinger lived a recluse life of restitution.

Chapter 1
The Mysterious Fisherman

Next year, I'd be in the eighth grade. Until then, I just wanted to play and rest my overworked brain. I figured I deserved a break without long division and history lessons. But a riddle would challenge me more than any subject I'd had in school.

It was a tradition for my neighborhood friends and me to swim at the municipal pool on the first day of summer vacation. We arrived early with towels over our bare shoulders. Already a crowd had gathered at the entrance.

I pushed my way through the mob to the front. "What's up?"

A younger boy pointed to a sign that hung on a chain-link gate. It read, Closed Until Further Notice.

A security guard appeared on the other side of the fence. "Sorry boys and girls, but we can't open. The water doesn't pass the chlorine test. We must have a severe leak." The crowd moaned.

As I turned away, I noticed Pippy and her younger sister, Cindy. They were friends from our neighborhood. I had a crush on Pippy, but she barely knew I existed. She looked nice in her swimming suit.

I approached the pair when a red Mustang convertible pulled up. A handsome boy was driving, and his oversized friend was the passenger.

The driver said, "Hi, Pippy."

Pippy said, "Hi, Sly. What's up?"

Sly glared at me. "Not much. Griff and I are just riding with the top down."

While sitting on my bike, I leaned against the car.

Sly said, "Hey, punk, get off of the Mustang."

Griff got out and examined the paint. He wiped it with a handkerchief and said, "Keep your mitts off."

I backed up.

Sly said, "Hey Pippy, what are you doing with these punks. We're going for a drive. Want to come with us?"

Pippy replied, "I'd sure like to, but Daddy won't let me ride with boys. He said I'm too young."

Sly said, "Your Daddy's not here."

Pippy turned and looked at her sister. Cindy shook her head. "I'll tell Daddy if you go."

Pippy frowned. "I'd better not, Sly."

Sly flashed his bright teeth. "Some other time."

Pippy smiled and waved as he sped away.

I wish she'd look at me that way.

Cindy said, "I can't stand him. He's a big jerk."

"He's a star on the varsity baseball team," Pippy said.

Cindy laughed. "He thinks he's hot stuff."

"I think he's gorgeous," Pippy said.

Cindy rolled her eyes. "He's a bully and never goes anywhere without Griff. The big man wouldn't be so tough without his bodyguard."

"Sly's got a nice car, though," Pippy said.

Cindy shook her head. "Forget him."

Pippy sighed as she watched Sly's Mustang disappear. I didn't say a word as the girls pedaled away, but I wished I were with them.

By evening, the tragic news hit the paper. The pool needed massive repairs. The mayor announced the unexpected expense was not in the city budget, and he didn't know if he could ever open it again.

There wasn't a lot else to do in our little town in 1967, so my neighborhood friends and I pedaled our bikes toward the lake. Clinging to fishing poles and trying to steer, we rode a mile on the country road. Heavy on the brakes, we rolled down the steep hill to the top of the dam. Once we parked, we bounced onto a floating dock.

An older gentleman sat on a folding stool at the end of the pier. He wore a floppy hat and watched a bobber in the water. The fisherman reached inside a bag and pulled out a handful of popcorn and pitched it. Small bluegill rose to the surface and gobbled up the feast.

The bobber sank, and he set the hook. His hat fell off. "He's a fighter. It feels like a big one."

The drag on the reel hummed. The line jerked to the left, and his pole bent. The fish made a beeline to the right and jumped into the air.

I rushed to the fisherman's side. "It's a bass. Don't lose him."

My buddies and I gathered around the older adult. He backed up, but the tension pulled him forward toward the edge of the dock. I grabbed his belt and pulled. Amidst our shouts of encouragement, he hung on until the fish tired. In a few minutes, the exhausted fish rose to the surface and floated into the fisherman's net.

"It's a keeper," I said. "Gonna have it mounted?"

The fisherman removed the hook and held the fish high.

When he dropped the whopper into the water, our chins dropped.

"Why d'you do that?" I asked.

The fisherman wiped his hands on a towel and began putting his tackle away. "The excitement as in the challenge. When I released him, we both lived to compete another day."

My year-younger brother, Marshal, said, "I'd have kept it."

The fisherman shrugged. "I've learned two things in my life. Take only what's yours and keep just what you need."

He folded his stool. "Say. Aren't you a Rardin boy?"

I nodded and pointed at my brother. "Him too."

The fisherman said, "I thought so."

I raised one eyebrow and twisted my head to one side.

He said, "I know your grandfather."

"Oh," I replied.

The fisherman nodded. "I read in the paper; the police arrested you for shoplifting at the dime store."

I lowered my head and felt my face blush.

"He didn't do it!" Marshal cried.

Einstein added, "He was famed."

His brother, Butch, rolled his eyes and slapped his forehead.

"Framed, Einstein. Not famed," Butch said.

Angel clenched his jaw. "Someone slipped it into his backpack. Patton wouldn't steal anything. What a dirty joke."

3

The fisherman removed his hat and rubbed his bald scalp. Then he placed his hand on my shoulder. "Even if people don't believe you, believe in yourself. Your past doesn't have to dictate your future."

"Yes, sir," I replied.

Einstein, unable to follow a conversation for long, pointed across the water. "Is that Dillinger's Island?"

Everyone looked.

The fisherman said, "It's what some people call it."

Einstein said, "I heard there's gold over there."

My brother, Marshal, added, "Loot from a bank robbery thirty years ago."

The fisherman rubbed his chin. "It's a rumor I've heard, but I don't think so."

Marshal said, "We could swim over and look for it."

The fisherman stared at us. "What would you do with the gold if you found it?"

Marshal stood tall. "I'd live like a king for the rest of my life."

The fisherman glanced at me. "And you?"

I shrugged. "I don't know."

"How about you, mister?" I asked. "What would you do if you found Dillinger's gold?"

The fisherman adjusted his hat as he looked upward at a passing cloud. "I suppose I'd try to do some good with it."

He folded his canvas stool. "I'll leave the popcorn for you, boys."

I said, "Thanks."

I watched him depart down the dock. Not until later did I realize the fisherman's past would have such a profound effect on my future.

Chapter 2

Tip's Good Fortune

In 1933, a homeless man knocked on the alley door of Tommy's Billiard Hall. Tip stood straight, adjusted his shabby coat and hat, and tried to appear suitable. He hoped his stubby whiskers weren't too noticeable by the glow of the quarter moon. Through a peephole, apprehensive eyes scanned his face and torso. When the bouncer allowed the familiar vagrant into the speakeasy, Tip sighed. Booze was hard to buy during prohibition, but this was one place in Greencastle, Indiana, where he knew he could find it.

Inside, the mood was more celebratory than usual because a party was in progress. On pushed-together tables with white linen tablecloths sat a whole birthday cake. The half-dozen men were in business attire, and the celebrating women wore gowns—unusual for this working-class, midwestern town.

Tip staggered as he made his way toward the bar. In time, with effort, he climbed aboard his familiar stool. He wished to drink alone, disturb no one, and brood. But it was not to be. Since he arrived somewhat pickled, his inebriation intensified earlier than usual.

It was after the second whiskey, his inhibitions, a fickle friend, departed. Once he downed the third shot, the cat that held his tongue left too. Alone to fend for himself, a potential disaster loomed.

A silver-haired gentleman in a gray, two-button suit stood to speak. His crimson suspenders matched the handkerchief in his breast pocket. The businessman buttoned his wool jacket, cleared his throat, then raised a glass. Tip, through bloodshot eyes, recognized the speaker as Mr. Goldworth, the bank president, whom he despised. Their mutual disdain, fashioned years prior, had amplified.

"I propose a toast," the banker announced. "Happy birthday to my wife, Billie Jean."

A hearty cheer preceded the sipping, followed by applause. The husband removed a box from his jacket pocket and presented it. "A little gift for you, my dear."

"Oh, you shouldn't have."

As she ripped the tinsel paper, Tip examined the lanky spouse. He thought her salt-and-pepper bun added to her height and didn't do much for her long face, either. She reminded him of a horse he once owned when times were better.

Tip muttered, "He must have married for money."

In a flash, the decorative wrapping was off, and she dangled a gold pendant and chain before her guests. "Oh, a St. Christopher medal."

She held it to her neck, and her mate stood behind her, assisting with the clasp. The couple's flaunted wealth disgusted Tip.

She announced, "I love it. Thank you so much, dear. You're so kind."

Her husband rocked back on his heels and beamed at his ostentatious wife as she expressed her admiration for the gift. He cocked his head as he admired it. "You look wonderful, Billie. Gold is your color."

The banker grinned, proud of his not-so-humorous joke, and the guests applauded. As the town's eminent citizens wallowed in their affluence, Tip pulled the last coin from his pocket and ordered another whiskey. He stared into the liquor as if it were a crystal ball.

The drunkard saw no future for himself, just endless days of an arduous existence. Short-on-luck, but not lazy, he jumped at any work available during the depression. But full-time workers clung to positions tighter than a tick in a dog's ear.

He'd slaughtered hogs, bailed hay, and laid brick pavement for the government. It was unfortunate, but there were more men than jobs—even for nasty employment. His meager, infrequent income provided him with food and drink, and of late, less for both. Rent money at the flophouse had run out, and the proprietor evicted him posthaste. Homeless, he slept any dry place he could find.

While Tip pondered his unfortunate state, one partygoer slipped beside him and slapped a hand on the bar twice. Tip noticed his starched cuffs.

"Another bottle of champagne." The staggering socialite appeared intoxicated and braced himself. While holding onto the counter, he swayed as if the tavern were a floating ship. A wave rocked the saloon, and he smashed into Tip.

Though bumped hard, Tip politely steadied the unstable partier and recognized him as a cashier at the bank. Tranquil from his liquid sedation, Tip ignored the intrusion. For he too had sailed the rolling liquor seas on occasions.

"Keep your hands to yourself!"

Tip frowned at the uncalled-for comment but returned to his whiskey without a reply. Again, he pondered an escape from his meager existence in such times.

When the next imaginary wave tilted the deck, the banker rocked and plowed into him again. The collision spilled Tip's drink. Now aggravated, Tip shoved the unstable patron. The push, more forceful than necessary, was not as hard as possible. "Get off of me," Tip ordered.

The cashier stumbled but caught a chair. Then, he zigzagged over to the bar and planted both feet on the deck. "Hey! I warned you before to keep your hands off me."

Tip wanted no more trouble, so he turned to his shot glass.

"Don't ignore me!"

Tip's jaw twisted as an unexpected fist blasted a tooth from his gum. Catapulted from his chair, he crashed onto the pine floorboards, and resembled a turtle on its back. There was a profound silence. But when he regained his awareness, the elite celebrants had surrounded him.

"What a disgrace," the bank president scolded.

Tip blinked to improve his focus, but it didn't help much.

The senior banker pointed was pointing at him. "If you can't handle liquor, you shouldn't drink. Now you're bothering people. I should call the cops."

Tip could see the accusing finger, but the face was still blurry. He rolled over and rose to his knees as the rebukes continued. Added insults were thrown from the crowd.

"A worthless drunk."

"You're disgusting."

"Why do you demean yourself? You're a bum,"

Tip staggered as he stood and straightened. He rubbed his eyes, hoping to recover from the sucker punch while the elitists chastised him. He stroked his aching jaw as the room swayed. "What happened?"

His drunk assailant slurred, "I punched you. I told you not to touch me."

Tip studied his blood-covered hand front and back. The scarlet fluid had oozed from his mouth when he rubbed his throbbing jawbone. Faint, he lost his balance and steadied himself against the cashier. When he backed away, he left a red handprint on the banker's bright, white shirt.

When the junior officer saw the stain, he clenched his fists. "You, idiot! See what you've done!"

The bank president's wife placed both fists on her hips. "Get out, you're ruining my party!"

Tip blinked as he leaned forward and appraised the lady through blurry eyes. They were almost touching noses before he spoke. "Okay, sir. Which way to the door?"

Billie Jean swelled with indignation. "*Harrumph.*"

Without warning, she slapped him across his throbbing jaw.

"Billie's not a sir!" the banker snapped.

Tip responded, "It seems not! He slaps like a girl."

The banker puffed out his chest. "Did you hear me? I said Billie isn't a man. He's my wife."

She glared at him.

"I mean, SHE'S my wife."

He emphasized his point with a stomp on the wooden floor. The superior, in his own mind, had spoken and awaited Tip's response. The tavern was so quiet you could have heard a mouse burp. It was most unfortunate for my future grandfather. The cat that held his tongue had departed earlier.

Tip stared at the self-important lady, then at her husband. He patted Mr. Goldworth on the shoulder. "I understand your confusion."

The partiers bristled at his insult, and chaos ensued. The bouncer lifted Tip by the arm, then shoved him toward the exit. Tip's toes scraped across the threshold as he exited the illegal saloon. After a short, but scenic flight, he landed with outstretched arms and slid on his belly along the alley. His nose bounced on the dusty pavement for several yards.

Tip rose, then steadied himself against the brick wall. After regaining his stability, the homeless vagabond buttoned his stained tweed coat, which was too big. He misaligned the buttons, so an empty buttonhole dangled over his belt. The well-oiled drunkard fiddled with the garment, got frustrated, and quit.

Tip picked up his worn, shapeless hat and brushed off his floppy trousers. Shaken, he combed his hair with his fingers. His mop was brown but had black streaks — a remnant of the coal bin where he'd slept last. He placed the fedora on his head and pulled with both hands.

As he stumbled toward the main street, he leaned on garbage cans for balance. Unaware of a hidden critter, he stepped on a swishing tail. The cat shrieked, and Tip fell across a refuse barrel which knocked over two others. Bottles and other waste spilled over the stunned vagrant. He roused when a large raindrop smacked his face. His hat lay in the alley beside him. Lettuce adorned the brim, and a slice of red tomato rested on top of the salad bed. It was just the touch it needed. Simple but elegant.

Though on his back, he saw no stars in the murky, clouded sky. *Plop!* Another drop splattered his forehead. *Best head for cover,* he thought.

When he sat upright, fish heads tumbled from his coat. He surmised he was behind a meat market. In his lap lay a slimy, rotting catfish. He lifted it closer for examination. "So, no one wants you either."

Sniffing cats leaped from shadows. Tip had an idea. With Herculean effort, he pushed himself to a standing position. He held the fish by a finger in its mouth, and it dangled before him. "First, we need to dispose of your cut-up friends."

He up-righted the trash cans and returned the bodiless heads to the container. After securing the lid, he picked up the long-expired catfish and stared into its lifeless eyes — eye, one was missing. "Perhaps, my stinky friend, you won't be a total waste."

With the reeking thing swinging beside him, he crept from the alley. Feral felines rushed toward the sealed garbage can, but unable to find a single morsel, they followed the smell of the departing catfish.

Tip poked his head from the darkness and saw no one. At the curb sat a Packard automobile. The four-passenger beauty was unlocked, and the interior of the bank president's car still smelled new. As he looked both ways, Tip whispered to his one-eyed companion. "Let's give the aristocrats their comeuppance."

He thought the fish smiled, but he considered it might be the alcohol tricking his brain. He'd spent evenings conversing with things no more alive. Once, after a night of drinking aftershave, a debate with a hickory tree proved most memorable.

Their discussion turned into an argument, and Tip yelled, "You're nuts."

The glaring pun amused his hardwood friend, and they laughed so hard, and for so long, they forgot their disagreement.

But tonight, his thinking wasn't as foggy. Tip crept to the car, and the jokester slipped the slimy catfish under the driver's seat before rolling down the window and latching the door. He shuffled a crooked route across the street to the courthouse where, in the shadow of the pillars, he hid from view. He covered his giggle as he waited for the entertainment to begin.

Soon, a feline marauder appeared with an upturned nose. The gray tomcat identified the source of the aroma and leaped inside the extravagant vehicle. He dined alone until other uninvited guests approached.

A yellow tabby streaked from the alley, followed by a bushy-tailed black-and-white. The snickering human lost track of the feline count after the dogs arrived. A short-legged mutt circled the automobile as he assessed the situation, and a beagle and two unidentifiable mongrels soon appeared.

Tip smothered a giggle as he wondered if the mutts were after the cats or the fish. Then, a long-eared hound placed his front paws on the open window and howled. The brown-with-black-spots hunter bellowed bass tones. An unruly choir—sopranos and tenors — joined in chaotic harmony.

The fighting toms inside the vehicle resembled tossing clothes in a runaway washing machine. The cat screeches, heard between the almost continuous woofs and bays, attracted more canines. After a running start, a German shepherd leaped through the open window.

Colorful fur on four legs escaped the confined fury, then pounced on a howling, freaked-out beagle. The pup yipped as the tomcat clung to its back with needle-sharp claws. Like a bareback rider at a rodeo, the smaller animal dismounted the steed while the dog continued its furious getaway. Other cats leaped to escape the German shepherd. Once outside, they slashed wet noses, which dispelled the yelping canines beneath their front porches. The felines scattered down alleys and up trees, leaving a single canine on the backseat.

The prankster slapped the concrete as he rolled and laughed. Tip's side ached from the laughter. He'd about recovered when the bankers departed from Tommy's, and the president opened the car for the pretentious ladies.

"What a gentleman," Tip whispered.

His wife recoiled when greeted by the snarling beast which hovered over its smelly prize. The socialites retreated to the sidewalk, and the commotion attracted a nearby cop.

"What seems to be the problem?" the officer inquired.

The banker pointed at the vicious creature, so the policeman devised a plan. He opened doors on both sides of the vehicle and poked the animal with a nightstick. It snarled but soon yielded to the officer's wooden persuader. The German shepherd escaped down the street with remnants in its mouth.

Tip heard the loudest complaints as the banker assessed the damages. Scratches, rips, and smells were a sampling of the descriptions to the deputy.

While the gentlemen picked fish parts and fur from the seats and wiped the leather with their colorful, silk handkerchiefs, the bouncer provided newspapers for the seat. In time, the partygoers entered the vehicle, and with four open windows, the odorous Packard departed. The doorman returned to the speakeasy, and the cop headed down an alley. With all witnesses gone, except for a nearby treed cat, the mischief-maker emerged from the shadows and studied the threatening sky.

"We'd better find shelter," he advised a treed kitty.

Then he stumbled down away to escape the coming shower. His most likely opportunity would be at the Ebenezer Tabernacle. He called it the Holy Roller, All-Hypocrite Church. When he arrived at the rear of the building, he squatted and tried to raise a locked basement window. Unable, he tried another, but when he pulled, he lost his grip and fell backward. The expected raindrops pattered on his hat. He stood but slipped, so he crawled to the third sash, and this time opened it. By then, steady rain pelted the puddles, while downspouts strained to drain full gutters. He escaped the torrent by lowering himself into a Sunday school room and collapsed face-up on a child-height table.

For a few minutes, he lay in the darkness, but when lightning flashed, he saw someone standing above him. Tip's entire body flinched at the surprise.

11

He expected eviction, but the person didn't move or speak. Tip blinked, trying to see who hovered over him. In the next flash, a figure peered through him, not at him. Tip shivered. Were the goosebumps from his wet clothes or the penetrating stare, he wondered.

A bolt streaked across the sky, and he concentrated on those eyes. Were they angry for his trespass, or were they kind? It seemed both. Who was this enigma who expressed both anger and forgiveness for a reprobate?

For an unexplainable reason, he felt both shame and hope. Could it be the booze confusing his mind? No, something else was happening, but what? In a moment of clarity, he decided, whatever it was, he would succumb. Like a dog on its back exposing its weak underbelly, Tip yielded to the enticing invitation.

Outside, the heavens opened, and rain fell in sheets, washing streets and alleys clean. Grit, grime, and morsels of fish swirled into the storm sewer grates and took Tip's troubles with them. As he lay, almost passed out, a warmth penetrated his body and his soul too. He was unaware then, but it was his last drunken night sprawled prostrate wherever he landed.

In the morning, he awoke with hunger, but not for alcohol. His yearning, the first in forever, was for bacon and eggs.

Coffee, he smelled it brewing. There was a thud, and he suspected someone else was in the church. So, he slipped from the table and peered into the main room. An old farmer in bib overalls tossed chunks of coal into a pot-belly stove, then he lit a rolled-up newspaper and pitched it in too. It was late September and colder than average.

After a while, others arrived and poured themselves a cup of coffee, then huddled around the heater. They talked about crop yields and beef prices. Someone told a joke, and one man spat his drink. Once the room warmed, the men removed their jackets. A distinguished gentleman in a well-tailored suit entered. It was Tip's nemesis, Mr. Goldworth. He approached the podium. "Let's begin, but first look around to see we're alone."

Tip hurried into a closet. The hinges squeaked twice as someone peeked into the classroom, then left.

"No one here," the man reported.

Since the door was ajar, Tip tiptoed over and peered through the narrow slit. The speaker rose to his feet, and with both hands, he strained to lift a salesman's sample-case onto the table. Then Mr. Goldworth removed a black velvet bag. He loosened a string, allowing the material to drop. A foot-tall, solid-gold eagle glared at the crowd.

"Wow!" Tip whispered. "It's worth a fortune."

Mr. Goldworth slammed a gavel. "Since everyone is present, I call this meeting of the Saint-Gaudens Society to order."

Quiet settled on the crowd as stragglers found seats, and Mr. Goldworth raised his arm. "As you know, four months ago, President Roosevelt issued an executive command which made it illegal for private citizens to own gold, and he ordered it surrendered. We believed his misguided efforts were unconstitutional, so we ignored his directive. But going forward, the penalty for hoarding is stiff, so we must be cautious."

Tip strained to listen.

"As chief officer of the bank, I've learned the revenue officers are planning a raid. They'll open safe-deposit boxes in search of violators."

A gasp, followed by murmurs, preceded the president's motions for quiet. "Everyone in this room has gold in their lockbox, which exceeds the limit. If the agents find it, you'll face a prison term."

One man exclaimed, "I'm getting mine out of there this morning."

Several made similar comments and stood as if to leave.

"Wait, a minute." Mr. Goldworth waved his hands in a downward motion. "Sit down, please. We founded the Society not just to share our disdain for government intrusion but to protect the members. We can't surrender the gold because we didn't claim the income on our taxes. Don't forget Al Capone went to prison for tax evasion."

Several arched their eyebrows and nodded.

Mr. Goldworth glanced at his pocket watch. "Gold is too dangerous to hide at home because desperate, unemployed men would kill for those coins."

As murmuring ensued, Tip watched the speaker use his finger as an imaginary knife across his throat. "It's why we have the gold in safe-deposit boxes. No one, including bank employees, can access it because it takes two keys—the cashier's and the customer's key."

"How will revenue officers unlock them?" asked a member.

The president responded, "They'll force the owners to open the box and arrest them if it has over a hundred dollars' worth of gold in it. If the holders don't show, a locksmith will break the lock and replace it with a new one."

"Well, what keeps criminals from breaking into the bank boxes?" someone shouted.

"They can," replied the banker. "But it takes too long. Thieves prefer to get the cash and make a quick getaway. They're aware most of the contents are just papers such as wills and life insurance policies."

"So, what's your idea?" a participant asked.

"As you know, two of our members are officers at the bank." The speaker pointed at businessmen seated in the front row. Tip recognized one as the man who sucker-punched him last night.

The banker continued, "Only we bankers can enter the vault. In there, we keep the large bills in a free-standing safe."

The tellers nodded.

"Next to it, we stack bags of coins. We receive them from the mint marked as pennies, nickels, dimes, and quarters. We open them as needed."

"Get to the point," someone interjected.

The banker leaned on the table. "Revenue officers won't check the penny sacks, so we'll hide the coins there."

He smiled at the speechless crowd. "If robbed, a thief won't steal pennies, so it'll be safe."

Mr. Goldworth raised straight and pulled his suspenders forward with his thumbs.

Someone exclaimed, "Brilliant!"

Others nodded and chuckled while the banker clipped the end from a cigar and lit it. He allowed the chatter to continue for a while before he continued. "Each of you come to the bank, one at a time not to raise suspicion. Once you gain access to your box, bring it to my office. I'll verify the amount and place it in a penny bag. Once full, a teller will sew it shut."

His cigar went out, so he lit it again while everyone waited. After a few puffs, he continued. "We'll hide our eagle in plain sight where they'll never suspect it's gold. You'll see it each time you enter the bank."

After a brief discussion and a vote of approval, the members departed. The farmer in the bib overalls dumped the coffee pot, rinsed it, and exited.

Once alone, Tip sat on the low children's table to rest his legs. His knees ached—oh yes, the bouncer tossed him out of Tommy's last night. *That'll hurt awhile.*

When he checked his other joints, they seemed uninjured. His fingers massaged the back of his neck while he pondered the things he'd heard. While preparing to stand, he looked up and saw a portrait on the wall. The eyes reminded him of his mother's — God rest her soul. Even when he misbehaved, her loving gaze always expressed her unconditional love.

Through the foggy hangover, the events of the night emerged and clarified. He remembered lightning dispelling the darkness, the down-to-the-bone warming, and the person standing over him. *Oh, it was just a picture.*

But was it? How could he dispel with logic the earlier feelings? It was too much to understand all at once. He would ponder the experience at depth, later.

He removed the portrait from the frame, rolled it, and slipped it into his coat. Tip crept through the basement then up the back stairs. The former drunk tiptoed up the steps and scanned the alley before darting into the morning chill.

He couldn't wait to tell his cousin about the Saint-Gauden's Society and their secret stash of gold. John Dillinger would find this information most valuable.

Chapter 3

John Dillinger Robs the Greencastle Bank

A few weeks later, John Dillinger parked a stolen four-door, Studebaker Commander on Jackson street alongside the Central National Bank in Greencastle, Indiana. Four men in long wool topcoats rushed up the incline and rounded the corner to an oak-framed, glass door. A bucktoothed Jack-O-Lantern sat on the limestone stoop, a sign of the season. Harry Copeland stopped outside to stand guard while the other three gangsters entered the bank. Though the bell announced their entrance, none of the busy employees or patrons paid attention.

A short, aging lady in droopy nylons and a worn tweed coat stood near the front, counting her money. She ignored the men who brushed past her.

Black poster-board cats and ghouls hung on the walls and wished a happy Halloween to the customers. Dillinger glanced up at the empty security guard's cage suspended above the entrance and continued into the lobby. The scaffold was new since they cased the bank a week ago. Getting right to business, Pete Pierpont walked to a teller window, removed a sawed-off shotgun from his long coat, and raised it. The cashier, busy counting money, didn't notice the deadly weapon pointed at him.

"Next window," the banker ordered. Pete cleared his throat, and the banker looked up from his work.

Charlie Makley, a natural-born killer, pulled a Tommy gun from his topcoat and surveyed the bank. A sun-tanned farmer wearing a straw hat stood with a cash deposit shaking in his hand. His wife shuffled behind her husband, but their tall son concentrated on a lollipop he was licking. Dillinger paused before the suntanned man. "Put your money away."

The frightened farmer slipped the bills into his pocket and raised his arms.

Dillinger added, "We're bank robbers. We don't want your money."

He lifted a businessman's necktie to admire his tie tack. "That a real pearl?" he asked.

The man nodded, "It was a gift from my wife."

"Nice."

Dillinger dropped the tie and walked away. The shabby lady near the door snapped her purse shut and hurried onto the sidewalk.

As she brushed past, Harry snapped, "Hey, you! Stop!"

She marched on and didn't respond as Dillinger walked to the door and watched her leave. "Stop, I said!"

"I'm going to the dime store. You jump in the lake," she hissed in a German accent.

Harry, unwilling to draw attention, let her go. "This is your lucky day, lady," he mumbled.

Harry leaned against the sparkling limestone facade. As the criminal lookout held a cigarette in his left hand, Dillinger noticed him caressing the 38 Smith and Wesson he always kept in his right coat pocket. Dillinger glanced across the street toward the courthouse and the Sheriff's office.

He turned and pulled a .38 revolver from a shoulder holster. With renewed focus, Dillinger hurried across the marble floor and kicked open the gate to the teller's cage. Splinters scattered from the top rail and post.

Six wide-eyed customers concentrated on Charlie as he waved the tommy gun. Charlie looked inside a cloakroom while the hostages held their hands high. "Get in the closet."

"Why, Pa?"

Before his father responded, Charlie, poked the muscular, bib-overall-clad, young man with the gun barrel. "Because I said so; get inside there."

The boy's father pulled on his son's overalls. "Please don't hurt him. He doesn't mean any harm. He's simple."

With one arm still in the air, the weathered farmer yanked his son toward the closet. "Relax, son. Just do as he says."

His plump wife followed her husband, and the other bystanders shuffled there too. Charlie placed a chair under the knob then walked toward the two bank tellers while brandishing the tommy gun.

"Don't want a farmer being a hero," Charlie explained. "How about you bankers, are you brave?"

"No, sir, don't shoot."

"I'll only plug you if you make me."

As Charlie guarded the two nervous tellers, an office door opened, and the bank president and his wife appeared. Charlie spun and pointed the machine gun at the pair. "Freeze, or I'll cut you in half!"

Neither of them moved.

"Hands up and get back in that office."

"Yes, sir."

Charlie spun around and motioned for the other bankers to enter the office too. "No fast moves." The four moved as Charlie followed.

Meanwhile, across the room in the teller's cage, Pete removed cash from the drawers, which he stuffed into his oversized pockets. Nearby, Dillinger entered the unlocked safe and removed a few bundles. Disgusted, he dropped them. "Just small bills!"

Pete stooped to pick up a bundle of tens and stuffed them in his overcoat. "Not much of a bank."

"Don't waste your time," Dillinger snapped.

Dillinger saw stacked coin bags and stooped to pick up one. The mint had stamped One Cent-United States Currency on the white, cotton fabric. He placed the sack on the waist-high safe and pulled at the seam. Unable to see inside, he cut the stitching with his pocketknife. When he peeked into the slit, he smiled a pearly-white grin. "Just as Tip said, gold coins."

Pete said, "Beee-uuuu-tiful."

Dillinger handed the bag to Pete. "Give this one to Harry."

Dillinger watched as Pete carried the stolen loot outside and set it beside the lookout who shuffled sideways and hid the bag. Harry tossed his cigarette on the sidewalk. A grocer glared at the stranger as he stomped on the butt then swept it into his dustpan.

Meanwhile, Dillinger took a canvas sack to Charlie, who stood guard over the bankers in the office. The hostages' noses were down, and the soles of their shoes pointed upward. Charlie harassed them. "Look at the oak floorboards."

Dillinger saw the woman. "Let the lady off the floor."

"She's a snotty one," Charlie warned.

"But she's a lady."

Charlie arched his eyebrows and shook his head. "Okay, ma'am, you can stand."

The well-dressed socialite rose and wiped the imaginary dust from her dress with her white-gloved hands. "It's filthy."

She straightened her feathered hat and tugged her garments as the gangsters watched. "Who do you think you are?"

Dillinger flashed his teeth, ignoring her scornful glare. "I'm sorry, lady. We're bank robbers. Sometimes, we forget our manners."

Peeved, the female ignored his sarcastic apology and stepped closer. "You must consider yourself a big man, but you're TRASH."

Her harsh comment roused instant anger, and Dillinger's smile dissipated. "I'm John Dillinger."

Charlie raised his Tommy gun. "Told you she was snotty, let me shoot her."

Veins in Dillinger's neck bulged. "Lady, I'm trying to be nice to you."

She raised her nose and turned her head to one side. "*Harrumph.*"

A red flush on Dillinger's neck crept up onto his face. He took a step closer and spied her necklace — a pendant on a chain. "Does it have special meaning to you?"

She grasped the medallion as if to protect it. "It's a birthday gift from my husband."

"Hand it over, lady!"

She held it tighter, emboldened beyond reason, and refused him. "No! It was a gift."

Dillinger glanced at the men on the floor. He stepped a few paces toward the prostrate hostages and poked the president with his pointed, shiny shoe. "Is this your husband?"

"Yes."

Dillinger kicked her spouse hard enough to break a rib. The banker groaned.

"Hey!" she cried.

"Do you know why I kicked him?"

Her haughty expression evaporated. She shook her head.

"Because I try not to hit women."

Her wide-open eyes showed her shock, but she said nothing. Dillinger walked toward her with an outstretched hand. "Give me the pendant."

She clung to it, but her eyes expressed fear. Dillinger waited a few seconds, then turned and stomped away. "We don't have time for this."

She smirked at Charlie as if she'd won. Dillinger stopped and looked back. "Go ahead, shoot her!"

It could be a woman never removed a necklace so fast. It was Charlie's turn to smirk as she handed him the chain. Charlie raised the Tommy gun, and she looked cross-eyed into the barrel.

Charlie said, "Now, get on the floor."

Dillinger joined Pete in the vault, and each man grabbed a bag.

"They're heavy," Pete said as they departed.

As Dillinger passed a black statuette on the cashier's desk, he stopped. Pete bumped into him.

Dillinger said, "The eagle."

Dillinger tried to lift the bird with his free hand but couldn't. He dropped his sack on the desk to examine the figurine, tipped it backward, and scratched the bottom with his knife. The sliver glistened. "Look at that chunk of gold!"

Pete whistled then responded, "Geez, Louise!"

Dillinger said, "It's too heavy for me to carry both this and the bag, so let's get the boy."

Pete looked puzzled.

"The farmer's kid."

"Oh," Pete said. He followed Dillinger into the cloak closet.

Dillinger asked, "What's the boy's name?"

"Sherman," his father replied.

"Sherman, I need your help. Will you carry something for me?"

He glanced toward his dad for instruction.

Pete said, "Don't worry, Pop. We won't hurt him."

The farmer looked worried, so Dillinger put his hand on his shoulder. "I promise."

He examined Dillinger's face then nodded his approval.

Dillinger pulled at the boy's shirt. "Sherman, if you help me, I'll buy you an ice cream."

Sherman opened his eyes wide and turned to his father for permission.

"Go ahead, son, but you come right back here when you're done."

The farm boy towered over the gangsters as he followed them to the teller cage. Dillinger smiled at the bulky boy and pointed to the eagle. "Can you lift it?"

Sherman wrapped his large hands around the statue and lifted it with little effort.

"Can you carry it?"

He nodded then tucked it under one arm. Dillinger patted him on the back. "Attaboy, now follow us."

Before departing, Pete stomped into the office where Charlie was guarding the bankers. His stiff leather soles thumped on the hard floor. He stood over them as he gave a warning. "If any of you move in the next five minutes, I'll come back here and kill everyone!"

No one replied. Charlie tapped the president with his shined, pointed shoes. Charlie asked, "Did you hear him?"

"Yes, sir. Five minutes."

After tucking their weapons inside their coats, each man carried a bag to the stoop. Sherman followed behind with the eagle. The grocer next door scooped his debris and dumped it into a trash can. Sherman exited and walked toward him, but the gang headed in the opposite direction.

Sherman said, "I'm getting ice cream."

The busy shopkeeper hadn't seen the departing thieves but stopped when Sherman spoke to him. "That's nice."

Harry hurried back while the other gangsters waited. "C'mon, Sherman."

The grocer pointed at the black-and-white eagle. "What've you got, son?"

Before Sherman could answer, the apron-clad grocer reached into his back pocket.

Harry yelled, "Gun!"

In a flash, Harry withdrew his pistol and smacked the firearm against the grocer's head. Injured, the man dropped unconscious to the sidewalk with blood oozing from a small cut above his ear. A handkerchief fell from his hand. Harry glanced both ways, but no one had seen the altercation.

"Why d'you do that?" Sherman asked.

"He doesn't like ice cream," Harry replied.

Sherman scowled at the blacked-out grocer, then kicked him as Harry pulled him away. The crew rounded the corner and carried their heavy load a short distance down the hill. Once they reached the Studebaker, they paused. In earlier robberies, they'd slipped inside with a few bags of paper money, but this weighty score presented an unexpected problem. They placed their loot on the rear floorboard of the trunkless car.

Once loaded, Pete and Charlie crawled into the backseat with their knees to their chins. The car squatted to its frame. "This won't work," Pete said.

Dillinger pointed to a pickup truck across the street with a few dozen pumpkins in the back. The old Ford had wooden sideboards and pine planks for a bed.

"Use the Ford," Dillinger ordered.

After pulling themselves from the backseat, each man removed a bag. The gangsters rearranged the pumpkins then strained to load their fortune. Sherman placed the eagle on the truck bed and turned to Pete. "Ice cream."

As Harry and Charlie made a hasty getaway in the stolen truck, Pete pulled a coin from his vest pocket and handed it to Sherman. "Here's the money, boy. Buy yourself an ice cream."

Sherman grinned and gripped the quarter.

Pete continued, "Once you get the treat, go back to your parents. If anyone asks where we went, tell them Chicago."

Dillinger started the engine of the Studebaker. "Pete, get in the car."

Sherman clung to the coin in one hand and waved goodbye with the other. As Dillinger departed, he glanced at two deputies exiting City Hall. Deep in conversation, they didn't notice the bandits.

In a few minutes, the getaway car rolled into the little town of Manhattan, where Tip sat on a wooden fence next to a farmer's boy. The teenager teased a dog with a stick, and the mutt snarled and growled each time he poked him.

Dillinger nearly passed the pair before he saw Tip waving. He braked hard, and the Studebaker slid to a halt on the gravel road.

"Get in," Pete instructed.

The dirty-faced boy looked puzzled as he scratched his scalp.

"Why? Who are you?"

"He's not talking to you, dummy. He meant me," Tip explained.

"Who are you calling dummy, dummy?"

Tip dropped from the fence then turned to the shirtless farmhand. In a flash, he yanked the stick from the boy's hand.

"Hey! That's mine. Give it back."

"Here! You can have it."

Tip shoved the walking stick into the boy's chest. The youngster flipped backward and landed as the penned hogs squealed and scattered.

"C'mon! Quit messing around," Dillinger commanded.

Tip scurried toward the getaway car but hesitated. He motioned and whistled. "Here, dog."

With ears and tongue flapping, the mutt dashed into the car, and Tip followed. Before he slammed the door, Dillinger smashed the gas pedal.

The farmer's boy rose and stared at the disappearing vehicle and coughed from the cloud of dust. Then he noticed his manure-covered hand. He shook it and wiped it on his filthy denim pants.

"We've got half the county after us, and you're messing with a boy and a flea-infested mutt!" scolded Dillinger.

"That'll teach him not to tease a dog," Tip muttered.

Tip scratched his new pet's ears, and the mutt panted. As the gang sped toward Terre Haute, John Dillinger looked in the rearview mirror. "Cousin, you're a softy to a fault."

Tip smiled as if he considered it a compliment.

Dillinger continued, "It was as you said. We got four bags of gold and a solid gold eagle."

Tip sat taller. Dillinger tossed a pendant over his shoulder into Tip's lap, and Tip held the chain up and studied it.

"What's this?" Tip asked.

"A reward from the bank president's wife — what a snob."

Tip smirked as he admired the gold St. Christopher medal. He remembered the night her husband gave it to her. He flipped it over, and the back was blank. "I think I'll get it engraved."

He placed it around his neck and showed it to the dog. "Stick with me, boy. We'll start a new life together."

By the time the Studebaker reached Route 40, they'd spotted Harry and Charlie in the stolen pickup truck. Together, they glided westward on the concrete highway past fields of brown, ready-to-harvest corn.

Chapter 4

President Goldworth Robs His Own Bank

Back in Greencastle, the bank president lay on the floor with the others. Mr. Weble, the elderly security guard, climbed the steps from the basement where he'd been stoking the furnace. "Anybody here?" Mr. Weble shouted. "Must be the rapture — and I missed it."

The banker rose to his knees. "That deaf, old goat is a worthless guard."

Mr. Goldworth jumped to his feet and peeked from his office. The guard was staring at the fractured railing and wood splinters.

"That's not right," Mr. Weble muttered. He pulled his revolver and aimed it at the vault. Mr. Weble crept a few feet forward. The bank president touched his shoulder. The startled guard pulled the trigger. The bullet ricocheted around the vault before coming to rest in a stack of ledgers. Both men dropped to the floor and covered their heads. When all was quiet, the banker looked up at the guard. "Are they gone?"

"Who?" Mr. Weble asked.

Mr. Goldworth scanned the lobby then rushed to look out the window. He turned and hurried back to his office. "Get up, everyone, they've left."

Looking confused, the guard slipped his pistol into his holster. "Who left?"

The bankers brushed off their suits. One proclaimed, "The customers, I'll let them out of the closet."

As he hurried to the lobby, the president followed. "Weble, go to the courthouse and tell the Sheriff there's been a robbery."

"Robbery?"

"Yes, robbery."

While shaking his head and scratching under his cap, the guard rushed toward the door. "Robbery and I missed it."

The president muttered, "It's a good thing. If he'd been here, he'd have gotten everyone killed."

Mr. Weble left for the sheriff, and the president locked the door and flipped over the Closed sign. The hostages left the closet, and Mr. Goldworth motioned for them to gather. Mrs. Goldworth joined them in the lobby.

The bank president said, "Stay here. The police will want to talk to you." He turned at the tapping on the glass.

Sherman smiled and waved. The president unlocked the deadbolt and opened the door. Grinning, the man-child entered with an ice cream cone. The banker saw the grocer sitting on the sidewalk, rubbing his scalp but ignored him. He slammed the door and locked it.

When the authorities arrived, a detective interviewed the customers in the lobby. The sheriff questioned the employees in the president's office, while another officer stood guard outside alongside Mr. Weble.

The sheriff turned to a deputy as he closed his notepad. "Go to the office and radio the state police. Tell them to watch for a car with four men."

The deputy left, and the sheriff picked up the telephone and rested his hand on his hip. "Operator, get me the FBI in Indianapolis."

After a short conversation, he hung up the phone and turned to the bank president. "Let's go to the lobby." Once there, he approached a deputy who was interviewing the final customer. "Got everything you need?"

The deputy nodded. "Yes, sir, Sherman heard them say they're heading to Chicago."

While ignoring the conversation, the child-man downed the last of the cone. The sheriff pointed to the customers. "Let 'em go."

Once the patrons shuffled outside, he turned to Mr. Goldworth. "While we're waiting on the FBI, take an inventory."

"Sure thing."

The banker motioned for the tellers. "Count the cash drawers."

A tall assistant entered the teller cage as the shorter employee followed his boss into the vault.

"Oh my God, it's gone!" the president whispered.

The shorter teller steadied himself. "They've taken the gold."

Both men stared at the missing bags. Then, the president dropped to his knees and opened the free-standing safe. Next, he removed a panel in the back, revealing a hidden compartment stacked full of large bills.

"Don't mention the secret chamber or the money," he whispered. "To anyone." In a hurry, he replaced the board just before the sheriff entered.

"How's it going?" asked the sheriff.

Still, on the floor, the banker flinched and looked over his shoulder. "We're making progress, but it'll take a while."

"Fine, I'll be in my office. I'll return in an hour when the FBI gets here. An officer will be outside standing guard."

"Okay, thanks."

The taller teller returned from the cage. "Nothing but coins in the drawers. They took the bills except a few scattered on the floor."

The president announced, "They stole the gold."

"Oh, my God." The taller teller gasped.

He rushed out of the vault and then returned.

"They took the eagle too."

The trembling man removed a handkerchief and wiped his brow. "What now? The club members trusted us."

"Pay attention," Mr. Goldworth said. "We have precious little time. I can't report the gold stolen, but the government insures the cash. Let's hide the bills and say Dillinger stole it."

"Hide it? But why?"

Mr. Goldworth responded, "So the FBI won't find it."

"But where?"

"In safe-deposit boxes. We've got several empty ones. Hurry and move the money before the FBI arrive."

As the tellers moved the bills, Mr. Goldworth typed two falsified safe-deposit cards. When the sheriff arrived, Mr. Goldworth slipped them into his watch pocket. "Are you done?"

"Yes, Sir," the president replied.

"How much did they steal?" the sheriff asked.

"$74,802."

As he wrote the figures on a notepad, the sheriff whistled.

"That's a load of money."

27

The bank president nodded. "It's Parent's Weekend at DePauw University, so businesses deposited more cash than usual."

The sheriff slipped his pad in his back pocket and headed toward the door. He turned. "The Feds will be here soon. They'll want to talk to each of you." The bell clanged when he left, and the president rubbed his sore ribs as the three awaited the FBI.

Chapter 5

Summer, 1967

Butch asked, "Is it possible the Dillinger treasure is on the island?"

I replied, "Grandpa Tip said John Dillinger camped there after robbing a bank in Greencastle, Indiana"

Marshal said, "It's a hundred miles from here. Sometimes, he'd hide in Chicago after a robbery."

I interrupted, "But after the Greencastle job, he came here, instead. The island was a park then, and Grandpa Tip said there was a campground. Once they built the dam, the new lake flooded most it."

Marshal and I often completed each other's sentences. When I inhaled, Marshal continued the tale. "When Dad was a kid, his family picnicked there. There were hiking trails, and there was a flat-top hill. It was bare except in the center there was a huge oak tree."

"Dad said everyone called it Eagle's Roost because eagles nested there in the spring," I added.

Marshal pointed toward the land across the water. "Now, just Eagle's Roost protrudes from the lake."

From our location, we saw trees around the perimeter with grass in the middle. In the center, towering high above the others stood an expansive oak tree. Near the top was a large eagle nest.

"Did your grandpa ever meet John Dillinger?" Einstein asked.

"Yep, he knew him," I responded.

Angel asked, "Oh man, did he help Dillinger rob any banks?"

Marshal answered, "No. Dillinger needed a sober gang. Grandpa Tip drank when he was younger." Marshal imitated a drunk man while he pretended to drink from a bottle.

I added, "Dad said, Dillinger, joined Dad's family reunion on a Sunday afternoon. No one in the park except my father's family had any idea it was John Dillinger and his gang. Dad was just a ten-year-old boy, but he remembers John and the three strangers."

When I stopped to swat a fly on my arm, Marshal grasped the opportunity to continue. "Dad was young, but he said Dillinger and Grandpa Tip discussed the bank robbery in Greencastle."

Angel stared across the water. "Man, there's nothing on the island."

Angel had a habit of saying "man" in most sentences.

Marshal interjected, "I told you before, Dad said a treasure might be on the island or in the surrounding water."

I continued, "Grandpa Tip said John Dillinger buried a treasure after the Greencastle robbery. He planned to return but got killed in Chicago."

Angel interrupted, "If the gang buried the bank loot, the bills would have rotted by now. Besides, people have searched for it, so they'd have found it."

"Aren't you curious?" Butch asked.

No one answered as they stared at the island just a short distance away.

Butch said, "It's not far."

Marshal said, "We could swim over and see what's there."

Einstein scratched his scalp. "I've swum further."

Einstein's droopy eyes and gaping mouth explained why his brother nicknamed him after the genius, Albert Einstein. It was an insult, but Einstein never complained.

It didn't matter to us. Proximity, not intelligence, was the only condition for membership in our neighborhood gang. Butch removed his shoes.

"This isn't a good idea, man," Angel warned.

Butch stripped off his clothes, except for his underpants. "Who's going with me?"

Angel said, "Man, it might be dangerous 'cause we might get sucked into the city-water intake pipe."

"I can do it," Marshal responded. "It's not far."

Everyone except Angel and me stripped. Soon, I felt the pressure and removed my shoes.

Angel whined, "Are you sure? I'm not."

Before long, Angel shed his clothes too. He said, "Man, this isn't a good idea. I bet they catch us."

Though a year older than me, Angel was less daring. He earned his nickname because he confessed too readily when caught misbehaving. The flaw frustrated me because his honesty sometimes ensnared me.

Butch shouted, "This man's going for a swim. You boys can join me if you've got the nerve."

Butch, the oldest, was a year older than me. He stood with his fists on his hips and displayed his more muscular body. He dove and paddled toward the island. Soon, other boys followed close behind our leader. The rippling, radiating waves, resembled a bullseye on a target.

I didn't want my friends to leave me behind, so I dove into the crisp lake. As I slipped through the water, goosebumps formed on my arms and legs. I paddled toward the intake tower for the city water supply. Never had I swum with such urgency.

Angel lingered behind as the other boys swam toward the concrete tower. "Man, this is crazy." Then, he jumped too.

When I arrived at the water-works intake, the feared water suction to the water treatment plant wasn't there. The other boys who had arrived before me were grasping rungs of a metal ladder. I read two signs with red letters which stated, No Swimming By Order Of The City Council and Danger, Authorized Personnel Only.

Angel grabbed a steel rung while gasping as if he'd swum the English Channel. "Halfway there, man. We can make it."

Einstein added, "Can't turn back now."

We clung to the ladder, and I waited for someone with the courage to proceed.

"Here goes," Butch yelled.

He slipped away, followed by Einstein and Marshal. Angel and I hesitated. As Angel clung tight, I climbed a few steps higher to get a better view. Across the bay, Butch reached shallow water and stood upright. Then Marshal and Einstein arrived and walked onto dry land. They climbed onto a tree jutting

31

over the bank. Years earlier, the waves had eroded the soil around the roots, which caused the tree to lean horizontally. The new growth turned skyward, so the trunk was L shaped with its crown above the water.

Three adventurers walked on the trunk and jumped, then they swam to shore and returned. The fun enticed me to. "Come on, Angel. I'll swim with you. If one of us gets in trouble, we can help each other."

Together, we released our grip and paddled until we reached shallow water and stood on the clay bottom. Relieved, I rested before joining my friends. After we crawled up the horizontal trunk, we jumped into the water. Butch ended our frolicking when he walked away. "We have an island to explore."

As he entered the trees, he glanced back to see if we were following him. When we reached the center, we found a treeless place with knee-high grass. In the clearing was a tall lone oak, and high above was an abandoned eagle nest.

As we walked through the tall grass, my legs itched. "I wish I had insect repellant"

Butch said, "*Wa-wa, you want your mommy?*"

Not wanting to sound babyish, I stopped complaining. I was embarrassed to explore the island in my underpants. It was more private when submerged in the murky lake water.

Mid-step, I stooped and broke off a stalk of wild grass and placed it in my mouth. Everyone else imitated me, and we stood in the clearing as proud as if we'd climbed Mt. Everest.

"Looks desolate," Butch commented.

He rotated as he scanned the city-owned island. We found a shady place under the large tree to drop and rest.

I was glad I'd followed the others. I thought it was our private paradise as I lay on the carpet of grass feeling more independent than ever. Exploring a forbidden isle was the most adventurous thing I'd ever done, and the timidity of my childhood slipped away.

A voice from a megaphone interrupted my tranquility. I couldn't make out the words, but we stood and turned to listen. "Man, who's that?"

"Don't know," Butch answered.

We walked toward the sound. We left the grassy clearing and headed back through the woods. As we traveled closer, the voice became more understandable. "Hello, anyone there?"

Butch crouched behind a tree and hid. As we peered toward the dam, we saw a sheriff's car. My heart skipped a beat, and I felt a strange sensation. Panic was a new feeling for me. A parked cruiser sat next to our bikes, and the deputy spoke into a microphone.

"He's trying to find the owners of our bikes," Butch whispered.

The deputy shrugged his shoulders, got in his car, and left. His patrol car climbed the steep hill and disappeared around the curve, so I breathed a sigh of relief. "I hope he left for good...."

Marshal finished my sentence, "... but I bet he comes back."

Butch rose to his feet. "So, what?"

Butch oozed of confidence. I'd never hidden from a policeman before, and it made me nervous though.

"Let's explore. We'll walk around the edge this time," Butch said.

I followed him but glanced back. I didn't confess my apprehension to the others. In a duckling line, we tailed our leader along the shore. At one point, he dropped to the ground, and we did the same. A boat with two fishermen puttered past looking for a fishing hole. They stopped a few hundred feet from us and cast their lines, so we crouched awaiting Butch's lead.

I don't know why we hid. An ant crawled on my leg and bit me. I flinched and swatted it before it struck again. Butch gave me a dirty look, but the fishermen didn't react to my noise.

The driver reached into an ice chest and removed a bottle of cola. Soon, the other fisherman appeared impatient and reeled his bait. As they rested and finished their drinks, their muffled conversation was within my earshot. Then the driver pulled on the motor rope, and the engine started. In a minute, they disappeared into the bright horizon.

Once they were out of sight, Butch stood, and we followed. We shadowed him halfway around and discovered a lagoon. A thick vine hung from a tree, and Einstein pulled the lower end free.

He tugged a few times then swung above the lake and jumped from a height of ten or twelve feet. Einstein pierced the water feet first while we admiring friends applauded and bellowed our approval.

When the vine returned, Angel rushed to be next. He backed up more and ran toward the lake. The vine swung higher, so Angel dropped from fifteen feet, dove headfirst, and soon surfaced. "Man-O-man, that was great!"

Convinced I could beat him, I grabbed the vine, backed up further, and ran faster. My friends cheered as I flashed past them. I left the ground with a hard push and soared five feet above the lake before ascending. My flight was higher than Angel's, but I lifted my feet to increase my altitude even more. At the apex of the arc with my feet stretched outright, the vine broke. For an instant, I hung midair then dropped while still clinging to the useless vine. Before I had time to adjust my flailing limbs, I smashed onto the water on my back. "Ouch."

Marshal cried, "Dang!"

While holding the vine, I sank. My back stung from the hard landing, so I didn't swim. I just floated to the top. My friends paddled to help, and Butch reached me first. "Are you okay?"

I didn't answer. Then, Einstein towed me to shore. I didn't even help as he pulled me onto the bank. With my eyes closed, I lay on the clay bank. When the pain eased, I opened them. Einstein was above me with a worried expression, but after I looked up, he smiled a goofy grin. "Wow, that must've hurt."

I moaned, and my friends gathered around me.

"You okay?" Marshal asked.

"Let me lie here a minute."

My friends dropped beside me as I sprawled on the beach.

Marshal said, "Someday, you'll think it's funny."

Butch said, "Yeah, I already think it's hilarious."

The boys took turns retelling their version of my catastrophe and poking fun. They exaggerated the tale each time told since I had accomplished a feat worthy of any teenager's recognition.

Not since I'd pierced a dead hog with a sharp stick had I received such praises. Last summer, I popped the swollen animal, and the fumes gagged us. Daily, we returned to the farm to test our ability to endure the putrid smell. Each day it became more unbearable and more covered with flies and maggots. Our farmer-neighbor grew tired of our trespassing, so he buried the unfortunate farm animal which ended our daily gag-endurance ritual.

In a while, even I was laughing at my painful landing. Meanwhile, Angel lay on his back and saw something in a tree. He stood and pointed at a nest on a sturdy, leafy branch. "There's a bird nest, man."

In a flash, he was on the limb, balancing himself and resembling a tightrope walker. He nearly reached the nest, but he slipped and plunged into the lake.

"Almost had it," said Butch.

Without a word, Angel tried again, but he hesitated when he heard a motor in the distance and stretched to see.

"Who is it?" asked Butch.

"Don't know, man." Angel stood on the limb and peered across the water. "Man, are those fishermen back?"

We dashed into the cover of the thick bushes, and Angel crouched lower to hide among the leaves. "Oh, man, they're coming this way."

My heart raced fearing the cop had called the game warden. "Should we make a run for it?"

"Don't move," Butch whispered.

The engine stopped, and the boat glided into the secluded lagoon. Speechless, we viewed the occupants, four gorgeous college-age girls wearing bikinis of various colors. I felt *sooo* naked crouching behind a tree in my wet underpants.

"See, I told you this place is awesome and private," the tall blonde declared.

A petite brunette stood and raised her arms above her head to pull her hair into a ponytail causing Marshal to make a soft wolf-whistle.

"Woof...," Marshal said.

"... look at her," I added.

The brunette's head turned owl like as she admired the swimming hole and removed her wrap. "You're right; it's a perfect place to sunbathe away from staring boys."

Little did she know, five pairs of male eyeballs ogled every inch of her fantastic body. Two other girls climbed from the seats and onto the bow. The watercraft was a large, white vessel with red and blue stripes, and I recognized it. It belonged to a neighbor, and the blonde driver was his daughter, Linda, who attended the local university.

The attractive Linda and the shapely brunette jumped feetfirst as the other teenagers spread towels on the fiberglass bow to bask in the summer sun. The pool was neck-deep to Linda, but the shorter brunette had to tread water.

"We're stuck for a while," I whispered.

Butch tilted his head forward and peered down his nose. "Who cares? I'm not going anywhere."

My wet, tidy-whitie briefs clinging to my skin exposed too much for my comfort. "I don't want them to see me in my underpants."

"Hush, I'm trying to concentrate." Butch turned to examine the beauties while the giggling coeds shared a bottle of suntan lotion. For a blissful eternity, they massaged their arms and legs. As we gazed from our hiding place, they smeared the cream on each other's backs and shoulders.

Butch appeared entranced by the girls. The primary source of his devotion seemed to be the babe in the yellow bikini. She lowered her shoulder straps to allow her friend better access with the lotion. The sunlight glistened off her oily skin. The shining bronze goddess frowned as she examined the white lines on her shoulders. "I hate these strap marks, I plan on wearing a strapless dress to the fall formal, and these will look awful."

Linda bobbed in the lake while watching her friend fiddle with her straps. "Take it off, we don't mind you if skinny dip."

The missy in the yellow two-piece tilted her head to one side and appeared to ponder Linda's suggestion. After looking around at the private setting, she elevated her eyebrows and shrugged her shoulders. "Why not?"

As she reached behind her back, five boy's jaws dropped. Angel stretched to see through the leafy branches, lost his balance, and fell. I gasped, but he caught himself before plunging into the water. He dangled for a few seconds then swung his legs around the limb. The young ladies didn't notice the hanging sloth. Instead, they were focusing on their friend trying to remove her top. "I'm having trouble with this hook."

Butch said, "I'll help her."

Just then, clumsy Angel lost his grip and hung by his legs. Still, they didn't notice him.

"Got it," she said.

At the same moment, Anel dropped with a splash. The stunning beauties froze as they watched him flail. Angel dog-paddled to shore, then waded on to the bank in his underwear glory.

After a brief, awkward moment, Angel smiled and waved. The bikini-clad babes shrieked. In a hurry, the squealing girls wrapped themselves in beach towels. Linda dropped into the driver's seat, glared at the nearly naked, still-waving adolescent boy, and started the engine. When Linda gave it the gas, the outboard motor roared from the lagoon. Butch exited his hiding place, so we followed and stood beside Angel.

"Nice going, Angel," Marshal said.

"Thanks," I added.

Einstein said, "That was amazing."

Butch stared at his brother with a mystified expression. "What was so amazing?"

Angel smirked. "Well, they almost skinny-dipped."

Butch threw his arms up and flipped his head back. "Idiot."

"Well, almost," Einstein responded.

I stared dejected at the departing speedboat. "Too bad."

Five disappointed adolescents standing at the water's edge, wearing wet underpants, watched the girls flee. As the propeller's radiating wake splashed across my toes, I sighed.

We flinched when another boat approached, and we dropped behind the bushes again. They cut the engine, and it slipped into the lagoon. The sun had settled behind the tall trees on the hill.

As the boat drifted to a stop, a large man dropped the anchor. He was taller and huskier than the man scanning the water. The smaller male shifted from one side of the boat to the other as he peered over the edge. Meanwhile, a sturdy woman sat behind the steering wheel, smoking a pipe.

I asked, "Is that a woman…?"

Marshal continued, "… smoking a pipe?"

After lighting cigarettes, the men gazed into the deep. The smaller male had both hands on his hips, and the big one spoke as he lowered the anchor rope. "Not too deep."

Einstein poked his head from a bush and whispered a question to his brother. "What are they doing?"

Butch put his finger to his lips. "*Shh.*"

The larger stranger helped his friend put a scuba tank on his back. Then the diver pulled a mask over his face and fell backward into the water.

After tapping the ashes from her pipe, the oversized woman stuffed it with fresh tobacco. But before she put the bag away, she removed a wad of leaves and placed them in her mouth.

Butch shook his head. "Geez, she's a tough old bird."

She chewed awhile then spit brown juice overboard. After she clawed the wad from beneath her lip, she flicked it across the lagoon. Then, she lit her pipe.

Marshal remarked, "She's rough as a sailor…."

"… in the merchant marines," I concluded.

Soon the diver came back to the surface. "It's too dark down there."

The woman pointed at the slanted rays striking the hilltop. "Mack, the sun is behind the trees, so let's return in the morning when there's better light."

Mack peered at the trees. "I guess you're right."

She said, "We'll come back under better conditions. In the meantime, let's check along the hilltop."

Mack pulled the diver from the water and helped him remove his tank. "I'll raise the anchor."

Mack pulled on the rope and placed the anchor in the boat. She turned the key, and the engine sputtered then roared. As she spun the craft in a tight circle and sped from the lagoon, the engine left a trail of oily smoke. As they headed toward the distant boat ramp, we rose.

"Man, what was that about?"

I said, "We may never know."

Einstein brushed his hair out of his droopy eyes while pondering. "Was it too late for fishing?"

Butch rolled his eyes. "They weren't fishing. They had scuba gear."

"Well, they might have been spearfishing."

"Idiot!"

Only Butch could call Einstein names. He'd thump anyone else who insulted him. "It's getting late. We've explored enough today, so let's head home,"

Butch led us across the island, then we swam toward the intake tower. With more confidence on our return trip, we swam with leisure. Upon reaching the concrete structure, we stopped to rest.

In a few minutes, we continued toward the dock and grabbed ahold. After a brief rest, we climbed the ladder. At the top, we scared off a flock of birds which were eating the popcorn.

Angel picked up his shirt. "They were walking on our clothes."

I was exhausted and sat to dry. The others joined me. I gazed upward toward the wooden lookout platform jutting from Hillside Park. Someone was standing far above us on the deck. Blind as a bat without my eyeglasses, I sat them on my nose. "Oh, Crap!"

"It's that cop," Marshal said.

Everyone looked.

"Oh, man. He's got binoculars. We're dead."

As I hurried to get dressed, I jumped on one leg, struggling to get into my shorts. *Why was it harder to pull on clothes when in a hurry?* I pulled on my shorts, shirt, socks, and shoes. "Let's get out of here…."

"… before he comes," Marshal finished my sentence.

Butch pointed up the hill. "Too late. Here he comes."

The police car rolled down the hill. We rushed to our bikes, but I realized there was no escape. With just one road, and the officer on it, he trapped us.

"I'm not sticking around to see what he wants," Butch yelled.

He ran toward the wooded hill below the lookout. I surmised, other than going back into the water, Butch's path was our only route of escape. Leaving our bikes behind, we hastened too. We split and climbed different directions on the steep incline. I figured the policeman couldn't catch everyone if we separated, and it appeared the others had the same idea.

The squad car rolled to a stop on the dam. When the officer got out, he didn't even close the door. He got back inside and drove back up the hill.

Once high above, he walked out on the lookout deck. We saw him, but he couldn't see us as we hid behind trees and underbrush. Two teens crawled left, and others scurried to his other side. Those on the right side bypassed the park and hurried toward the paved road beyond the officer's view.

I chose a path farthest left of the officer separating me from my buddies. It was longer, but I felt it was the safer route. I walked on a trail along the lake

39

then I climbed. It seemed almost vertical and required me using hands and feet. I grabbed saplings and pulled myself upward along the steep incline. When I came to the top, I found the trail. Now exhausted, I took a chance. Before committing to descending gullies and climbing more hills, I opted to check the park for the policeman.

With caution, I traversed the trail and slowed my pace as I neared the lookout. While stepping light-a-foot, I saw the observation deck, and it was vacant. No one was in sight, so I sighed. I left the privacy of the trail and ambled onto the gravel parking lot. "Oh, boy!"

The officer was in his car, and our eyes met. I whirled around to run when he started the engine. He shot my direction. I didn't go far before his braking tires slid on the loose gravel behind me. When the door slammed, I knew he was in hot pursuit.

I ran as fast as possible on the trail which snaked along the ridge above the lake. His footsteps grew louder. "Halt, police!"

His shouts didn't convince me to stop. As I ran, my lungs burned, but I tried to outlast the deputy. Though he was taller with longer legs, I hoped he'd enjoyed too many donuts and would tire before me. Now gasping for air, I realized I wouldn't last much longer.

Ahead, I saw a woman observing two men digging. The men pitched dirt from a knee-deep pit the size of a grave. Their heads turned in unison as I approached.

Too winded to speak, I flashed past the trio.

"Who was that?" the woman asked.

I glanced back and saw them still staring at me. They didn't seem to notice the approaching officer. In a while, I realized there were no footsteps behind me, so I stopped. I bent forward, with my hands on my knees and panted. I wiped the sweat from my brow with my T-shirt and licked my dry lips. Once rested, I became curious of the gravediggers.

Being careful, I crept back. Once close, I stepped off the dirt path and inched toward a tall maple tree.

The multi-year ground-cover of brown leaves crumpled under my and a branch snapped. I hesitated on my way to my hiding place. My lungs still burned from the chase, but I breathed shallow and didn't move.

40

They didn't appear to notice me, so I slipped behind the trunk. With my back to the tree, I panted to catch my breath. Sweat burned my eyes and matted the hair on my forehead. I wiped my face with my T-shirt and stared ahead until I mustered the courage to look.

When I peeked, I saw they were the boaters I'd seen earlier. The two men, with their dusty shoes planted in the hole, sat as the officer interrogated the female. In the quiet of the woods, I could hear them.

The officer had his hands on his hips. "This is public land. You can't dig in a park."

"Oh, is this a park?" she asked.

The officer raised an upturned palm. "Well, you can't dig a hole in private property, either."

"I didn't think it'd hurt to dig in the woods since we planned to put it back as it was."

"Fill it up." The deputy removed his sunglasses. He pulled out a handkerchief and wiped his face. As the interlopers filled the hole, he took off his hat and fanned himself. His crimson face paled to a flesh tone after a while. "Why were you digging?"

"Just looking for Indian relics."

"There weren't Indians around here."

She replied, "We're looking for Civil War items too,"

"You won't find those, either. There weren't any encampments or battles in these parts."

She shrugged her shoulders. "I guess we're just wasting our time."

The officer frowned. The two men stomped on the loose dirt to complete their task.

A motorboat hummed by on the lake below us. Fifty feet above me, two playful squirrels chased each other, causing leaves and twigs to drop onto my head. When they jumped to an oak tree, a dead limb fell onto the forest floor. When the deputy glanced up, I pulled back. I heard his warning, "I could arrest you."

The woman said, "Sorry, it won't happen again."

"It better not."

"Thank you, officer."

41

I exhaled in relief and peered from behind my hiding place. The deputy followed the violators to the parking lot and watched until they departed. Then, he pitched his hat in the backseat, climbed in the squad car, and left.

I darted across the gravel lot to the paved road and ran downhill. I rounded a curve toward the dam. In a few yards, Marshal joined me then Einstein emerged from the woods too. We hurried down the incline, and I tried not to stumble. When we ran across the dam to our bikes, Butch was waiting. "Who were those people?"

I replied, "It was those scuba divers. They were digging, and I interrupted them."

Butch brushed his long dark hair from his eyes. "They'll hold a grudge."

Einstein looked left and right. "Where's Angel?"

I scanned the steep, tree-lined incline, but didn't see him.

We waited for his return until Butch pedaled away. He said, "Let's leave before the deputy returns."

Einstein followed Butch. "Yeah, I bet Angel's home by now."

At the base of the hill, we jumped from our bikes. It was difficult to push our bicycles to the top. Then, we hurried along the mile-long road leading from the lake to our neighborhood.

Our path became shady as we entered the tree-lined road. The overhanging hedge apple trees on both sides shielded us from the hot sun. Honeysuckle intermingled the tree limbs with wiry stems and broad leaves which formed a canopy making an eerie path. Gnarled trunks resembling super-sized, twisted vines, created a natural fence along the road. Pastured horses wouldn't wander through the thicket because of the sharp inch-long thorns. A long forgotten husbandman planted the hundred-year-old trees as livestock barriers before barbed wire existed. Over time, the neglected trees had grown forty feet tall with long, leafy branches. We took care to avoid the grapefruit-sized Osage oranges on the road. The green fruit was as hard as baseballs and could trip our bicycle if we hit one.

The limbs above my head reminded me of the grasping witch's fingers I'd seen years earlier in an animated movie. The made-for-children film made me cover my eyes as my older brother teased me. Any minute, one of those branches may reach for me. I flinched when a crow cawed an ominous warning, and the uneasy sensation running up my spine intensified. I wondered if a black cat may cross my path to make it spookier, but an opossum jumped from the ditch, instead.

When the pointed nosed, creature saw us, it flipped onto its back and, played dead. Its defense-mechanism caused its enemies to ignore it. The term playing possum described well its odd behavior. An animal, with four paws sticking up and a tongue hanging from its gaping mouth, added to the scary setting of the tree-tunnel, so I pedaled faster.

A spider's nest, large enough to trap a bird, encased a limb and its leaves. Insect shells hung from a basketball-size clump. Sucked of their soft guts, the spider left them as trophies like a hunter would hang a deer head above a mantle. A foot away, a dragonfly struggled while a spider encased it with netting. A chill ran through me as I passed below the ugly fight.

At last, we exited the nightmarish stretch into the bright daylight, heading toward the final curve.

"Close to home," Butch shouted back at me.

Warm sunlight baked on my back, causing the chilly, unnerving feelings to evaporate. Ahead, Butch and Einstein slammed to a stop, and when I reached them, I learned the reason. The deputy and Angel were standing beside the officer's parked car.

The officer shouted, "You might as well come on in boys because Angel gave me your names."

Our shoulders sagged in unison.

Butch raised his fist. "The rat."

"Angel just can't keep his mouth shut," Einstein added.

It was futile to run or hide, so I pedaled toward the deputy. "Let's go."

The others joined me for our surrender. Once handcuffed, the deputy stuffed the five of us into the backseat of the patrol car.

Butch whispered, "You rat fink."

"Man, he made me talk, man."

"How?"

Angel hesitated then mumbled, "He asked."

Butch scowled at Angel. "When I get out of these handcuffs, you'll be ratting through a split lip."

"Man, he made me."

"Shut up, you fink."

43

My stomach knotted as I pondered my plight. What would Mom and Dad think, especially after the shoplifting incident? My parents would ground me for the rest of the summer, or worse.

Another car approached, so I twisted to look out of the rear window. A tall, stocky man with broad shoulders unfolded himself from the vehicle and stood. He examined me as he passed. "What have you got, deputy?"

The deputy remained seated. "Well, Sheriff, these boys were swimming around the intake tower, and they avoided arrest."

The sheriff stooped and looked over the seated officer's shoulder to examine his prisoners. "What's your plan, Deputy?"

"Well, I'll take them downtown."

The sheriff glanced toward the bicycles then back at the younger cop. "And you want me to load those bikes?"

The deputy exited the car and stood before the taller officer. "Yes, sir, I'll help."

"Then, what?"

The deputy hesitated, studied us, chewed his lip, and tugged up his belt.

"Well, I don't know for sure. I guess I'll call the boys' parents."

The sheriff tilted his head back. "What will you say?"

"Well, I suppose I'll tell them, their children were breaking the law."

"Okay."

"Then I'd tell them they need to come to the jail to bail them out."

The sheriff tapped his fist on his holster, then pointed at me through the open window. "You son, what have you got to say for yourself?"

I flinched as if he'd shot me. I didn't expect an interrogation. I assumed we'd go straight to the firing squad. With eyes as big as quarters, I couldn't think of anything.

Impatient, the Sheriff arched his eyebrows. "I'm waiting. Why were you swimming in the lake?"

"Well, uh," my mind raced for an answer. "The city pool is closed."

The sheriff lifted one eyebrow and asked, "Why didn't you go to the beach?"

I replied, "It's too far to the other side of the lake, and the only road is a busy highway. We can't ride our bikes there."

Angel said, "Yeah."

When the sheriff looked at the timid teen, Angel shrunk his head back in his shell and stared at the floorboard.

Butch whispered from the side of his mouth, "You witty, dog."

The sheriff sighed as he scanned us and rotated his head from side to side. He made a *tsk, tsk, tsk* clicking sound with his tongue. When the Sheriff stopped shaking his head, he said, "You can only swim at the beach."

The senior officer turned to his deputy and put his hands on his hips. "Clarence, have you ever swum on a hot summer day?"

"Uh, yes, sir; I suppose so."

"Felt good, huh?"

"Yes, sir, but Sheriff…."

The sheriff removed his hat and wiped his brow with his arm. "I'd like to take a dip right now."

"But, Uncle Willard…."

The senior officer stomped his foot. "Don't call me Uncle Willard at work. Call me, Sheriff."

"Sorry, Sheriff, but these kids broke the law."

The sheriff put on his hat. "Maybe they did, and maybe not."

"But Sheriff, it's posted No Swimming."

"Don't pettifog, Clarence. You sound petty when you quibble over trifles."

Marshal and I smiled at each other. The older officer reached into his uniform pocket as if for a cigarette but appeared disgusted when there was none.

"You're trying to quit," the deputy reminded him.

The sheriff frowned. "I know."

He pulled a stick of gum from his pant pocket. He wadded the wrapper and pitched it on the ground. The deputy picked it up and pushed it into his pocket.

"Deputy, there's something I want you to remember."

The sheriff folded the stick and put it in his mouth. "My job is an elected office."

He pointed toward himself. "In this county, the sheriff, that's me, appoints the deputy."

He pointed at the deputy. "That's you."

The sheriff looked toward me. "These boys' parents are voters, and they voted for me to protect their families from vicious criminals."

45

The senior officer opened the car door and motioned for us to exit the vehicle, so we slipped and slithered out with our hands behind our backs.

The sheriff sighed. "Deputy, remove the handcuffs."

Once Clarence freed me, I scratched at the bug bites around my waist. There were even welts lower in my pants. The other boys scratched too.

The sheriff pointed at us. "Clarence, do these boys look like vicious criminals?"

The shorter deputy stood speechless with slumped shoulders and shook his head.

The sheriff placed his hands on his hips. "So, Clarence, if a deputy arrested these kids for swimming on a hot summer day, their parents might think the sheriff's office was overzealous. Shoot, a mama might even think I'm needlessly picking on her little boy."

Clarence's shoulders slumped lower as he tilted his head. He resembled a scolded dog. I tried to hold still, but the itching made me wiggle.

Sheriff Jones pointed at me as his voice crescendoed. "I can hear his mother telling her friends the police should chase real criminals instead of harassing her little darling."

The boss paused and rubbed his forehead as if massaging a headache then spoke like a teacher to a student. "Clarence, do you want this boy's mother to criticize the sheriff's office to her neighbors and friends?"

"No, sir."

The sheriff's penetrating stare may have caused the deputy to burst into flames if he wasn't his nephew. "Good. I'm glad we had this little chat."

Then, the sheriff turned our direction and hooked his thumbs on his belt, while we boys reached into our pants and scratched. "What's wrong with you, ants in your pants?"

I reached down to my crotch. "Bug bites. I think something came from the birds."

He said, "When you get home, take a soapy bath and rub calamine lotion on those bites."

As I scratched under my waistband, I nodded.

Sheriff Jones stepped nearer. "Before you leave, I've got something to say."

While towering overhead and leaning forward, he was an imposing man. The sheriff's hat made him seem even taller. Intimidated by the black leather gun belt and a large pistol, I wilted. The matching black boots were the largest I'd ever seen. The patch above his pocket had the same name as his deputy, Jones. After sighing, he opened a pad and wrote each of our names and phone numbers.

"I've got their names," the deputy interrupted.

The sheriff ignored Clarence. Once he had our information, Sheriff Jones slipped the notepad in his back pocket and began his lecture. "Men, I've memorized your faces, so no swimming near the waterworks, do you understand?"

We responded in unison. "Yes, sir."

The sheriff placed his fists on his hips. "Since it's the first time we've met, I'm Mr. Nice Guy. But don't mistake kindness for weakness because I can drop on you like a ton of bricks. You'd best stay out of trouble."

If he intended to scare me, it worked.

"I'm going to call your parents and say you were swimming near the city intake tower. I'll explain my concern for your safety, but I'll let them handle it."

The sheriff turned and walked toward his car. *He's hard-boiled but a good egg.*

I whispered, "Dad will kill me."

Marshal added, "Me too."

When the sheriff made a U-turn and drove away, the deputy puffed up again. Butch said, "Here comes Officer Friendly."

I swallowed a giggle, but Einstein snickered then laughed as the inexperienced officer approached. It seemed to anger the deputy who glared at us. "I'll be watching you, boys."

Deputy Jones whirled around and stomped to his car. Then he rolled down the window and stared. "Remember, I'll be watching you."

As the officer's car rolled away, we said nothing, but fidgeted. Angel moaned as he reached elbow-deep into his pants and scratched. "Man, I told you we'd get caught."

Chapter 6

Downtown

In a few days, after our bug bites stopped itching, my brother and I rode our bikes downtown. We pedaled past hazy rows of soybeans sweating off the morning dew. A haze hovered over the rows of knee-high plants. Later, we passed fields of waist-high corn with long leaves chattering in the breeze. As rhythmic gusts blew across the plants, it resembled green ocean waves. In another month, the sturdy stalks would be taller than me. Marshal and I left the row crops behind as we neared the business district.

A few blocks before our town square, we stopped at the barbershop. The candy-cane colored pole spun outside, as men inside waited for their haircuts. Painted on the window was Ben's Barbershop. Ben had been my barber forever. A bell clanged as we entered.

Mature customers waited in chrome chairs with red vinyl upholstery. A sign on the wall stated Liar's Section—Only Two Lies, And One Fib Allowed Per Visit. Few obeyed the warning. Ben waved and greeted us as gossiping patrons ignored our entrance. "Hi, boys!"

We responded in unison as we took available seats amongst the talkative fellows. "Hello."

We sat without more comments. I was intimidated by the older men. The smoke from cigarettes, cigars, and pipes, fogged the room. Ben removed a hot towel from a reclining customer's face, then applied shaving cream with a brush. He lathered whiskers without a drop of soap in an eye. I loved the sound of him sharpening his straight razor with a rhythmic slapping on a leather strap.

As the lady departed with her sheared youngster, two men entered. Ben splashed aftershave on his client as he greeted the new arrivals. "Have a seat, and we'll be right with you."

I recognized them as the hole diggers at the lake. Mack, the tall one had a masculine physique. His flattop haircut and square jaw made his head resemble a box. His nose twisted off-center, a result of a fistfight, I assumed. He wore a T-shirt stretched around his chest, which made his slender waist look even smaller. *He must lift weights.* A few of the observant male customers tried to hold in their flabby bellies.

His shorter associate, Petey, had an average build and sported a red ball cap. He removed the lid and exposed jet-black hair, and I recognized him as the scuba diver. I hoped their glimpse of me at the park wasn't enough for them to remember me.

The larger one sat beside me, so I picked up a magazine and turned away to avoid eye contact. A feeble old man leaning on a cane examined the pair. "I don't recognize you. I've lived here my whole life, but I don't believe I know you. Are you visiting someone?"

The shorter stranger looked up. "We're just here for a few days, nothing important."

The genial interloper's name was Horace, and he often sat in the barbershop without getting a haircut. He was sloppy, not abnormal for old men, with a dab of egg yolk on his shirt. His face displayed a couple day's growth of stubble. Horace often deposited himself at Ben's and interjected himself, uninvited, into conversations. Most patrons tolerated his amiable interruptions with graciousness.

The senior citizen peered at the pair. "I'm the oldest resident with a sound mind in this town. I'd be glad to help if you have a question about our fine city."

Petey asked, "Did you say you've lived here your whole life?"

"That's right, born here in 1880."

Petey leaned forward. "So, do you remember before they enlarged the lake?"

"Shoot, yes. We needed more water, so the city built a dam across the river.

Petey said, "Someone told me there was once a park near the old lake. Is it underwater now?"

"Yep." Horace lit his tobacco. "The whole valley flooded after they built the dam."

He sucked the pipe and exhaled as he pondered. "Well, there's a tiny part above water. Eagles Roost was a high point. It's now an island near the water plant. You can still see it. Townspeople call it 'Dillinger's Island.'"

Petey leaned forward. "Dillinger's Island, why?"

Horace puffed on the pipe. "Rumor is John Dillinger buried a treasure there."

Petey scooted forward in his seat. "Did anyone ever look for it?"

"Sure, most of the town poked around there. Shoot, I even dug a few holes."

"So, no one found it?"

"Nope."

Ben removed the cape from his client, shook it, then laughed. "Dillinger's loot is a fable. You'd have a better chance of finding gold at the end of a rainbow." The barber brushed the clippings with a powdered brush.

Horace whispered, "I bet, it's real."

After Ben's client paid, the barber picked up the cape and waved it matador style. "Which long-haired soul will sit on my throne?"

I jumped into the chair and was soon caped and pumped higher. As he clipped and combed, Petey interviewed Horace. I couldn't hear much from the barber chair with Ben yapping in my ear.

Soon trimmed, we were on our way toward the city center. We pedaled past farmers in bib overalls who sat on benches outside the courthouse. The county built the buff, textured-stone building after the Civil War. A young attorney, Abraham Lincoln, represented clients in the old courthouse. They razed the wooden structure to make room for the masonry one.

We stopped to rest at the Civil War monument on a corner. Inscribed in stone was a quote by Abraham Lincoln, "A house divided against itself cannot stand. I believe this government cannot endure permanently half slave and half free."

Across the street, teenage boys leaned against their hotrods and discussed their modifications. The vehicles weren't much, but to a boy on a bike, they were incredible. I longed for the day I'd be old enough to drive.

The older teens ignored us as we pedaled past. As we passed a hamburger joint on the corner, the aroma made my mouth water. The little shack cooked the best burgers in town. Good Food Fast was the slogan on the sign at Snappy's. Hamburgers, fries, and chili was the entire menu, except for drinks.

We continued a few blocks off the square toward our grandfather's hardware store. On summer afternoons, he paid us to clean. After we parked our bikes, we rushed past the wooden Indian on the front stoop.

When I entered, I could smell urethane. Tongue-and-groove planks gleamed because each summer Grandpa Tip added a fresh coat of varnish to the floorboards.

Grandpa Tip had a white, paper bag full of hamburgers and fries sitting on a round table. He'd stopped at Snappy's to my delight. The thin burgers on toasted buns and shoestring potatoes were my favorite. "Boys, don't wait on me; dig into those burgers."

We removed the delectable treats from the bag. Grandpa Tip pulled colas from a machine. His body had become frailer in the last year, and the short trip across the room winded him. He dropped in a chair and rested a minute before he moved again. Then he brushed his snow-white hair back with his hand and reached for a burger.

Grandpa Tip's attire was classy. His usual dress was a long-sleeve, starched shirt with French cuffs. The cufflinks weren't expensive but matched his necktie pin. His wool pants were charcoal gray with cuffs. He didn't perspire, even in such warm clothes. When outside, he'd wear a dressy hat with a colorful hatband.

Sweat trickled from my chin. "It sure is hot."

"Yes, very," Grandpa Tip replied.

"Did you ever consider air conditioning the place?" I asked.

"Nope. It's been this way for thirty-four years. Besides, it's only hot in the summer."

Marshal wiped sweat from his forehead. "Grandpa Tip, would you have more business if the building weren't so hot? A lot of businesses are installing air conditioners these days. Times are changing, change with them."

"Well, boys, I may not keep the store open much longer. No sense spending a bunch of money on an A/C unit."

I stopped chewing on my burger. "Close it, why?"

"Yeah, why?" Marshal repeated.

"It's a simple answer. I'm getting old. My doctor said my ticker is wearing out."

"But you've always had the store," I said.

"It won't be the same," Marshal continued.

Grandpa Tips said, "I love the business, but everything ends."

We sipped our beverages which no longer seemed sweet.

I asked, "What'll happen to the wooden Indian out front?"

Grandpa Tip set down his hamburger. "Son, she's a special Indian. Her name is Liberty."

"Like the Statue of Liberty?" I interrupted.

Grandpa Tip took the opportunity during my interruption to draw on his cigar. "Yes, but this Miss Liberty wore a bonnet of feathers, not a crown."

He giggled when he saw my puzzled expression.

Marshal said, "Squaws don't wear war bonnets. Chief's headdresses had feathers."

"This one did," he said. "I've made many riddles for you and Marshal since you were small, and I even wrote one that involved the wooden Indian."

"Her?" I asked.

"Yep, but you aren't to solve it until after I'm gone."

"Gone where?" I asked.

He said, "Gone, like dead."

I frowned. "I don't want to think of you dying."

"Boys, everyone dies. It's part of living, so I'm prepared for it. In my will, I leave most everything to your father, but I left something for you two."

"What is it?" I asked.

Grandpa Tip grinned. "Well, I'll tell you this much, Jesus is the key to unlocking the puzzle. He 'll lead you to the Indian named Liberty."

"Jesus? What's He got to do with it?" I asked.

Grandpa Tip replied, "He helped me, once, and He'll help you."

Marshal cocked his head sideways like a puppy listening to a strange sound.

Our grandfather said, "He's the great finder of the lost."

He rose and hobbled toward the electric switch then turned on the ceiling fans which stirred the hot air. I loved lunchtime with Grandpa Tip even with the intense heat. Though cleaning the store afterward was less enjoyable. It made me feel grown-up to have a job.

After lunch, Marshal swept as I emptied stinky ashtrays. In 1967 many adults smoked cigarettes because they didn't know it was harmful to their health. Many men got the habit during World War II when soldiers got free cigarettes. At the time it was courteous to have ashtrays on hand for guests.

After I wiped the ashtrays, I dumped trash cans. While we worked, Grandpa Tip did paperwork in his office. He kept the door closed because he owned a pet rhesus monkey which he didn't keep in a cage. Grandpa Tip named him Babe after the famous home run hitter, Babe Ruth. Babe was feisty, so Grandpa Tip seldom allowed him out of the office.

He nicknamed the monkey Babe for a good reason. When Grandpa Tip shouted, "Batter up," the little monkey would swing a miniature bat at an imaginary ball. One of the few people allowed to play with Babe was Sparky.

Sparky was taller than average with a thin build and never-combed, gray-and-white hair. His short, salt-and-pepper beard matched the chin hairs of the monkey.

I hung a rag on a hook in the storeroom. "We're done,"

I washed my face and hands in the sink. The dust and sweat had formed a dirty, beaded necklace, so I wiped it with a wet towel. The water was a refreshing respite from the heat. When I placed a damp cloth on the back of my neck for a few moments, Marshal shoved me aside with his hip. "Move it, give me a chance."

I dropped on a chair and awaited Grandpa Tip to pay us. We called him Grandpa Tip because we had two grandfathers and Tip was his nickname. Grandpa Tip emerged from his office and leaned against a chair to steady himself.

"You okay?" I asked.

Without answering, he continued his unsteady gait toward us. He laid cash on the table then dropped onto a chair. "How long will the money last?"

"Not long, I suppose," Marshal answered.

"I bet it'd be nice to have more than I could spend," I added.

Grandpa Tip replied, "Money doesn't buy happiness."

I said, "I'd be willing to try."

He leaned forward and tapped the table with his index finger. "Listen, boys, money can make you happy, but it can also cause misery."

Marshal and I politely smiled and nodded. Grandpa Tip pulled a paper from his pocket and laid it on the table. "So, I've got a riddle for you to solve."

He was a prolific writer of riddles. We'd taken part in many of his treasure hunts.

"Is this a hard one?" Marshal asked.

I leaned over to read the note. He'd scribbled the following words:

> A cowboy on a stallion white,
> This afternoon, gunmen he'll fight.
> On the main street, they'll meet at noon,
> After previews and a cartoon.
> You pay admission to view
> The grand adventure awaiting you.
> The prize awaits beneath the eagle.
> Two passes for the picture Regal.

Marshal shot up and slapped the table. "That's easy, reviews, cartoons, cowboys. It's a movie!"

"At the Regal Theater!" I added.

Our grandfather chuckled.

I jumped up. "The prize is admission tickets."

Marshal continued, "They're under the eagle."

We rushed to the office door but stopped. "Is it Okay?"

Grandpa Tip nodded his approval for us to enter. "Careful, don't let Babe escape."

Marshal peeked inside then hurried with Grandpa Tip and me close behind him. Babe sat on the windowsill watching people pass outside. The black-and-white bird sat on a waist-high safe beside stacks of papers and ledgers.

Our grandfather once tried to keep his office tidy but gave up after he bought Babe. The monkey hated neatness, so Grandpa Tip was always picking up after the creature. In time they seemed to agree on an acceptable amount of dishevel for their mutual comfort. Then, there was peace. Marshal tilted the heavy eagle as I pulled on the tickets.

"Thanks," I said

Marshal hugged Grandpa Tip. "You're the best!"

Grandpa Tip grinned then adjusted the figurine to its original position.

I asked, "You're particular with the eagle, where did you get it?"

Grandpa Tip dusted it with his handkerchief. He stuffed the hankie back in his pocket as he admired the bird. "It was a gift from a friend. It has a lot of value to me."

"Sentimental value, maybe," Marshal whispered.

"Is it concrete?" I asked.

"No, solid metal. I painted the bird myself, or I should say, I repainted it since it was black when I got it."

Its body was black, and he painted the neck and head white. The yellow beak wasn't the right color, and the eyes didn't match. His pinpoint-pupils appeared crossed.

Grandpa Tip said, "Someday, this will be your father's."

I forced a smile, but I doubted Dad wanted it. The junkyard purchased metal. I doubted Mom would want the cross-eyed bird in her house. A pendant on a gold chain hung from the eagle's neck.

"What's the medallion?" I asked.

Grandpa Tip lifted it from the statue and admired it. "A St. Christopher medal."

He placed it in my hand, and I read the inscription on the back, "To Tip from Jackrabbit."

"Who's Jackrabbit?" I asked.

"Someone I knew when I was young."

Someone inscribed, "What Goes Around, Comes Around," in smaller print on the perimeter.

"What does it mean?" I asked.

Grandpa Tip said, "It means whatever you do, it comes back to you. It's a law of the universe."

I nodded but didn't understand. "Why don't you keep the medallion in the safe?"

Grandpa Tip patted the steel box. "I don't want to keep it in Ole Linclas. I keep it out to admire it."

"Linclas?" Marshal asked.

"It's my nickname for my safe." Grandpa Tip grinned as if he was giving us another riddle.

Marshal said, "It's a funny nickname. How d'you name it?"

Grandpa Tip sat down.

"Will this take long? We have a movie, you know," Marshal whined.

Grandpa Tip loved to tell stories, but we didn't have time for a long one. Driven to brevity, he turned toward the safe. "This safe has been in Charleston since before the Civil War. Once a staunch Democrat owned it. Thirty years later, a dedicated Republican had it for his business. These days, I put the cash inside at the close of business, and the bills come from Republicans and Democrats, alike."

"So, I still don't know how it got its nickname," I said.

Grandpa Tip pointed to an artist's pencil sketch on the wall behind his desk. "It's Abraham Lincoln and Stephen A. Douglas at the debate. A Republican and a Democrat met in Charleston and made history together. They were quite a combination, so I call it Linclas."

Grandpa Tip grinned.

"That's it?" I asked.

"It's Lincoln's and Douglas' names combined, but there's a more important combination I want to explain to you."

Marshal glanced at his watch. "The movie will start soon."

"We should go," I replied.

I handed the medallion back to Grandpa Tip. "Okay, we'll finish this after the matinee."

We darted out the door and ran toward the theater across the square.

"Is everything a riddle with him?" Marshal asked.

"He'll explain it later," I replied.

I noticed Pete, Mack, and a large woman conversed with men on a bench outside of the courthouse.

"What do you suppose they're doing?" Marshal asked.

"Still snooping around town."

More nosey than cautious, and hoping to eavesdrop on the conversation, I crossed the street. My brother followed. As casual as possible, we approached as Petey questioned an old man seated and leaning on a crutch. Upon arrival, I saw the senior citizen was missing a leg.

Petey asked, "So, do you believe the Dillinger's treasure rumor?"

The one-legged man crossed his stump over his knee. "I saw the Dillinger gang at Lakeside Park on a Sunday afternoon when I was younger. So, I suppose he could have hidden the money."

"Are you sure it was Dillinger?" the woman interrupted.

"I wasn't then. I was playing baseball when a Studebaker drove past us. We didn't see big cars often, so we stopped playing to check it out."

"What makes you think it was John Dillinger?" she asked.

"The men inside were strangers, and it had Indiana plates."

"That's not so convincing," she replied.

The one-legged man said, "I heard rumors the next week that Dillinger had spent the night in the park. Then, I read in the newspaper, he'd robbed a bank in Greencastle, Indiana. They got away in a black, four-door, Studebaker Commander, like the one I'd seen."

"It could have been them, Marge," said Petey.

She spat brown tobacco juice on the sidewalk then wiped the drool from her chin. "Do you think he hid the loot around here?"

"The FBI seemed to think so. Agents from Chicago showed up a few weeks later and searched the park."

"How d'you know it was the FBI?" she asked.

The one-legged man adjusted on the bench. "They requested help from the local authorities. A blabber-mouthed deputy leaked it to the press, and the next day, a hundred men with shovels dug holes everywhere."

Another old man in jeans with rolled-up cuffs leaned forward. "They found nothing. The park had more pits than a battlefield. I hadn't seen so many foxholes since the war."

I noticed a man standing behind the bench who was a silent observer. I elbowed Marshal and whispered, "Hey, that's the fisherman from the lake."

The one-legged man said, "I told an agent what I saw. He didn't confirm or deny if it was John Dillinger and his men. But, if he hid the loot, it wasn't in the park. Otherwise, someone would have found it."

"Maybe someone did," the man in rolled-up jeans responded.

"What do you mean?" Marge asked.

"The federal men appeared interested in a new resident who came from Greencastle."

"Is that so?"

"Yep. quite a coincidence, huh?"

"Maybe not," Marge surmised. "Where can I find this man from Greencastle?"

The man with rolled-up jeans pointed. "Couple blocks that way. He owns Tip's Hardware."

Marge's smile showed her tobacco-stained teeth.

Marshal poked me and whispered, "The movie begins in ten minutes."

"Shouldn't we warn Grandpa Tip?" I asked.

Marshal replied, "Naw, he can deal with those treasure hunters. C'mon, or we'll miss the cartoons before the show."

As I entered the theater, the air conditioning chilled my arms. The previews of coming attractions were on the screen as I dropped in my seat. For the next two hours, John Wayne shot black-hatted outlaws while we devoured buttered popcorn.

As we exited the theater, it felt like an oven. So, we walked to the Rexall drug store for a milkshake in air-conditioned comfort. We lifted ourselves onto the red vinyl stools at the bar. A lady in a pink waitress outfit adjusted her white cap.

I said, "Two chocolate shakes."

She didn't respond until her cap satisfied her. "Two shakes on the way."

She reached for heavy glasses then halted. She turned and stared at me with an odd expression. Without preparing our drinks, she slipped to the pharmacy and returned with a man in a lab coat.

The pharmacist asked, "Are you Tip's grandsons?"

We both nodded. The druggist cleared his throat and wavered, as the waitress covered her mouth and watched with agonizing eyes. "Boys…."

He hesitated, again, and placed a hand on each of our shoulders. "Boys, something happened at Tip's Hardware."

He glanced toward the lady who shook her head without speaking.

He said, "It's your grandfather. I think you should call home."

We leaped from our seats and bolted toward the entrance.

"Wait a minute," the pharmacist shouted.

We ignored him and hurried through the aisles. We ran past the shoppers on the sidewalk and rushed past Snappy's. Parked outside of the hardware store were two police cars, and a deputy stood on the stoop next to the wooden statue. We rushed past him.

"Hey!" he shouted.

We dodged an officer who was interrogating a customer and rushed into the office. Babe stood on a filing cabinet in the far corner. He was shrieking and swinging his miniature baseball bat as two officers argued how best to subdue him. Clarence sat in a chair holding a handkerchief to his bloody forehead.

I asked, "Where's Grandpa Tip?"

Sheriff Jones spun our direction with a shocked expression. "How'd they get in here?"

His eyes darted behind the desk. I followed his gaze and saw Grandpa Tip on the floor with his head next to the safe.

"Grandpa Tip!" I shrieked.

When I rushed to him, he didn't move, even after I shook him. "Grandpa Tip, wake up, get off of the floor!"

Our attempts to revive him were to no avail as the chaotic room became quiet. Even Babe halted his ear-piercing shrieks to watch. The sheriff's heavy-hearted expression answered my silent question before he spoke. "He's dead. I'm sorry."

My eyes filled with tears as I rose. "How?"

No one spoke as the sheriff removed a handkerchief from his pocket and handed it to me. A deputy did the same for Marshal.

Sheriff Jones said, "It's possible the monkey went berserk and hit him on the head. He's got a cut on his scalp so it could be from the bat."

"Babe wouldn't have hurt Tip," said Sparky.

What's he doing here?

The monkey jumped from the cabinet, ran across the room, and leaped into Marshal's arms. He shivered as Marshal calmed him.

Sparky said, "See he's just scared and upset."

The sheriff pointed to the unkempt man and said, "Sparky found him."

A deputy entered with a sheet and covered the body while the senior officers nudged us out of the office.

Sparky followed us. "Babe wouldn't have hurt Tip."

Clarence held a bloody handkerchief up and tilted his bleeding head forward to display his wound. "Look, he's vicious."

Sparky responded, "Can't you see he's upset. Something happened here. He must have seen it."

Sheriff Jones said, "Nothing appears to be missing. His billfold was in his pocket."

Marshal said, "But he was lying in front of the safe. Did someone try to get him to open it?"

The sheriff asked, "Do you know what's in the safe?"

Marshal shook his head. "No."

I said, "I don't know if anyone besides Grandpa Tip knew the combination."

The sheriff rubbed his chin as he contemplated the clues. "As I said before, his billfold is here, so it's most likely not a robbery."

Sheriff Jones asked, "Are you aware of anyone who might want to hurt your grandfather?"

I shook my head. Dr. Morton, the coroner, exited the office and motioned for the sheriff. They turned their backs as the coroner whispered, but I could still hear him. "He has a bump on his scalp with a minor cut. The monkey could have struck him, but more likely, he hit his head when he fell. My opinion, he died of cardiac infarction."

The sheriff squinted his eyes.

"A sudden heart attack," the coroner explained.

"Oh."

I stepped toward the coroner. "He was unstable. He could have fallen."

Marshal wiped his wet cheek. "Grandpa Tip fell sometimes."

Sparky nodded.

"It could be an accident, but more likely a coronary. It's what I'll put in my report," said the coroner.

Chapter 7

The Riddle

We didn't return to the store for several weeks after our grandfather's death. In time, we had to clean it because Dad planned to sell the contents and the building. I dreaded the somber task.

But, on a Saturday morning, Dad drove us downtown. I stood beside the wooden Indian as my father unlocked the deadbolt. I propped the door open as my father walked across the store to a closet. Inside was an electrical panel with a large handle on the side. When Dad lifted the lever upward, I heard a loud click when the contacts snapped, and I could smell a whiff of ozone, electrified oxygen.

Marshal flipped a switch, and the lights came on. Slow ceiling fans began a lazy twirl which stirred the dusty odor. Dad pushed up on steel rods to open the six transoms above the plate-glass windows. Though closed only a few weeks, the dust had already settled on everything.

"A man is coming to make an offer on the contents," Dad explained. "Today, I want you boys to clean the cellar. First, bring all the boxes up and stack them here."

He pointed to a large oak table.

Marshal said, "Boy-o-boy...."

"... it's hot," I completed his thought.

"It'll get hotter, so let's hurry and finish this morning," Dad replied.

Dad turned and stepped toward the office. He said, "I'll clean out the desk."

Our father paused at the door. "Throw nothing away until I scrutinize it."

He entered the office as we headed toward the basement stairs. The temperature dropped with each step downward.

61

"I'm glad to be working down here," Marshal commented.

"Yeah, but it's hard to see."

Two light bulbs hung from cords. The first box I opened contained Christmas lights, and the next had ornaments. Good for us, Grandpa Tip had installed a small freight elevator, so I loaded the items and rode the lift upstairs. We had to press and hold the button for it to run without stopping, but it was better than carrying everything up the narrow stairs.

After placing the stuff on a table, I went back to the basement to help Marshal pack more. We repeated the trips for hours.

After bringing a load upstairs, we dropped onto wooden chairs and rested. My father was still at Grandpa Tip's desk. I walked to the office to get further instructions and leaned on the door frame. Dad was flipping through a photo album and smiling. He wiped his eyes with his handkerchief as he flipped the pages. When he saw me at the door, he motioned for me to join him. "See what I found? It's an old photo album."

Dad pointed at a snapshot. "This is your grandmother, my mother."

She wore a dress and sat in a rocking chair.

Dad said, "When they took this picture, women wore dresses and open-toed leather shoes every day. Grandma was snapping beans from the garden. She was sitting on the cool porch."

He flipped the page. "Here's my father in his World War One uniform."

Several pictures were of Grandpa Tip with soldier buddies who were leaning on each other. They looked drunk.

Dad said, "This was most likely taken in France while they were on leave."

The next page had a picture of Dad as a child. In another shot, he was standing next to his younger sister. Both children were wearing bib overalls and were barefoot. Next was a photo of my father in his Navy uniform beside his sister again. He was a grown-up and was handsome, and she was pretty in her dress with white socks. Dad flipped the page.

"Wait! They took these pictures when I was a boy. We were at a picnic at the lake. The man beside Grandpa was John Dillinger. I didn't know it then, but he was a bank robber from Indiana."

I leaned closer for a better view. Dad stretched back, brushed his hair with his hand, and said. "I didn't know we had these photos."

In one image, Dad, as a boy, was sitting on a stack of bags with John Dillinger and a few others. All the men were smiling, and Dillinger was messing up Dad's hair. Grandpa Tip was much younger, and I didn't recognize the others.

"Hello!"

We swiveled our heads toward the voice which came from the front entrance.

Marshal answered, "We're closed."

The man shouted, "Abe?"

Dad stood and answered, "Yes."

Two strangers entered and introduced themselves with outstretched palms and friendly smiles.

"I'm Bill, with Family Hardware."

My father shook his hand.

Dad said, "We spoke on the phone. Look around."

Dad pointed to us. "These are my sons, Marshal and Patton."

Dad said, "Marshal, show Bill the inventory."

Bill opened a pad and pulled a pencil from his pocket. While he counted, Marshal returned to the office while the other stranger introduced himself.

"Hello, I'm Robert Richardson with the newspaper."

Dad shook his hand. Robert smiled and tipped his hat to my brother and me. "Boys."

We nodded our recognition of his greeting.

Robert said, "This store has been a stable business for many years, and the community respected your father as a businessman and a philanthropist."

Dad replied, "Thank you."

The man continued, "As a tribute, I'd like to write an article about him and this store. It would make an interesting public interest piece. Would it be okay with you?"

Dad answered, "Sure."

"Good."

Dad said, "It's fortunate, I just found photographs which may interest you."

He sat and scooted the chair to the side as he motioned for Robert to look at the scrapbook. "How about a photo of my father with John Dillinger?"

"What!?" the reporter exclaimed.

Dad grinned. "Yep!"

"John Dillinger, the bank robber?"

Dad nodded. "He was my father's cousin. I was about ten when John came to visit. He camped at what was then Lakeside Park, and we had a picnic. It's underwater, now. All my family was there, and Dillinger had friends with him who were strangers to me."

Marshal interrupted, "I didn't know John Dillinger was Grandpa Tip's cousin."

Dad replied, "He's not a relative we're proud to claim."

"How cool," I interjected.

Dad peeled the photos from the scrapbook and handed them one at a time to Robert.

Robert said, "Not many photographs of John Dillinger exist, but these photos resemble him. Can I take these to have them authenticated?"

"Sure, but I want them back."

"Of course."

Robert flipped through the photos. He examined one longer than the others. "Who is this?"

Dad leaned forward. "It's me with my father, Tip," Dad pointed. "That's Dillinger, but I don't recognize the other men."

"You met John Dillinger?" Robert asked.

Dad nodded. Robert stared at my father, then returned his gaze to the photo. "Holy smokes, it's the Dillinger gang!"

Dad asked, "You think so?"

"I'm not aware of a photograph of the whole gang together, but I bet it's them."

The amazed reporter shook his head. "These are worth a fortune."

The reporter leaned closer to the pictures. "What's in the bags you're sitting on, Abe?"

Dad took the photo and stared. "I don't know, but they look like flour or sugar bags, but why would they be at the park?"

Dad handed the snapshot back to Robert, who studied it awhile. Then, Dad gave him another picture. In this one, Dillinger and Tip were both standing by the driver's side of a car, and each man was holding a large coin. Someone wrote, "Hettie" on the border of the photograph.

Dad handed him another photo. It was a closeup shot of the coin with the word "Hettie" scribbled along the edge. The reporter reached into his jacket pocket and removed a magnifying glass. "Reporters are investigators," said Robert.

He examined the photo with the lens for a while, and under his breath, mumbled to himself. "Hmm, Hettie."

The reporter tilted the picture and moved the magnifying glass in and out.

Dad stared at the ceiling as he concentrated. He repeated, "Hettie, Hettie."

His eyes lit up, and he snapped his fingers. "I've got it. Follow me."

We followed him out the open entry door to the wooden statue. Dad said, "Look, the coin resembles this Indian!"

He handed the photo to the reporter who compared the faces. Mr. Richardson scratched his scalp. "I'm not so sure."

Dad said, "Grandpa Tip called this Indian Hettie, which I thought was a dumb name for a squaw."

"Why is she wearing a chief's warbonnet?" I asked.

Robert asked, "So, is there a connection between this wooden squaw and the Indian head coin?"

"Yes," Dad said.

Dad turned the statue around and pointed to the back of the headdress. Someone had burned the word "Hettie" in small letters. "There must be a relationship."

As we conversed, Bill exited the store. "Abe, I've got a good start. I'll come back later with a helper."

"Sounds good."

Bill continued, "So you're admiring my grandfather's work."

"What?" Dad asked.

"My grandfather carved the wooden statue for Tip," Bill answered.

"Really?"

"Yes, sir. He was an art teacher at the college, and for extra money, he made these chief statues. They were popular."

"I didn't know," Dad replied.

"My Grandfather didn't care for this one because Tip wanted it to have a woman's face."

Bill rubbed the arm of the statue then shook my father's hand.

"Well, goodbye, I've got to go. I'll get back to you, Abe."

Dad turned his attention back to Robert, who was still comparing the wooden Indian to the picture of the coin.

Dad said, "We may never know the connection. Grandpa Tip was secretive. He didn't talk much about Dillinger and never told me he had photos."

Robert put the pictures in his sport jacket pocket. "I'll research these. I'm also interested in why Dillinger had those coins."

Then Robert changed the topic. "This has been an unexpected twist to the story, but I'd still like to interview you about the hardware store and Tip."

"Sure."

"It's my understanding your father's store was once the city jail."

"Yes, that's right."

"Any remnants of the old jail exist?"

"Yes, there's a cell door with steel bars in the basement. Also, there's a tunnel between the old jail and the courthouse several blocks away. Deputies once escorted prisoners underground."

I was surprised.

Robert raised his eyebrows. "No kidding, is it still there?"

"Yes, unless it collapsed," Dad answered.

"Any construction overhead that would have destroyed it?" the reporter asked.

"No, I don't think so."

Dad placed his hands in his rear pockets and leaned back a little. "I was only in it once. They made the arched tunnel of brick, and it was dark and damp. When I reached the other end, I found a locked door. After I exited, my father locked it and place a large cabinet in front of the door. He told me to stay out."

"Wow!" exclaimed Marshal. "You never told us Grandpa Tip's store was the old city jail, or there was a passage under the town square!"

Dad declared, "It's locked for a good reason. The tunnel is dangerous."

Robert took photographs as Dad gave him the tour, and we followed. The reporter said, "Boys, let me get a picture of you two standing behind the bars."

We stood inside the cell and imitated pitiful convicts.

After the reporter left, Dad instructed us to continue cleaning the basement. Then, he went on an errand. We emptied the tall cabinet which contained old paint cans and cleaning supplies. After we cleared it out, we tried to move it, but it was too heavy.

We gave up and took the contents upstairs via the freight elevator. Once done, we carried empty cardboard boxes back to the basement where Grandpa Tip had stacked hundreds of shop towels on wooden shelves. He never threw the old ones away. He'd just put them in the basement when they got worn. We loaded several boxes then stopped to rest. We sat and surveyed the room.

An aging Franklin stove was in a corner—a remnant of the jail-house days. A furnace stood nearby next to a coal-oil tank. Protruding from the tank was a spigot. I turned the valve, and coal-oil dripped out.

"Still has fuel in it," I said.

Marshal replied, "Well, leave it alone. You've got it stinking in here."

I returned to work. While loading towels into a box, I discovered a gallon-sized glass jar with a metal lid. "What's this?"

Marshal asked, "Pickled eggs?"

Grandpa Tip always had a jar of pickled eggs on the sales counter, so maybe this was excess inventory. I studied the container, but it wasn't food. "No, something else."

I carried it closer to the light. "Firecrackers! It's where Grandpa Tip kept his fireworks."

Marshal rushed to my side. Our grandfather loved fireworks on Independence Day. He'd pitch firecrackers under the chairs of unsuspecting patrons. As people became more familiar with his antics, he developed more devious schemes.

One year he dipped a string in wax and made a long fuse which he tied to a bundle of firecrackers. He taped the pack with its winding fuse under a chair and lit it. It took half an hour for it to explode. By then, an unsuspecting man had occupied the stool. The entire store erupted in laughter when the rapid series of explosions caused the flailing patron to flee. I stuffed a few packs in each of my pockets. "I'm taking some."

Marshal put some in his pockets too. "Get the string, too."

When I returned the jar, I found two cardboard tubes. "What's this?"

When I removed the metal cap from the end and tilted it, a roll of glossy paper slipped into my hand. Once unfurled, I admired the picture above the dates, which was a scene of a grist mill on a babbling creek. Below the image, in bold letters, was the date 1954. Imprinted further down were the words Tip's Hardware.

"It's an old calendar. Grandpa Tip must have given these out for advertisement."

Marshal said, "It was the year we were born."

I pulled another tube from the shelf and removed the metal cap. "This one has something written on it."

"What?"

I read the text out loud. "It says Patton and Marshal's Great Adventure." I looked up. "Grandpa Tip said he was working on a new treasure hunt."

I tipped the tube, and something slipped out and clanged at our feet. Marshal jumped backward.

"What's is it?" I asked.

Marshal bent and picked up a skeleton key. It was about eight inches long and made of black steel. It was the kind I'd seen in the movies for prison doors. "Could this lock the cell door?"

Without answering, Marshal ran into the open cell and pushed the key into the lock. It turned but seized, so he reversed the key and pulled it out.

"It might help to lubricate the tumbler," I suggested.

He ran to the coal-oil tank, opened the spigot, and allowed a small amount of kerosene to rinse the key. Then he inserted it in the lock, and this time it moved further. He rotated the key, and with each turn, it became easier.

"It's working better," he said as he locked then unlocked the tumbler.

We looked at each other and grinned.

"Do you think it fits the tunnel door too?" I asked.

"Maybe, but the cabinet is in the way, and it's too big to move. We'll need help."

I replied, "Let's get someone and come back."

"Okay, I'll put the key back in the tube."

68

When Marshal looked inside the cardboard cylinder, he wrinkled his brow. "Something else is in there."

When he tilted and shook it, a roll of paper slid out a bit. He pulled it from the container. It was a newspaper with a string tied in a bow. Marshal released the string and removed the newspaper wrapper. Inside there was a roll of thick paper. I unfurled it to find a portrait of Jesus.

I cried, "Grandpa Tip said, 'Jesus is the key to the puzzle.' This must be the riddle!"

I held the picture toward the light and examined it.

Marshal said, "There's writing on it!"

Someone had scribbled an inscription. I read it aloud, "To the Best Cousin Ever. I Trust You with My Treasure—John Dillinger."

Our eyes met, and together we announced, "John Dillinger's treasure!"

I held the picture higher.

Marshal shouted, "Look, there's more writing on the back."

When I flipped it over, the ink and penmanship differed from the Dillinger signature. I tried to hold it steady as Marshal read,

"Oh, Liberty, created by a saint,

Your name emblazed on your headband!
Roosevelt giveth and Roosevelt taketh away.
A Squaw with a feathered head,
And the tail of an eagle.

"Your halo has thirteen stars, and
Your belt once forty-six, now forty-eight.
The belt surrounds your golden glory.
The eagle watches your back
Bearing arrows for war and an olive branch for peace,
It announces, 'In God We Trust.'

"Born in the city of Brotherly Love,
Resembling Hettie.
Like Moses, hidden from destruction
And saved."

"What do you suppose it means?" I asked.

"It could be a code. I think the handwriting is Grandpa Tip's."

Since our earliest memories, our grandfather had written riddles. He'd hide candy and make us solve challenging clues to find it. As we grew older, he made the riddles more difficult. We'd become adept at solving his mysteries, but this appeared to be the hardest yet. After examining the document, we heard footsteps upstairs.

I said, "Don't tell Dad about the riddle, yet."

He nodded his agreement as he returned the picture to the tube. We stacked boxes on the freight elevator then went upstairs.

"That's half of the towels," Marshal said.

"We'll get the rest later," I added.

Once upstairs, we placed the cartons on a table. Dad sat at a desk in the office. "You boys are getting filthy. It looks like you've been in a coal bin."

He wiped sweat from his forehead with his blue, paisley handkerchief. "We're all dirty and tired, and it's late, so let's head home. Your mother will have dinner ready soon, so we'll clean more another day."

With no argument from us, we rushed outside, and Dad followed. As our father locked the front door, I examined the wooden squaw and realized her name, Hettie, was in Grandpa Tip's riddle. I'd solved the first part of the mystery.

I whispered to Marshal. "It said the treasure resembles the wooden Indian."

"What?" Dad asked.

"Oh, nothing."

After our baths and meal, we retreated to our room to discuss the riddle.

"Marshal, I wonder if our Indian, Hettie, has something to do with the mystery. Grandpa Tip said Liberty resembled Hettie."

Marshal asked, "Who would name a treasure Liberty, and why does she resemble a wooden Indian? Also, why does she have a halo?"

For a moment, I considered his questions.

I said, "She has a halo of thirteen stars. Could it be a constellation like the big dipper?"

Marshal lay on his bed with his hands behind his head. "What has thirteen stars?"

I slapped my knee. "I've got it. The first American flag. One star for each colony."

Later in bed, questions bounced inside my head. Sleep overtook me as I pondered the stars on the halo and the belt.

Chapter 8

The Numismatist

A week later, the article appeared in the evening newspaper. The two-page spread appeared on the second and third pages. The reporter focused on the Dillinger gang and printed large pictures of them posing with my grandfather and my ten-year-old father. He said we discovered photographs of a criminal group. Robert had researched the outlaws and identified Dillinger's accomplices as Pete Pierpont, Fat Charles Makley, and Harry Copeland. Copeland was the sole member convicted of robbing the Greencastle bank. Police had killed or executed the other members for previous crimes.

There was a picture of Dillinger holding the coin and an enlarged shot of the gold piece. Robert reported that the government called the twenty-dollar currency the Indian head double-eagle. A photo showed the "head" side with the Indian wearing a warbonnet, and the article explained the reverse side displayed an eagle.

The third page told how the hardware store had once been the city jail. It contained present-day photos along with one during the Civil War. The picture of Marshal and me behind bars made us laugh. Dad smoothed the newspaper on the kitchen table, and we all leaned forward.

After he read it aloud twice, our parents retired to the living room.. I concentrated on the coin since I'd only seen the original photographs for a moment.

"Count the stars," Marshal said. "There are thirteen."

I responded. "Look at the headband! It has letters on it. L-I-B-E-R-T-Y spells Liberty!"

"Like in the riddle," Marshal replied.

"Marshal, there's a connection between the coin and the riddle. Seems if we get more information about the gold piece, we could solve the mystery and find the treasure."

"Let's ask Pappy." Marshal said.

"Yeah, he might know."

Pappy was a coin collector in our neighborhood. We pedaled our bikes a few blocks to Pappy's house and found him sitting on his front porch. As we approached, he lowered his newspaper and gazed over his reading glasses.

"Well, they let you out of jail."

"So, you saw our picture," Marshal replied.

Pappy lifted the newspaper from his lap so we could see it.

"Yep, got it right here, and it's quite an article. I see your grandfather was John Dillinger's cousin."

"Yes, sir," I answered. "What about the coin?"

Pappy removed his spectacles and slipped them into his shirt pocket. "It's the most intriguing photo of the bunch."

"The government minted the coin in the first part of the twentieth century. Teddy Roosevelt ordered the design, and later, President Franklin Roosevelt destroyed it."

"Destroyed it, why?" Marshal asked.

Pappy shifted in his chair. "Franklin Roosevelt was the president, and we were in a financial depression. Frightened people were hoarding gold, and even sneaking it out of the country, but Roosevelt believed we needed money in circulation. So, in March 1933, he ordered it surrendered to the government."

I asked, "Did they destroy all the gold coins?"

"Yep, except for rare collectibles and collections. Otherwise, a citizen could keep only a hundred dollars' worth. The government melted it and sent the bars to Fort Knox.

Pappy stood and motioned for us to follow him inside his house.

IIis barking beagle greeted us. "Hush, dog, these boys won't bother you."

We followed him into his living room, where he had stacks of coins, proof sets, and numismatist books. His sizeable wooden desk sat below the picture window, providing a resting place for two cats.

Content and basking in the sunlight, the cats ignored us as they lounged in various locations. Three were on the floor, and one was on a plastic-covered

73

couch next to a stack of magazines. Another was on top of a bookshelf, and I wondered how many pets lurked in the shadows.

I asked, "How many cats do you own, Pappy?"

"You don't own cats, they own you."

He didn't seem to want to answer the question, so I dropped it. After moving a cat from a shelf, he removed a book, and we followed him into his dining room. Coins he'd been cleaning covered the table.

His wife worked in the adjacent kitchen. She offered us sweet tea, which we accepted. Pappy made space on the table as his wife sat the drinks on coasters.

He put on his reading glasses, flipped through the book, and stopped at the section about the Indian Head coin. He studied the page. "*Hmm*, it says here they named the twenty-dollar, gold coin the Indian Head double-eagle. They minted a ten-dollar gold piece too. Teddy Roosevelt commissioned an artist named Saint-Gaudens to come up with an image."

I recognized the clue at once, and Marshal's expression indicated he did too. Together we said, "Saint."

Pappy ignored us as we nodded at each other. He continued, "Saint-Gaudens was a famous sculptor and used Hettie Anderson as his model for Liberty on the face of the coin."

"Hettie!" my brother exclaimed.

I smiled. By now, we were standing as Pappy read. The expert paused and gazed at us over the top of his reading glasses.

"Go on," I urged.

He continued, "Teddy Roosevelt insisted the designer place an Indian war bonnet on Lady Liberty to make her an authentic American. Most everyone at the mint thought his instructions were ridiculous."

Pappy laid the book on the table and pointed at a color photograph of the coin. It was our first good view.

I said, "Look, you can see the stars better in this picture. There are thirteen."

Pappy said, "It also has stars on the edge which is unique. They had forty-six stars when first minted, but they added two more when Arizona and New Mexico became states.

"The belt!" Marshal exclaimed. "It's the edge of the coin!"

I add, "Forty-six, now forty-eight, like in the riddle."

Pappy looked at me with a questioning expression. "What riddle?"

"Never mind. It's not important." I responded.

"What else does the book say?" Marshal asked.

"Oh, yes. You'll notice the coin in this picture doesn't have a mint stamp. If minted at Denver, it would have a letter D, and if made in San Francisco, a letter S. Since it lacks a mark, it's a Philadelphia coin."

He removed his glasses. "Boys, I grew up in Philadelphia. Would you like to learn something interesting about the city?"

We both nodded.

"William Penn named the city after he immigrated to America. He got Philadelphia from two Greek words. Philos means love, and adelphos is the word for brother."

Marshal and I smiled because we solved another part of the riddle. It seemed Grandpa Tip was describing the Indian head gold coin. His puzzle stated it came from the "city of brotherly love."

"Tell us about the reverse side," I requested.

Pappy ran his finger under a picture of the "tails" side of the coin. "An eagle is standing on a bundle of arrows and holding an olive branch. Stamped beside are the words IN GOD WE TRUST."

All the clues were there. Grandpa Tip had described the Saint-Gaudens Indian Head gold piece. Pappy picked up the newspaper and opened it. He put it on the table, and he pointed at the photo of my father as a little boy sitting on the bags.

Pappy asked, "Do you see those sacks?"

We leaned forward to get a better view.

"If you look closer, you can see the letters U.S. printed on one. Those appear to be from the United States Mint."

"Are you positive?" I asked.

"Can you boys keep a secret?"

We nodded.

"For safety's sake, don't tell anyone."

"Okay," Marshal replied.

"Let me show you what I mean."

Pappy rose from his seat. He walked to the basement door, stopped, and turned. "It's something few people have seen."

"Are you sure?" his wife asked.

Pappy nodded and winked. "It'll be fine."

His wife hesitated, then nodded her approval. He opened the door and started down the steps, so we followed. Once at the bottom, he flipped the light switch. He'd stacked more white canvas bags than I could count onto skids. Pappy had piled them six high along narrow paths. All had U.S. Mint printed on them.

"These are United States coins," he explained.

My jaw dropped as did Marshal's. Pappy weaved down the aisle to the center of the room, pointing as he went.

"I've got pennies, nickels, dimes, and quarters, in the original bags. I've been collecting them all my life."

In amazement I scanned the room. "Why do you collect full bags?"

"I know it's silly, but I've always loved coins. I worked at a bank when I was young, so when the government released a new coin, I just bought a bag."

"Why new coins?" I asked.

"All coins were once common, even the rare ones. So, I figured, why not collect new ones and one day they might be worth something?"

"Are any of them valuable?" Marshal asked.

He chuckled. "Well, yes. I have pennies now worth two cents, so I've already doubled my money."

I said, "I guess you have a point."

He continued, "One thing about it, robbery is unlikely. It'd take a week to carry these out of here."

Then he placed his hands in his pockets and appeared solemn. "So, I wonder why Dillinger had four bags in the picture. Your father was sitting on U.S. Mint bags, but Dillinger was holding a twenty-dollar gold piece. Those didn't come in large sacks; they came in small boxes."

Pappy sat on a stack. "I'm certain Dillinger didn't steal pennies, nickels or dimes. He wouldn't even have taken quarters. Could those bags have been full of gold coins?"

Pappy stood and proceeded to a corner room and unlocked a steel door. A workbench and a safe were the few furnishings. He turned the combination lock, pulled down on the handle, and opened the safe. Inside were neat stacks of small, cardboard boxes. Pappy pulled one out and laid it on the bench. He opened the box and removed two gold coins in clear plastic pouches.

"I cleaned and stored each Indian Head in a sleeve," he said.

He placed one before me and another for Marshal. Upon examination, we saw they were twenty-dollar gold coins just like in the picture.

He said, "I bought these from your grandfather."

I picked up the coin and examined it with new interest.

Pappy continued, "Most people know I collect coins, and one year at Christmas, Tip knocked on my door and asked if I'd be interested in buying a gold piece. I'm disinclined to buy gold because of the expense, but his was of good quality."

I asked, "Why'd he sell it?"

"He said it was the Christmas season, and his cousin wanted to buy presents. He explained his cousin couldn't come in person, so he was selling it for him."

Pappy lifted one of the gold pieces to admire it.

"I paid a premium since it was of exceptional quality." He sat on a stool. "After our transaction, we relaxed at my dining room table, had a cup of coffee and a cookie. We discussed the spirit of Christmas. He claimed he loved the season because it was the one time of year when people weren't selfish. After a pleasant conversation, he thanked me and left."

"What a neat story," Marshal said.

"A few days later, an officer from the Salvation Army sold me a gold coin too. He said someone dropped it in the Christmas kettle. Upon examination, it was like the one your grandfather sold me."

I said, "Cool."

"Every Christmas season after that, Tip sold me a coin, then we'd have coffee and cookies. Most years, I'd read the Christmas story from the Bible before he left. Then, a few days later, just like clockwork, the Salvation Army officer would arrive with a coin from a bell-ringers kettle."

Marshal said, "How neat."

Pappy picked up a coin and held it up for us to see. "Here's the last one I bought from your grandfather. Last year, he came as usual, but he seemed more introspective. So, I asked him the question I'd always wondered, 'Who is your cousin?' Tip answered, 'His name is John. He did bad things, and he's trying to make up for it.'"

Pappy sipped from the tea glass. "I asked Tip what he was doing with the money he got from the sale of the coins."

I leaned forward anxious to hear the answer.

"Here's what Tip said: 'Every Christmas morning I watch as my family opens presents, then in the afternoon we have a feast. But in the evening, I go to my store and unlock the doors for the men and women who don't have relatives or aren't welcome there. I serve them turkey that's been roasting since early morning. Afterward, I distributed gloves, hats, and socks.'"

Pappy rolled the coin in his palm. "Tip wiped a tear from his cheek and said, 'I was a drunk once, the same as those people. My mother never stopped praying for me, though. One day I had a run-in with Him — Him with a capital H. It wasn't the experience Mom expected, but He changed me. I quit drinking and started a business.. I've been doing it for thirty-four years.' It's what he said, boys."

Pappy placed the coins back in the box. Marshal and I bowed our heads as we pondered the side of Grandpa Tip we'd never seen.

Pappy continued, "Your grandfather showed more brotherly love than most of my church friends."

Neither Marshal nor I spoke. Pappy replaced the lid and returned it to the safe. Then he closed the heavy door and spun the dial. "Boys, from what I learned from the paper today, Tip's cousin was John Dillinger, and there could be more coins somewhere, possibly a lot more."

I'd already come to the same conclusion. We exited the secure room, followed by Pappy, who turned out the light and locked the door. He led us through the maze of bags then upstairs where we said goodbye.

As we rode our bikes toward home, we discussed what we'd learned. The riddle was without a doubt about the coins and connected to John Dillinger. Next, we had to find where he'd hid them.

Chapter 9

We Meet Marge and Her Gang of Outlaws

We rose early and hopped on our bikes. As we approached Angel's house, he greeted us on his bicycle. He said, "What a cool article in the newspaper."

We rode to the hickory tree at the corner, and sat in the shade.

Angel said, "I didn't know you were related to John Dillinger."

"Yep...," Marshal replied with a grin.

"... he's my Grandpa Tip's cousin," I added.

Butch and Einstein approached from a distance and appeared to be racing. Butch braked hard and slid to a stop, but his brother flew past us. Once Einstein crossed the road, he dropped into the deep ditch.

Einstein crawled back to the road and examined his bike for damages, but neither he nor the bicycle had suffered injury. "I won," Einstein announced.

The Miller girls approached on their bicycles. They wore matching shorts and T-shirts.

"Here come those pesky girls," Butch said.

Pippy stopped beside me and smiled. We called her Pippy, short for Pipsqueak because she was short. Pippy had dark hair, and Cindy was blonde.

"Hi," I said.

They both waved. They pulled combs from their hip pockets and combed their hair. In earlier years they didn't worry over out-of-place hair, grass-stained shirts, or bloody knees. But now, I liked them in those crisp, pressed outfits. Their white bobby socks contrasted their tanned legs, which were longer than I remembered.

Cindy said, "We saw your picture in the paper. The shot of you in jail was groovy."

79

Pippy added, "I'm surprised you're related to John Dillinger, and it's amazing he was at our city park once."

"Yeah, neat," Marshal replied.

"What about the coins?" Cindy asked.

Marshal replied, "Hidden somewhere, and we want to find them."

I wrinkled my brow and glared at him. I turned and expected them to mock our treasure hunt, but they didn't.

Marshal continued, "We found a clue if you're interested."

I cocked my head and gave Marshal an exasperated expression.

Wide-eyed, the girls said, "Sure, it sounds exciting."

Everyone heard, so the secret was out. I turned to the eavesdropping boys and sighed. "You guys interested?"

"Sure, man."

"You bet," Einstein replied.

"Count me in," Butch added.

So, we now had a team of treasure hunters.

I said, "Well, the best place to start is Grandpa Tip's hardware store where we found a clue."

"Cool," said Pippy.

For the first time I noticed her hazel eyes. My chin began to sag.

Marshal said, "Close your mouth before a bug flies down your throat."

I flinched back to reality. Pippy smiled and looked down. Her cheeks grew red.

Marshal pulled a key from his jeans and displayed it with a grin. "Hey, are you guys coming?"

Thus, we embarked on the treasure hunt. A block before the square we passed Ben's Barbershop. Then, we reached the town square and dismounted.

We walked on the sidewalk past the courthouse where old men sat and talked. As we strolled by benches, we were privy to short bits of conversations. One pair discussed their crops while a farmer spat tobacco juice. I pointed so the others were careful to avoid the splattered mess. Then we passed a group sharing fishing stories with hands spread further apart than the truth.

When we crossed the street, older boys sat on their cars outside of Snappy's, the hamburger joint. The smell of the crisp, thin hamburgers with onion was enticing. I often spent my meager funds there, but today I was in a hurry.

Once past the square, we boarded our bikes and rode the two blocks to Grandpa Tip's store. We parked outside and walked to the entrance. As Marshal unlocked the door, the girls examined the wooden Indian on the stoop. Marshal pushed the front door open, and we strolled into the stuffy display floor.

"It stinks," Pippy commented.

"It's been closed for a while," I replied.

Marshal went to the closet to find the electrical panel. When he pushed the large handle up, the lights lit the room. "We'll need lights. The clue is downstairs."

I motioned for everyone to follow me. "Let's go."

We descended the stairs to the damp basement. I pulled the string on a lightbulb hanging from the ceiling, which gave us minimal light, and Marshal pulled a chain on another bulb.

I removed the cardboard tube from the shelf. I tucked it in my armpit and tilted it, so the picture slid into Marshal's arms. He slipped it from the newspaper wrapper, unrolled the thick paper, and turned it to the light. "It's a picture like we have at church."

Einstein added, "What's so amazing? Every church has one."

Marshal said, "Look closer at the handwriting."

While straining to see in the semi-darkness, Cindy pushed Marshal's hand toward the light, and read it aloud. "To the best cousin ever. I trust you with my treasure."

Her head snapped up with a shocked expression. She said, "John Dillinger signed it.

Pippy cried, "It says 'treasure.'"

Marshal flipped the picture so the others could see the reverse side.

"There's a riddle on the back written by Grandpa Tip."

Cindy pushed the paper toward the light and read,

"Oh, Liberty, created by a saint,

Your name emblazed on your headband!

Roosevelt giveth and Roosevelt taketh away.

A Squaw with a feathered head,

And the tail of an eagle.

"Your halo has thirteen stars, and

Your belt once forty-six, now forty-eight.

The belt surrounds your golden glory.

The eagle watches your back.

Bearing arrows for war and an olive branch for peace,

It announces, 'In God We Trust.'

"Born in the city of Brotherly Love,

Resembling Hettie.

Like Moses, hidden from destruction

And saved."

When Cindy finished reading, Marshal rolled-up the picture. Butch scratched his head. "What the heck does it mean?"

Marshal said, "We've figured out the riddle is about the gold coin in the newspaper."

I continued, "We think there may be lots of them hidden, but we have to figure out where."

Einstein asked, "How? They could be anywhere."

"It's what the riddle will tell us if we can just solve it," Marshal replied.

Pippy asked, "Is there a clue in the photographs?"

Marshal said, "We have a newspaper upstairs. Let's check it out."

Marshal put the cardboard tube back on the shelf between stacks of shop towels. Angel was first to the stairs with Marshal chasing close behind him. Halfway up, Angel stopped, which caused everyone to collide. While laughing, Angel went up again, taking one hesitating step after another. Butch followed Marshal and pinched his upper leg. Marshal reached behind and swatted Butch's hand away as he pushed Angel. I pinched Einstein. We scurried upstairs to avoid further tweaks. The girls trailed behind, shaking their heads at our childish antics.

Hurrying through the lounge, Marshal led us into the office where there was a newspaper on the desk. He smoothed out the sheets and pointed at the photo. "There's the coin."

I tapped on the picture of our father as a boy. "Dad was sitting on bags, and we think they were full of gold coins. If so, they're worth a fortune."

Pippy leaned over me and placed her hand on my shoulder. Her hair fell across my cheek, and it smelled of flowers.

A different odor interrupted my reverie. Was it brimstone? A voice behind me said, "So, you're looking for bags of gold coins."

We spun around, and a woman my father's age was entering the office door. I recognized her from the boat, and she was with the two men.

"Can I help you? I asked.

"Well, I hope so," she said. "I saw the newspaper article."

We didn't respond as she stepped closer.

"My name is Marge Pierpont, and my large friend is Mack Makley."

She pointed toward the shorter man. "That's my little brother Petey."

I nodded.

"We're interested in those coins too." She said, "We've been searching for a long time."

83

They moved closer until her tall friend, Mack, towered over us. Petey stood silent a few feet behind them. I felt daunted by their presence. I saw a purple bump on Mack's forehead and a bandage on Petey's ear.

She continued, "My father was Pete Pierpont, and Mack's father was Charles Makley. You might recognize those names from the newspaper article. Our fathers robbed the Greencastle bank with John Dillinger."

My gut clenched.

Einstein blurted, "They're John Dillinger's relatives."

"I read it in the paper, so we should be friends," she responded.

Her smile was imitation and insincere, and her voice was three lumps of sugar-sweet when two may have been more convincing.

I asked, "What coins are you looking for?"

She replied, "After the Greencastle robbery, the cops captured my father and Mack's and extradited them to Ohio for murdering the sheriff. While Dad was in jail awaiting his execution, my mother visited him. He told her of the gold and where he hid it."

"Wow, your father was one of the Dillinger gang!" Einstein blurted.

"Dillinger gang, hah!" Marge snarled and stepped closer to Einstein. He leaned backward. She showered him with spit as her resentment spewed.

"My father was the leader of the gang. Dad didn't want his name in the newspapers, so he let John take the credit. Fancy John loved the attention." Then she emphasized, "Dillinger was an attention-seeking double-crosser."

Einstein asked, "double-crosser?"

"You heard me." She poked her finger into Einstein's chest, and he stepped back. "Once, our fathers broke Dillinger out of jail, but Dillinger ignored them when they got locked up."

Mack spoke. From his barrel chest, a baritone voice rolled out.

"They waited for Dillinger, but he never came. They tried to escape, but the cops killed my father and wounded Marge's. He was so shot up, they carried him to the electric chair."

Marge, now whipped into a frenzy, backed away from Einstein and directed her next comment to everyone. With her arm outstretched, she skimmed her pointed, bony finger above us. "The gold is ours. It belonged to our fathers, and if you have any idea where it's hidden, you'd better tell us."

The two girls wilted behind the boys. I figured Einstein might be the next to speak, but it was Angel. "Well."

I poked him hard with my elbow.

He said, "I can't help it, man."

Marge stepped toward Angel and stared into his eyes like a hawk descending on a mouse. "Well, what?" she asked.

Again, I elbowed him, but harder. It wasn't my nature to be brave, but I didn't want her to have Grandpa Tip's gold. Though Butch was the oldest of our gang, that day, I was the alpha male. "Shut up, Angel."

Angel glared at me with furrowed brows while rubbing his aching rib, but he stopped talking.

Marge said, "You don't have to answer my questions, but maybe, you'll tell Mack."

Marge took a few steps back, and Mack stepped forward. Angel cowered below the king-size intimidator and gulped.

I said, "He won't hurt you; he's bluffing."

Mack took one step nearer and stepped on Angel's shoe. Angel stared at the large boot atop his flimsy sneaker, then back at Mack's toothy grin. As the giant increased the pressure, Angel's eyes enlarged. Mack spoke with the low tone of a boat horn in a fog. "I don't hurt my friends. Do you want to be my friend?"

I said, "Don't let him scare you!"

Mack stared at his young captive. Angel broke from his hypnotic gaze and looked at me. His grimace told me he might soon yield to the torture.

Mack applied more pressure and squinted through snake-eye slits. "I asked, are you my friend?"

Angel nodded his approval with a tight-lipped smile and high-pitched whimper. "Uh-huh."

"Good."

Mack removed the weight, and Angel blew through puckered lips. Then, true to his nickname, he sang. "Their grandfather left a clue in the basement, man."

Mack placed his arm around his much smaller, new friend. He stood beside Angel and squeezed him. "I'm so glad we're pals."

Angel grimaced as Mack crushed his shoulders. "Me, too, man," he squeaked.

Then, Marge pulled a hidden revolver from her belt and waved it. I gasped. The boys leaned back as the girls withdrew behind us.

She lowered the weapon. "I just thought you'd want to see the gun my father used to rob banks."

"Is it loaded?" I asked.

"Maybe."

I giggled a nervous reply. Marge tucked it under her belt and pulled her extra-large, floppy shirt over it, then she displayed a wicked smile.

Einstein said, "Can I see it, again?"

Marge hesitated then held it for him to see. Einstein scanned the long barrel several times. When he grabbed her wrist to steady the revolver, she looked at me and pulled the weapon away.

"He's not right, is he?"

I shook my head. The girls peeked from behind us.

As Marge waved the gun, she said, "We've hunted for the gold a long time, so it's ours. Let's go to the basement. You, Mack's friend, go first."

Angel led the way as we obeyed. One by one, we descended the stairs with our captors following us. Once at the bottom, Angel pointed toward the shelf. "Man, it's there."

Marge replied, "That's a good boy. Now, get it!"

Angel pulled the cardboard cylinder from the shelf. When he removed the cap, the picture slid out. Petey grabbed it, and he pulled off the wrapping paper. He tossed it to the floor then held the portrait to the light. "It's just a church picture."

Angel said, "Look at the bottom, man. John Dillinger signed it."

"Well, so he did," Petey replied. "But, where's the clue?"

"Turn it over, man."

Petey sized up Angel.

"How come you say 'man' so often?"

Angel didn't answer.

Petey rolled the picture over, and his lips moved as he read it to himself. "What's this?"

Angel said, "The first part describes the gold coins, but we haven't figured out the last section."

"Let me see it," Marge demanded.

Petey turned the document so she could read it.

Petey said. "Dad said they buried it in Lakeside Park."

Marge's head snapped his direction, and she glared at him. "Shut your mouth!"

Petey dropped his gaze to the floor.

I heard Marge whisper to Petey, "Someone must have moved it."

Marge turned and said, "We're taking this picture with us."

"Hey, it's mine," I complained.

"I'm just borrowing it."

Petey asked, "What about the kids?"

"Don't worry about them. Let's go."

The three adults climbed the stairs, and when they reached the top Marge stopped. "I'll lock up as I leave." She laughed and slammed the door. Then, the lights went out.

Chapter 10

Our Tunnel Escape

Butch tiptoed up the steps and tried the knob, but it wouldn't open.

"Why'd they lock us down here?" Marshal asked.

I answered, "She's just mean."

It was so dark I couldn't see anything.

"No windows or doors," Marshal said.

"How about the elevator?" Einstein asked.

"Geez," Butch sighed. "There's no electricity."

"Oh, yeah."

As we stood in the darkness, I heard sobbing. Einstein said, "I don't like the dark."

I heard a smack, and Butch scolded his younger brother. "Geez, a gun in your face—no response, but the dark makes you cry?"

Butch pulled a book of matches from his jeans and struck one. The small flame was the single source of light, and it wouldn't burn long.

Butch said, "Find something I can set on fire."

Everyone searched the dark room until the match burned Butch's fingers. He lit another while Marshal grabbed a shop towel from the shelf and held it over the fire. The cloth ignited, and Marshal held it with an outstretched arm. The flame spread up the fabric, and Marshal dropped the rag.

I said, "Quick, make a torch."

I remembered a fire poker near the Franklin stove and rushed through the semi-darkness, fumbling along the wall, until I found it. Then I hurried to the shelf for another towel. After wrapping it tight on the top of the poker, I dipped it into the flame. It ignited but didn't burn well after it charred.

Marshal asked, "How about adding coal-oil?"

I shook the flaming cloth onto the floor. Then I rushed to make another torch and soaked it in coal-oil. I dipped it into the flame. "Success," I said.

In the light, I saw the worried expressions of my friends.

Einstein wiped a tear from his cheek. "What now?" he asked.

"Now let's get out of here," I responded.

Butch pointed to the stairs. "They locked the door, I tried it."

Pippy's lower lip began to quiver, and I tried to comfort her. "Don't worry, Pippy, we'll escape."

She responded, "No one even knows we're here."

Pippy and Cindy faced each other with glassy eyes, and it seemed contagious. Einstein's bottom lip quivered.

Butch, smacked him on the back of the head. "Knock it off."

The way a dog at the end of his chain scowls, Einstein curled his lips and snarled. Then, he held his fist in his brother's face. "You thump me again, and I'll punch you!"

His change of attitude seemed to bolster the attitude of the group. Even the girls ceased their crying and dried their eyes on a towel.

"Hey, don't get those all wet. We might need them for torches," Butch complained.

Cindy picked up the newspaper and raised it in the air. "Here, burn this paper."

"Wait a minute," Pippy shouted. "It's old, so it might be historical."

Cindy unrolled the newspaper while Marshal took the torch for a closer look.

"It's a Greencastle, Indiana paper. The date is February 14, 1934," Marshal announced.

Pippy read the headline, "Harry Copeland returned for trial."

Pippy took the torch and held higher. Everyone huddled close to see the old news article. Like a runt hog nudged from the trough, I got shoved to the side, so I walked around to the backside of the paper. Pinpoints of light shined through the newsprint like stars in the sky.

Hmm.

Pippy continued to read as I examined the opposite side. As I concentrated on the twinkling lights, I wondered if they formed a pattern, maybe a constellation? Could this be another of Grandpa Tip's clues?

I closed my eyes then opened them wide. Then I saw how the pinpricks formed letters.

"L-O-O-K," I read a letter at a time. Then I read the next line, "I-N-T-H-E."

"Look in the... Look in the tunnel!" I shouted.

Pippy lowered the newspaper and peered at me with a puzzled expression.

"Look at the backside."

She reversed the paper.

Pippy said, "It's an ad for baking powder."

"Marshal, hold the light behind the newspaper."

Marshal moved behind the paper as I rushed to Pippy's side.

"There are pinpricks of light coming through it," I said.

"Oh, Wow!"

"But, what does it mean?" she questioned.

I pointed toward the large cabinet.

"There's a tunnel back there."

"Oh, yeah," Marshal replied.

I said, "There's an old tunnel to the courthouse. Grandpa Tip's clue is telling us to look in there."

"Let's move the cabinet," Butch cried.

Excited, we all moved toward the tall hutch. It was about seven-foot tall with two full height swinging doors and stood on four short round legs.

"We'll never move it. It's too big," Pippy complained.

"Maybe we can," Marshal replied.

I added, "If we all work together."

Marshal cried, "Grab somewhere and pull hard."

Everyone got ahold. I yelled, "One, two, three...."

"Pull." Marshal completed my command.

The cabinet didn't budge. We tried again, but no matter how hard we tugged, we couldn't move it even an inch.

"It's no use; we'll never move it," Butch said.

"We can't give up," I pleaded.

"There's got to be a way, or Grandpa Tip wouldn't have left the clue," Marshal added.

"Let's lift and pull, man."

"It's worth a try," Einstein agreed.

So, the boys grabbed the corners, lifted, and pulled together. Cindy bent over and yanked from the front, but staggered and fell backward as the frame gave way. She held a board still attached on the other end. Pippy held the torch closer. "It's a lever."

Cindy pulled, and it seemed to swing on a hinge. "Help me."

Together they pulled, and the lever inched forward. As they pulled, the cabinet raised, revealing casters.

"It's on wheels, pull harder," Marshal cried.

The girls pulled again, and it raised more.

"Let's try to move it now," Butch suggested.

This time, the cabinet rolled. We pushed the large unit sideways and found a door made of vertical tongue-and-groove wood planks. It had a small opening with bars, but we couldn't see inside. I tried to turn the knob, but it didn't budge. "Locked."

Upon a closer examination, I saw a keyhole about the same size as the one in the jail door, so I retrieved it.

"Let's see if this key will unlock it."

It slipped into the hole but wouldn't turn. I complained, "It's rusted."

Marshal said, "Maybe it just needs to be lubricated."

I rushed to the coal-oil tank and wetted the key, Then I hurried back and inserted it into the seized lock, "Let's hope this works."

The key turned a little. Marshal said, "It needs more oil."

He scanned the shelves and grabbed an empty bottle. After filling it with the fuel, Marshal rushed back. "I'll try this."

Marshal poured until it overflowed and seeped out around the edges. "Try it now,"

As I twisted, I could move it a quarter turn. I returned it to the original position and removed the key.

"It's working; put in more oil."

Again, Marshal poured more lubricant into the slot until it overflowed. "Give it a minute."

Cindy held up the torch and peered into the window in the door.

Butch warned, "Better keep the torch away from the lock. It's full of coal-oil."

She moved back some, and I tried the key. This time, it turned a little further.

"We're making progress," Marshal remarked. Then, he added oil to the hinges too. While it soaked, I examined the faces of my friends and saw hopeful expressions.

Pippy asked, "Will it work now?"

I answered, "Don't worry; we'll get it. It'll just take a while."

Butch added, "Maybe getting the door open won't matter if the tunnel has collapsed."

"Be positive," I urged.

"Okay, I'm positive it won't matter if the tunnel has collapsed," he replied.

I inserted the key, and it unlocked. As I glanced back at the eager faces, I smiled. When I twisted the doorknob, the door unlatched.

Squeeeeek.

The hinges squealed as they released their decades-old grip. It took several of us to pull the massive, wooden slab open. While grasping the torch, I plunged it into the darkness and saw brick walls and an arched ceiling still intact. "It looks okay, but we need to have plenty of torch material."

Marshal said, "Everyone put towels in your pockets. I'll bring a bottle of coal-oil."

We stuffed our pockets as Marshal refilled the bottle. Once well supplied, we hurried back to the entrance. I removed the key from the lock and slipped it into my back pocket. "In case there's a lock on the far end...."

I led the way, as everyone followed step-by-step. The tunnel was wide enough for a deputy to walk beside a handcuffed prisoner. The brick ceiling was so low I could touch it if I stretched. With caution, I eased forward with my anxious troop following close behind me. Cindy reached for Marshal, "Hold my hand."

Pippy followed her sister's lead, and she held mine. After we shuffled a few yards in the darkness, I noticed a lamp mounted on the wall. When I held the torch closer, I saw the round, glass base sitting in an iron ring. The circular bracket protruded from between two bricks. The reservoir was empty, but the wick seemed intact inside the tall glass chimney.

"I wonder if it works?" Pippy asked.

Marshal stepped toward the lamp but stubbed his toe. "Ouch!"

He hopped around on one leg while I lowered the torch and noticed a brown container on the floor. Marshal bent over, rubbing his injured foot and muttering under his breath.

"What's in the jug?" I asked.

Marshal lifted the pottery, removed a cork, and sniffed it.

"Kerosene, fuel for the lamp, I bet."

He filled the base, then turned the knob to raise the wick before he doused the fabric. "Okay, light it.".

Butch struck a match and touched the flame to the wick. *Flash*, it illuminated the tunnel thirty feet in each direction.

"Man, that's great."

"Cool," Butch added.

Pippy said, "It may be decades since last lit."

I nodded. "Maybe there are more lamps along the passage."

Marshal lowered the chimney to its normal position.

"Let's take the jug," I said.

Now with better light, we moved faster. Before leaving the illuminated area, we came upon another lamp. We repeated our procedure and lit it too. Every thirty feet, we encountered another one.

Marshal said, "We've been going downhill since we entered this tunnel. We're getting deep."

Just then, my torch hissed. "Water is dripping from the ceiling."

Marshal looked up at the arched ceiling. "A drop hit me on the head."

I said, "I need to re-wrap my torch."

I shook the wet cloth from the poker, pulled a towel from my pocket, and wrapped it on the end. Cindy applied coal-oil, and Butch lit it.

Now more confident, I walked faster. But soon, the tunnel widened and was dark. "Must be a lamp here somewhere."

When I eased forward, I saw one. I lit it to see we were in a chamber. A rope hung over a pit and dangled along one side. The hole had brick walls and floor and was about twelve feet across and twelve feet deep. I held the torch over the edge.

"What the heck…?"

Another lamp hung from a chain near the edge. Once lit, I saw three buckets on the floor below us. Two sat together with the third on the opposite side.

Pippy said, "What in heaven's name…?

Marshal interrupted, "If this tunnel connects the jail and the courthouse, what was this pit?"

"Looks like a torture chamber," Einstein interjected.

"I don't think so. I have a theory," Pippy replied. "This was a jail cell."

"What makes you think so?" Einstein asked.

"I'm in the history club at school."

Cindy added, "She loves to read history books."

"The teacher told us about a criminal named Corley Appleston, who lived in our town before the Civil War. She showed us a picture of him standing on the gallows just before they hung him. Corley was a bad man who menaced the community. He harassed everyone, and he killed his neighbor for kicking his dog."

We listened to her story while staring into the pit.

"She said they held him underground in solitary confinement for a few months awaiting his trial. I suppose this was where they kept him."

Einstein pointed. "Why'd they keep him down there.?"

"The man he killed was the sheriff's cousin."

Butch said, "Ouch. That was a mistake."

"Yeah," Pippy replied, "Corley paid for it."

"Dang," Einstein added.

"My teacher said the young attorney from Springfield, Abraham Lincoln, visited him once. Abe came to visit his parents, who had a farm a few miles outside of town. Corley's mother asked him to represent her son. But when Lincoln went to see him, Corley rebuffed his offer. He said he didn't like Abe's father, Thomas, who had chased Corley off the Lincoln property once."

Butch said, "It seems Corley wasn't just mean, but dumb too."

Pippy smiled. "Corley told Lincoln to leave, so Abe nodded. He said, 'Don't get your neck bent out of shape.' Abe stood and said, 'Well, unless you're found guilty.'"

Everyone laughed except Einstein.

Butch held his hand beside his neck and pretended to be hanging by a noose.

"Get it? Neck out of shape? Found guilty? They hung him."

Einstein smiled and nodded.

Pippy said, "Lincoln had a dry wit."

I said, "I like it."

Pippy continued, "After leaving the jail, Lincoln claimed there was never a meaner man born in Illinois, and he called him 'wormy to the core Appleston.'"

We chuckled at Lincoln's quick sense of humor.

"Imagine," Pippy said. "Abraham Lincoln stood right here looking into this pit and talked to Corley Appleston."

I pondered her words then Angel interrupted my thoughts.

"Why three buckets, man?"

Pippy answered, "I guess one was for water, one for food, and one was his toilet."

Einstein said, "I suppose he couldn't use the same bucket."

Then he grabbed the rope and teetered on the ledge. "I'm going down for a look."

Einstein wrapped his legs and arms around the rope and stepped off the ledge. It snapped, and he dropped twelve feet to a rough landing. Einstein sat on the floor, but soon he waved. Butch looked down and sneered at his brother as he shook his head.

"Find what you were looking for, brother?"

Einstein dropped his shoulders and looked embarrassed.

"It's not funny!" Einstein moaned.

"Well, I'm glad you're not hurt."

Einstein stood, brushed the dust off his jeans, and looked up at us "Hey, you guys, get me out of here."

Einstein struggled to find a toehold, but it was an unprofitable effort. He jumped but couldn't reach his brother's extended hand, either. Even when Einstein stood on a wooden bucket, he couldn't reach Butch's grasp.

"We need a rope, man."

I pondered Einstein's situation but couldn't think of a solution as I peered into the hole with my thumbs hooked in my back pockets. But when I felt a dangling towel, I had an idea.

"Give me your towels!"

I tied them all together to form a rope then dangled it over the edge. Einstein stood on the bucket but couldn't reach the end.

95

"We need something else." Butch shouted to his brother, "Take off your jeans."

"What? Are you kidding me?"

"No, I'll add it to our rope, so it'll be longer."

"I'm not taking off my pants."

"Well, I suppose we could leave and come back for you when we find a rope," Butch replied.

"Don't leave me!"

"Well, take off your pants, or we'll leave you alone until we return."

Einstein said, "You take off your pants."

Butch replied, "No, I'm not the one in a hole."

Einstein shuffled an indecisive dance. "Make those girls turn around first."

The girls giggled but turned away, so Einstein unsnapped his trousers.

"Toss them up," Butch shouted.

Einstein rolled the jeans into a ball and tossed them toward his brother. They fell short of Butch's reach, but he succeeded on the second try. Butch tied the makeshift rope to one of the pant legs and looked down at his brother. "This should be long enough. I hope the legs don't tear apart when we try to pull you out of there."

"He's skinny, so it should be fine," Marshal said.

Einstein was embarrassed and looked for something to cover his near nakedness. In a bucket, he found a cloth. Too small to wrap around his waist, the bashful boy tucked it into the front of his tidy whities. He looked like a native American wearing a loincloth.

Marshal asked, "Do you think we should rescue Geronimo?"

I answered, "I don't know, he looks mean to me. What do you say, Butch?"

"He looks more like a chicken than an Indian. Look at those bird legs."

"Knock it off funny guys and get me out of here."

Angel said, "Give us a shout so we can see if it sounds like a war-cry or a cackle."

"I'm warning you, help me or else."

Marshal nudged me with his elbow. "Get him out, I'm worn out from his begging."

Butch dropped the pants-and-towel rope, and Einstein grabbed it. I passed the torch to Pippy so I could help pull. She held the light but couldn't resist a look, and Cindy was soon watching too.

Einstein's toes left the ground as we backed up and pulled. Einstein ascended until we saw his knuckles.

"Pull, man! He's almost out."

Einstein's strained face appeared, which encouraged us. When only his legs dangled over the ledge, he clawed himself onto the brick floor. Einstein rolled on his back and breathed a heavy sigh. "I worried you'd leave me down there." Einstein laid motionless while staring at the ceiling and breathing hard.

"We almost did," Cindy said.

"Nice underwear," Pippy added.

Einstein jumped up and turned his back to the girls. He tossed his loincloth to the floor as he grabbed his pants. "It's not funny."

Cindy smirked and replied, "It's a little funny."

Everyone but Einstein laughed as he danced on one leg while struggling to slip his pants over his shoes. While Einstein wiggled into his skin-tight jeans, I picked up the cloth bag he had tossed aside. Upon closer examination, I saw it had something printed on it. "U.S. Mint." I said, "It's a United States Mint bag,"

"It has One Cent printed on it," Pippy added.

"Wow," Butch said. "I bet it's a clue."

"Inside, there's a note," I said. I removed two folded pieces of paper. "It's Grandpa Tip's handwriting. You're right, it's another poem." I read it aloud as everyone hushed.

"This bag held coins, but not one cent,
But, many a gold of which I've spent.
And now you wonder where they went,
To help my cousin to repent.

"In the season of Advent,
To the needy, I did present,
And make them somewhat more content,
A slight escape from their torment.

"In your quest, please don't resent
Losing a small percent.
Far more exists so don't lament
And don't from your intent.

Marshal said, "Grandpa Tip rhymed it well."
"But it seems ole Gramps spent a lot of the money," Butch said.
I added, "But there's still plenty more."
I flipped to the second page.
"There's another riddle here."
I read it aloud:
    "You are holding a paper compass,
    With clues made up of many holes.
    Hold this sheet on Lincoln and Douglas
    Like ancient script upon the scrolls.

    "Words will appear to understand.
     Find Lincoln on the courthouse plaque
    Next to Douglas in the rotunda grand.
    Good luck to find another sack."
"It seems the next clue is in the courthouse," I said.
Pippy said, "Lincoln and Douglas—it was an important debate. There must be a marker at the courthouse, and the riddle claims it's in the rotunda."
"We've headed the right direction," I said.
I took the torch from Pippy, and I led the way toward the darkness. We soon found another lamp which we lit. We continued lighting lamps and inching forward until we passed four more lights.
Pippy said, "We should reach the courthouse soon."
Within a few yards, the tunnel widened, and we stepped into another room. Two lanterns hung from hooks, and several sat on the floor. In the middle was a table with a large kerosene lamp on top.
"It looks like it could hold a gallon of oil," Cindy said.
"It'll burn long without a refill," Marshal added. "Look, it still has oil in it."
"Light it," Cindy said.

Marshal lifted the glass chimney then I poured a little coal-oil on the wick. When the torch touched the cloth, it ignited in an instant. The smoke curled to the blackened ceiling.

I surveyed the room and saw four chairs around the table and two others against a wall. Along the back wall, someone had piled thin mattresses.

Marshal pulled a feather from a hole in the fabric. He said, "These are feather mattresses. Grandma had one."

I dropped into a chair and rubbed my hands across the table. I felt impressions cut into the wood. Upon closer examination, I made out the letters M-O-S-E-S. "Moses," I said.

Someone named Moses carved his name. Then I notice other names around the edges. "Someone whittled Washington and Ruth too."

Marshal said, "I see Mary and Isaac carved on this side."

Cindy added, "Washington and Rebecca engraved their names here."

We found names carved all over the table, including the legs. When we turned it over, we saw more initials and a short, sturdy knife hanging by the tip.

"Why is a knife in jail, man?"

Pippy said, "This isn't a jail. Most likely, these are the names of runaway slaves. This was a safe-house in the Underground Railroad, and the sheriff may have been a conductor."

"Why, man?"

"It makes sense," she replied. "The mattresses, the names, even women's names. It's a known fact, the sheriff before the Civil War was an abolitionist."

"What's that?" Einstein asked.

"An abolitionist was someone who believed slavery was immoral. There were many in central Illinois before the war."

Angel said, "How do you know?"

"The newspaper editor wrote many articles opposing slavery. In history club we learned he helped runaway slaves escape."

Cindy said, "But we live up north. Slaves were free here."

"Yes, blacks were free in the north, but they returned runaway slaves—it was the law.

Cindy said, "So, the slaves weren't free once they escaped?"

"They had to go to Canada, but many returned to fight in the Civil War."

Everyone listened to our historian.

"The Underground Railroad ran through this town. It originated in Missouri and ended in Chicago. Then runaway slaves got on boats to cross Lake Michigan into Canada."

I said, "But, most slaves couldn't write. How could they carve their names?"

"Well, a few could write their names, and they must have helped the others."

While we sat and rested, I pondered the gravity of our find. "I'm glad it's not like that anymore."

Pippy replied, "The Civil War was a hundred years ago."

"Grandpa Tip said when he was a boy, he could recall two Civil War Veterans who sat most days on a bench at the courthouse. Both were just boys when they entered the war."

Marshal continued my story, "They carried water and helped the Union cooks."

"When you say it that way, it doesn't sound so long ago."

Butch said, "If we're gonna get out of here before these lamps run out of oil, we'd better get going."

Everyone arose and turned toward the narrow, unexplored section. Within a few feet of entering the darkness, we found another lamp. Once lit, we saw a door like the one at the other end of the tunnel.

Butch tried the knob. "It's locked, try the key," he said.

I pulled the key from my back pocket and inserted it in the keyhole, but it wouldn't budge. I removed it and backed away. Marshal removed the cork from the bottle and poured coal-oil into the hole.

I tried again with slight success. We repeated the process until it unlocked. When we pulled the heavy door, it wouldn't move, so Marshal poured oil on the hinges. I yanked again, and it seemed to yield some. Now everyone pulled, and the rusty pins released their grip while squealing their displeasure. With great effort, it opened a little so I could squeeze through the slight gap. It was dark, so I reached back around the door. "Hand me the torch."

Once I held the flickering flame, I found myself in a small hall. Spider webs were as thick as mosquito netting; however, I could still see a staircase beyond the silky strands.

"What do you see?" Marshal asked.

"It looks like a haunted house in here."

100

"I wanna see, man." Angel squeezed past the door then stood beside me. I swung the torch from top to bottom, cutting a swath through the sticky threads. Once I hacked a path, I started toward the stairs with Angel close behind me.

"Are you ready?" I asked.

Angel nodded. When I placed my foot on the first step, there was a grunt and a rustling in the darkness beneath me. Then, something rushed from underneath the wooden plank and brushed against my leg. Startled I jumped backward and bumped into Angel.

When it passed between Angel's legs, he screamed. In an instant, Angel climbed on my back like a bear was after him. In a flash, I had a boy equal my size on me with his legs wrapped around my waist. I staggered and spun around, trying to remain upright against the wall. "Get off of me!"

Marshal shouted from the opposite side of the door, "What's wrong, what's happening?"

The furry beast circled me then dashed through the cracked door. When the critter exploded through the opening and flew between Cindy's legs, she wailed a shrill cry. Pippy's reaction differed from her sister's.

Pippy's eyes rolled behind her flickering eyelids before her knees folded and she slid down Butch's leg. To prevent her head from hitting the floor, he grabbed her hand. But the erratic creature circled back around, and Butch danced as it scurried past him. Butch released Pippy, causing her head to smack on the dirty, brick floor.

Everyone in the tunnel danced to avoid the four-legged tornado which bounced off legs like a pinball. Einstein raised his arms above his head and spun like a ballerina. In a tutu, he couldn't have twirled a tighter circle.

Einstein yelled, "It's got rabies!"

Then it ran a zigzag path away from the howling teens and shot toward the safety of the tunnel. The gray tail with black stripes passed under the flickering lamp and past Marshal. In a second it slipped further away and disappeared into the semi-darkness.

Marshal shouted, "It's just a raccoon, calm down everybody."

Angel dropped from my back. Now able to stand upright, I glared at him.

He hung his head. "Please, don't tell the others, man."

On the other side of the door, Pippy awakened from her fainting jag to find herself on the cold floor. She looked around and appeared confused. While still sitting, Pippy placed her hand on her head, flinched, and moaned. "Ow, there's a bump on my head, what was that thing?"

Before anyone could explain, the striped-tailed animal returned from the darkness at full speed and rushed over Pippy's horizontal legs. She made a slight grunt before again losing consciousness. She added a twin lump to her scalp as her head once again smacked the brick floor.

The masked mammal with its claws clicking on the bricks headed straight for the cracked door. Marshal pointed. "Here it comes, again!"

Angel and I pressed our backs to the wall to allow it to pass. As it scurried over our shoes in the narrow chamber, Angel pressed his shoulders and turned head against the wall as if to make himself a little thinner.

"*Uggh,*" he gasped.

It slipped under the open riser of the first step, and then there was silence. Angel held his chest as if he had a heart attack. "How many are in here?"

I said, "It may just be one."

Angel peeled himself from the wall and peered toward the steps. "Let's check before we try again."

While I held the torch low to examine the open staircase, I could see a broad set of red eyes and three smaller pairs reflecting the light at us.

"She has babies!" I exclaimed. "It explains why she returned."

The mother hovered over her young.

"Let's go, and leave her alone," I said.

I moved toward the stairs and lowered the torch to inspect underneath. The creature didn't move, so I started upward. I stopped on each step to swat away the cobwebs.

When I reached the top, I stepped onto a dusty landing, but there was no door. I saw rough-sawn oak studs with horizontal pine boards nailed on the reverse side of the framing. "Someone boarded over the opening," I said. "I bet no one knows this tunnel is here anymore."

I heard Butch's voice from the tunnel. "Pippy, are you okay?"

Then he said, "Get up and let's go."

After my friends squeezed through the door, each one occupied a step in a single file line up the narrow staircase. I gave the torch to Angel then kicked the boards between the wood studs until my foot went through the opening. I continued until I made a large hole so I could slip through headfirst.

When I stood, I saw light coming from a small window across the room near the ceiling. Once my eyes adjusted, I saw I was in a basement. Step-by-step, I walked but bumped my head on a low hanging pipe.

While rubbing my sore scalp, I felt something brush the back of my hand. I jumped back, expecting to see a spider. "Dang it."

I shook my hand but realized it was just a dangling string hanging from a light fixture. When I tugged the line, the light blinded me. With my hand over my eyes, I raised my eyelids a little and saw a massive boiler. Large pipes wrapped in white tape protruded from the heater in all directions. In the winter, they'd deliver steam to the radiators. I surmised I was in the courthouse basement.

Then, I found another bulb and pulled the string. One by one, all my friends emerged from the Civil War era tunnel.

"Gotta be an exit somewhere, man."

"Spread out," Butch said.

Marshal shouted, "Over here."

When I arrived, he'd already climbed the steps. We followed, and soon we were standing in the courthouse. Above us was a circular balcony with another one above it. Busy people scurried up and down the stairs.

"We're in the rotunda," I said. I closed the door behind me. The word Maintenance was painted on it.

"What were you doing down there?" I spun around, and Deputy Jones was glowering at us.

"You seem to have trouble reading signs. I haven't forgotten your swim at the lake."

He looked at the letters painted on the frosted glass. "It says maintenance."

As my mind raced, I uttered only, "Uh."

Marshal responded, "It was just a wrong turn."

Pippy added, "Yeah, we didn't see the sign."

The deputy scrutinized the girls. "These boys are a bad influence; you should find better friends."

Deputy Jones scanned each of us boys with obvious disapproval. "These aren't boys your parents would approve of."

Butch interjected, "We aren't bothering anyone."

"You're bothering me, so get lost."

103

We rambled toward the exit. The deputy followed us outside and continued watching us as he walked to his car. Before getting in, he paused and pointed to his eye. "Don't forget, I'm watching you."

We rested on the courthouse steps as he left in his squad car.

"Jerk," Butch said.

Once he left, we rushed back inside to continue our search. I said, "Okay, we have to find Lincoln and Douglas, so spread out."

Everyone scattered to find a clue. In a while, we exhausted our first-floor search and met at the base of the grand staircase. I said, "Let's try the second floor."

We hurried upstairs and scattered. Though we examined all the bulletin boards, we didn't find a hint. Frustrated, I stepped into the County Recorder's office. "May I help you, young man?"

The lady sat behind a wooden desk while looking over her reading glasses.

"Do you know where I can find a Lincoln and Douglas plaque?"

"There was one on the first floor, but they moved it. Now it's outside on the west porch."

I rushed outside her office and gathered my friends. We hurried down the stairs past busy barristers and their clients. We only slowed once as we passed a judge in a black, flowing robe. On the main floor, I hesitated and tried to decide which direction was west.

"This way," Marshal said as he pointed.

The plaque was at eye level on the limestone wall. A raised profile of two heads was above the description.

Pippy read the eighth-inch tall letters:

> "On September 18, 1858, Abraham Lincoln and Steven A. Douglas debated in this city, for the office of United States Senator. The main topic was slavery. Twelve thousand citizens attended the debate. Lincoln, the Republican candidate, won the popular vote but lost the election in the statehouse. Lincoln printed the transcripts in a book which lead to his national recognition and eventual election to President of the United States. Freeing the slaves was President Lincoln's most honored accomplishment."

"It was more than a hundred years ago," Einstein said.

"One hundred and nine to be exact," Pippy replied.

"Let's look at the clue," Cindy urged.

I removed the folded paper from my pocket and held it over the brass letters. It made little sense.

"Try putting the first hole over the first letter," said Marshal.

I read the exposed letters one at a time, so everyone could hear, "I-N-S-T-E-E-P-L-E."

"In steeple," cried Pippy.

"O-N-B-E-L-L,"

"On the bell," Marshal shouted.

I spread the paper tighter and continued to read.

"E-A-T-F-I-S-H. Eat Fish?"

Cindy said, "That's weird."

Pippy leaned against me as she tried to see the letters over my shoulder. I sniffed her fragrance and glanced sideways. She smiled, and I swooned a little.

She read, "F-I-N-D-C-L-U-E."

Butch said, "Find the clue."

Pippy summarized, "In steeple, On bell, eat fish, find a clue."

I mumbled, "Steeple, bell, fish, clue. How are a steeple and a bell in common?"

"A church," Marshal suggested.

"Okay, what about the fish?" Butch asked.

"Maybe the church is by a river," Einstein blurted.

Butch responded, "I don't think so."

"You got a better idea?"

Butch replied, "No, but I bet it's not a river."

Einstein said, "Could it be the school lunchroom? They serve fish for lunch every Friday, and they ring a bell."

"The school doesn't have a steeple."

I snapped my fingers. "Aha, I've got it! We have fish every Friday for the Catholics. They don't eat meat on Friday."

Marshal said, "The Catholic church has a steeple and a bell."

"That could be it," Pippy said. She pointed toward the church a few blocks away.

Chapter 11

The Catholic Church Tower

Marshal launched like a rocket toward the steeple, and we followed. We arrived out of breath and stood on the sidewalk looking high above at the bell in the tower.

"How can we get up there?" Cindy questioned.

"Gotta be a way," I said.

Butch bolted up the steps, through the double door, and into the narthex as everyone chased close behind him. We saw no one as we tiptoed to the sanctuary doors. The swinging pair had small windows shaped like a cross. Marshal looked inside, but it was vacant. We crept into the nave and eased down the pew-flanked aisle.

"Hello." The voice startled me, and I jumped.

"Hello, can you hear me?"

We spun, and a priest was peeking from a curtain as a bent old lady waddled away. "It's nice to have teenagers come to confession. I'll be right with you."

The elderly monsignor hobbled out of the sanctuary.

"Oh, crap," Marshal whispered.

"He thinks we're here for confession," I said.

Butch said, "Someone's got to keep him busy while we get into the steeple. Who's a good confessor?"

Everyone turned to Angel. "Wait a minute, I'm not even Catholic."

"Yeah, but you're great at confessing. I've heard you do it," Butch said.

Just then, the priest returned. "Who'd like to go first?"

Butch shoved Angel forward. "Angel would."

The father placed his arm over Angel's shoulder and ushered him toward the confessional. "Angel, well, that's an interesting nickname."

When they disappeared behind the curtains, I headed toward the staircase. "It's got to be up there."

We rushed up the stairs to a balcony, hurried up another flight, then entered an attic. A Christmas manger was in one corner, and a rack of cherub robes hung nearby. Einstein turned the handle on a BINGO tumbler which caused balls to chatter as they spun.

"Leave things alone," Butch demanded.

Marshal pointed to a spiral staircase. "Bingo."

Marshal led the way to the top and opened a trap door. Three startled pigeons flapped away, but I followed onto the metal-covered floor.

"I can see the whole town from here," Einstein said.

My knees shook as I shuffled to the edge of the short bannister. It was an incredible view from the height. I saw across the top of trees with olive-green leaves. A few blocks away, the courthouse towered in the center of the city square. The library dome was to our left, and Eastern State College was behind us. Its castle-like administration building was visible beyond the stately old homes. The rising summer heat caused the stone turrets to wiggle in the distance.

Pippy and Cindy clung to the trap door rail and refused to venture to the edge. Four large speakers were facing different directions with the wires running through the floor.

I pointed. "The bell is fake. They play recordings."

Marshal reached up and touched the black steel bell. Spider webs packed with empty fly-shells draped between the clapper and the lip.

I said, "The chimes are fake, but the bell is still here."

"Quick, let's look for a clue before Angel finishes," I implored.

We circled the large metal object. The only visible marking was the name and company slogan in raised letters.

"What does it say?" asked Cindy.

I rubbed my hands across the letter to remove the dust. It didn't help much, so I spit on my palm then tried again. Einstein and Marshal helped by spitting on the bell and rubbing too. Then the words Northwest Bell Company appeared followed by The Tone Is Good As Gold.

They'd stamped Carnegie four places on the rim. Butch moaned and scratched his scalp. "I don't get it."

"It makes no sense," Pippy added.

Angel said, "I don't know, either man

My head snapped toward Angel. "What are you doing here?"

Angel responded, "I confessed and told him we're on a treasure hunt."

"What!" I cried.

"How could you?" Marshal asked.

"Man, you should have known I'd spill the beans."

"Relax, boys and girls." When I spun around, I saw the Catholic father reaching the top step.

"Angel told me you're hunting for treasure." The black-clad man limped to the railing. "Which of you boys are Tip's grandchildren?"

Marshal and I raised our hands. I said, "I'm sorry, we shouldn't be up here."

The gentleman smiled. "It's okay, children. I'll excuse you since you're on a treasure hunt."

I felt relieved he wasn't angry.

"You know, I've been expecting you," the priest said.

"Really?" I asked.

"Why?" Marshal added.

The pastor replied, "Tip said you'd come here someday to solve a riddle. Even after he's gone, you're still working on one."

The elderly priest lit his pipe, leaned back, and stretched.

"Look out, Father! Don't fall!" Cindy implored.

"Oh, no worry, child. I've spent many hours up here. In the past, I had to ring the bell four times a day."

"That sounds like a hassle," Pippy said.

The old man puffed his tobacco. "It was."

The priest crossed his legs and rocked on the ledge. "I was glad when they converted to the electronic chimes. I suppose they felt sorry for my tired, worn-out knees."

A gentle breeze swept his pipe smoke across the rustling leaves of the maple trees below us. "Tip and I often played checkers in the rectory. Sometimes, he'd ring the bell for me if my arthritis hurt extra bad."

The priest massaged his knees. "He sure loved riddles. Tip asked the same question each time he returned from this belfry."

"What question?" I asked.

The elderly clergyman drew deeply on his pipe, squinted his eyes, and gazed into the distance. "Well, let me think. Oh yes, If Carnegie is around, how is it Northwest? I never could solve it."

No one spoke, but everyone appeared deep in thought. Marshal stroked his chin, Angel scratched his head, and Einstein's chin drooped a little wider than usual. I walked around the bell and rubbed the rim as I pondered the riddle.

As my fingers ran across the letters, I chanted, "Carnegie, Carnegie, Carnegie." I repeated the puzzle, "If Carnegie is around, how is it northwest?

I knew Carnegie was a man who got rich in the steel business years ago. My aunt worked at the Carnegie Library, and she said he donated libraries to communities worldwide. As my hand rested on the raised letters, I studied the company name—Northwest.

"Carnegie, Northwest, Carnegie, Northwest." I paused as an idea developed. Is it possible, northwest wasn't only the manufacturer but also the direction? I spun toward the pastor. "Which direction is northwest?"

He lifted his finger toward the library a few blocks away. I clapped my hands. "I've got it."

As I rubbed the rim, my friends gathered closer. "The letters forged around the rim of the bell spell Carnegie."

The reverend limped toward me, removed his reading glasses from his shirt pocket, and studied the raised letters. "I never noticed."

"Look northwest," I instructed.

His surprised expression told me he understood. He said, "Carnegie! The answer is the Carnegie library."

He waved a finger in the air. "Eureka! With Tip gone, I didn't think I'd learn the answer."

My friends joined the celebration, but Einstein said, "I don't get it."

Butch explained the solution to his brother. "The word Carnegie is around the rim of the bell, but the Carnegie library is northwest."

Einstein nodded and smiled.

I said, "The library will most likely contain our next clue." Then, I pointed to the slogan which seemed to confirm my suspicion. "It says Good as Gold."

The priest shuffled back to the rail and sat. "I'd like to tell you something about your grandfather. Tip was generous."

He got my attention.

He said, "Tip funded our food pantry. About once a month for thirty years, he'd bring me a gold coin. He always said it was an anonymous donation from his friend. After reading the newspaper article, I suspected his friend was Dillinger."

My heart sunk a little when I realized Grandpa Tip had given more coins away, and I wondered if he'd left any treasure for us.

"How many coins did he give you?"

The priest stood and hobbled toward the stairs. "Come with me."

We followed him down the spiral staircase to his office where he removed a ledger from a filing cabinet. Once seated, he flipped a few pages and ran his finger down a column. "Eight-hundred-four coins over thirty years."

Butch whistled through his teeth.

I asked, "Do you have any idea where he kept the gold?"

The pastor said, "No. He never told me. But he gave me something to give to you."

The priest removed a bamboo tube and poked it toward me. It was about six inches long and about three-quarters-inch diameter, and Grandpa Tip had sealed it on both ends with candle wax.

The monsignor said, "Tip said someday after he died, his grandchildren may come here on a treasure hunt. Tip instructed me to only give it to you if you solved his Carnegie puzzle. I will say, I'm impressed."

"Thanks, but I've had a lot of experience with Grandpa Tip's riddles."

"Break it," the priest said.

I twisted the attractive, wooden tube until it cracked.

He said, "Inside, there's a message."

I broke the end off and removed the note. I unrolled the paper and read it to myself, then showed it to the priest. Grandpa Tip had written:

"A soldier dropped John Jenkins dead.
The shot meant for a Copperhead.
Where his body became cold
Is your next clue for the gold.
Follow the bell; it's where you should look,

110

Inside *The Charleston Riot* book."

Angel thrust his open palm in my face like a policeman stopping traffic. "Don't read it aloud; I don't want to hear it."

"Yeah, he'll blab it for sure," Marshal said.

We passed the note around, except for Angel, who stepped aside. I turned to the priest. "Did Grandpa Tip say anything else?"

"Nope, he said you'd figure it out."

Angel faced away with his fingers in his ears.

I said, "Grandpa Tip wanted us to find a book call *The Riot of Charleston* at the Carnegie library."

"So, it seems," the pastor replied.

Chapter 12

The Carnegie Library

We rushed from the church on our way to the nearby library. When I was a few steps from the street, a car pulled up and blocked my path. Marge was on the passenger side with her elbow hanging out the window. "What are you boys doing?"

I stepped back. "Nothing."

Her tobacco-stained smile troubled me. "We got off on the wrong foot," she said.

I didn't answer as she pushed the rolled-up portrait toward me. "You can have this. I hope you're not sore because I took it and locked you in the basement. You know I was joking."

Though I accepted the picture, I was wary of her bewitching voice. She seemed too sweet by half. "Thank you, I'm glad to have it back."

I handed it to Marshal as she wheedled me.

She said, "We might do better if we work together."

I didn't trust the beguiler. "Oh, no, thanks. We're not looking for the gold any longer. We don't think there is any."

The persistent woman squinted and her eye twitched. She looked suspicious as I backed off the curb.

I said, "Good luck with your search, though."

Marge never took her eyes off me as we walked down the sidewalk toward downtown. The car rolled behind us at a walking pace but never passed.

"She doesn't buy it," Butch whispered.

"Yeah, they're following us, man."

When we stopped on the bridge over a creek and leaned against the rail, the car stopped too.

Marshal said, "They're just sitting there."

Pippy tossed a pebble into the shallow water ten feet below, and it landed with a plunk. The splash in the brook gave me an idea. "Let's wade."

As everyone watched, I removed my shoes then stuffed my socks into one. "They can't follow us there."

Without an argument, the others pulled off their sneakers and followed me as I slid down the steep embankment. We stepped through the grass and teetered on the bank before stepping into the stream. The creek was low, a few inches deep, and the bottom was smooth, hard clay. Chilly, refreshing water rushed over my bare feet.

As we waded beneath the bridge, we slipped from Marge's view, but I never heard the car leave. "They're waiting for us," Butch said.

After listening for a few seconds, I motioned for everyone to follow me. "Let's lose 'em."

As I splashed upstream toward the library, my friends followed.

Einstein said, "Someone's coming."

Petey slid down the path then sat and removed his shoes and socks.

"He's following us," Butch said.

After Petey stepped a few paces into the creek, someone on the bridge yelled at him. "Hey, what are you doing down there?"

Petey shielded his eyes and looked up at the lawman. "Uh, just wading, officer."

"I suggest you don't because snakes swim in there."

"Snakes!" Petey cried.

The knave's head twirled like an owl as he searched the water's edge.

"Yeah, Copperheads — mean and venomous."

Petey pranced on top of the water as he made his escape. He scurried unshod up the steep embankment ignoring the cockleburs biting his ankles.

Before the retreating grifter reached the top, Pippy jumped on my back with her legs wrapped around my waist. With one hand she carried her shoes, and the other clung to the collar of my shirt. Following her lead, Cindy leaped onto Marshal, and he staggered to keep his balance. She resembled a rodeo cowboy riding a twirling bronco.

"Let's get!" I shouted.

Marshal added, "... and watch for snakes."

I tottered around a bend, out of sight of the officer, and gazed around for fanged water moccasins. I paid attention to the uncut weeds and swampy lilies on the opposite bank. Copperheads are mean by nature, but they're even more aggressive if someone disturbs their nest. The creek narrowed and stirred faster. Ahead, it cascaded over several small waterfalls creating a boiling effect, so I couldn't see below the surface.

Just then, Einstein yelled, "Snake!"

While Pippy squealed in my ear, she raised her feet higher and kicked. As I struggled to keep my balance on the slippery clay, she pedaled as if riding a bike. I thought I'd found my balance then I saw the black cottonmouth approaching in the rushing stream. My passenger must have seen it, too, because she raced her imaginary bicycle faster and squirmed more.

Unable to dodge the three-foot-long, venomous serpent as it swam toward me, my heart pounded. The treacherous head bobbed up and down as it rushed straight at me. Barefoot and with short pants, I was unprotected.

I tried to avoid the fanged demon, but Pippy wrapped one arm around my eyes. Then, I panicked and took a few steps, slipped on the slick clay, and fell backward. Pippy and I plopped into the shallow, bustling water. Now sitting on my bottom, with Pippy behind me, I was eye level with the approaching adversary.

Terrified, I kicked and flailed my arms to prevent a fatal bite as my fearless friends fled. Now, the riled demon was right before me. By instinct, I lunged and grabbed the slimy beast behind the head and held it with my extended hand. When I clasped, its long, slender body slapped against my legs.

With bulging eyes, I stared into its wide-open mouth, expecting to see fangs, but there were none. I saw an endless, black throat gulping and swallowing. "No fangs!" I cried.

I strangled the slimy attacker while Marshal stood a safe distance away.

"It's an eel," he shouted.

On top of its demonic head was a single horn. I raised the unknown creature with outstretched arms and tried to squeeze the life from it.

When Pippy, who was still sitting behind me, saw the slithering beast she squealed and scooted backward. "*Eek*! Kill it!"

"I'm trying," I cried.

I had both hands wrenched around my ebony adversary as it flopped. When Pippy flipped over and crawled away, I was alone to fight to the end of one of us.

I reached into the water with one hand and lifted its tail out of the rushing stream. Once out of the creek, it stopped flopping. Now satisfied, I had crushed the life from the beast, I held it nearer for a closer examination. My squinting eyes and puzzled expression telegraphed my confusion.

"It's not a snake," I announced. "It's a bicycle inner tube."

I looked closer and said, "The horn is the valve stem."

The harmless section of a rubber tubing had floated downstream into our path. Pippy was standing at the water's edge with water dripping from her matted, tangled hair. Einstein chased my shoe, which bobbed along until it beached. The others helped retrieve our socks hanging from weeds and bushes.

"I'm soaked," Pippy griped.

"Me too," I replied.

I shook my hair like a wet dog, and Pippy combed her dripping hair with her wet fingers.

"Let's get out of this snake pit," Pippy said.

"There's thick grass along the banks, and there may be snakes in there," Butch warned.

"Hey, man, it may be safer in the water."

So, we continued wading upstream while we scanned the uncut swampy edges. We walked around a curve, and I saw a promising gentle bank ahead. "It looks safe there."

Picnic tables and benches were on the grass-covered, sloping lawn behind the library. We stepped onto the soft bluegrass. Pippy and I sat in the sun while the others retreated under a shade tree.

"Our clothes will dry here," I said.

She was shaking, and her teeth chattered.

"Are you okay?" I asked.

"Yeah, the sun feels good, and I'm getting warmer."

I rubbed her arms. "Does this help?"

"Thanks, it does help."

115

After our clothes dried on the front, we moved to the opposite side of the bench so the sun could warm our backs. We baked until my scalp sizzled.

Pippy said, "I'm dry enough to go into the library."

I felt my socks. "They're dry."

I slipped them on my feet, then pulled on my shoes. I pulled a comb from my back pocket and removed the knots from my hair. Once I made myself more presentable, I handed it to Pippy. "All right, let's go," I said.

Everyone jumped up and followed me to the rear entrance. When we entered, the cooled air caused me to pause, and my damp underpants felt ice-covered. A glance at Pippy's chattering teeth told me she was cold too.

The library was as empty as a beach after Labor Day. In the summer, few patrons were there. An older couple sat in the periodical section reading magazines, and the room was so quiet I heard them turning the pages. We stepped toward the desk as a pencil-thin lady glared over her reading glasses. She had a long pin stuck through the gray bun on top of her head. I wondered if she used it to skewer teens who talked in her literary domain.

"Where's my Aunt Dottie?" I asked.

She removed her spectacles and allowed them to hang from the chain around her neck.

"Dottie? Dottie Reagan?"

I nodded.

"She's in the children's addition."

I flashed my most polite smile as I backed away from her desk. We shuffled past the reference section toward the children's reading room. My aunt was pushing a cart and placing books on the shelves when she saw us.

"Well, look who's here."

"Hi, Aunt Dottie," I replied.

"How are you?" Marshal added.

"Who are your friends?" she asked.

"Just kids from the neighborhood."

She smiled as she made eye contact with each one — a skill she developed from years of reading to preschool children. "So, what brings you into the library on this nice summer day?"

"I'm looking for a book titled *The Charleston Riot.*"

"Oh, studying our town's history. We'll go to the history section."

As I followed my aunt, I tugged at my uncomfortable damp underpants. Aunt Dottie stopped at the card catalog and searched in drawers by title and author. She wrote the Dewey decimal number on a scrap of paper, then proceeded to the proper aisle. Her eyes scanned the neat, shelved titles until she found it. "Here, you can take it to a table in the reference section."

"Okay," I said.

We followed her to a golden-oak table with solid matching chairs alongside. Aunt Dottie said, "It's all yours. I'll be in the children's room if you need me."

I said, "Oh, there's something else."

Aunt Dottie turned. "Yes, what is it?"

I extended the tube with the rolled portrait. "Would you mind holding this for me?"

"Sure, I'd be glad to keep it."

The Charleston Riot wasn't thick, but it was big. When opened, there were illustrations of citizens shooting at Union soldiers. Many eyewitness accounts filled the pages.

We learned the battle occurred March 28, 1864, during the Civil War. Though in a northern state, many residents had immigrated from the south and were Confederate loyalists. Union soldiers and local folks were drinking throughout the day. Many soldiers were from the Charleston area and home on leave. Over a hundred southern sympathizers brought a wagon load of weapons to town.

The rebels had trained under the leadership of Sheriff O'Hare who had replaced the abolitionist sheriff. They went by names such as "Copperheads" and "Butternuts."

The paramilitary band had been training north of town for weeks and came to the courthouse looking for trouble. Most of the Union soldiers had gone, but a few dozen remained. They were to leave the next day after the last of the Coles County volunteers had returned from their visits.

In the afternoon, a small quarrel between a soldier and a Copperhead escalated into a gunfight. The confederate sympathizers opened fire on the unsuspecting Union soldiers, and they fired over a hundred shots in just a few minutes. When the battle was over, nine people were dead or dying, and twelve injured. Most of the deceased were northern soldiers killed without their weapons.

The centerfold of the book was a map of the city square. The hand-drawn diagram must have been the reason for the extra-large pages. The eyewitness account listed details of how the battle progressed. Numbers marked the location of those killed.

"Where did John Jenkins die?" Pippy asked.

"Number seventeen according to the legend," I answered.

"Where on the map?" Pippy asked.

I ran my finger around the page until I located seventeen. "There, on the south side of the courthouse—the fourth store from the east. That would be...." I hesitated to visualize the current downtown.

"Hills Jewelry," Marshal interrupted.

"Yes, you're right," Pippy said.

I said, "According to the riddle at the church, it will be where we'll find our next clue. Let's go."

Chapter 13

Kidnapped

The summer temperature felt good as I exited the air-conditioned library. My damp underpants had caused my lips to turn blue in the chilled building. Pippy had goosebumps on her arms.

As we hurried toward the city square, I noticed the black car again. The full-size older Ford Fairlane had headlights projecting forward which resembled two eyeballs, and paranoid me wondered if those peepers were searching for me. A bird-shaped hood ornament resembled a dog's snout sniffing for its prey. Marge's gang drove past. They always seemed nearby. The one-way road went the opposite direction, but I knew they'd circle back. Before they spotted us, we ran across the bridge and didn't slow down until we darted into an alley. Before we slipped into the rear of the dime store, we hid behind a trash dumpster. The car eased by again.

We browsed in the store as the black Ford passed several times. Petey was driving while Mack and Marge scanned the sidewalks. I figured they were looking for us. I waited until I hadn't seen them for a while, then made my way toward the front.

Just then, Mack and Petey entered. I slipped behind a shelf as the others hid too. The men combed the narrow aisles. We retreated and huddled in the back. They appeared as we hid in the hair-care aisle. I bolted toward the rear exit with my friends fleeing behind me. When we rushed outside, Marge was waiting with both car doors open. I almost stumbled into the back seat when my friends rear-ended me.

She motioned with her pistol to get inside as her accomplices shoved us. We crammed into the kidnapper's car. Mack sat beside the girls and me in the backseat, and he pushed a gun against my ribs. Marshal lay on the floor with my feet on him. Butch and Angel squeezed between Marge and Petey who was driving.

Marge instructed, "Hurry, drive away from all these people."

When the car exited the alley, Marge motioned for Petey to turn left on a one-way street heading south from the city center. When I looked at Pippy, her worried eyes seem to say what I was thinking, *I can't believe I'm kidnapped.* Nobody talked as we passed the stately homes on each side of the narrow road.

As we sped along, the tires whined over the embossed pavers. In a while, Marge spoke, "I know you're looking for the gold. I've seen you sneaking around town."

She put her arm over Angel's shoulder and smiled at him. "You're the one who likes to talk. Tell me where you were going."

Butch had his hand under Angel's knee and squeezed a ligament.

"Well," she insisted.

Butch squeezed harder, and Angel grimaced.

"Cat got your tongue?"

Angel moaned.

"What's the matter, need a bathroom?"

Angel shook his head, but Butch didn't relent from his pinch.

Marge insisted louder, "I asked you a question."

As the car slowed for a stop sign, the whining tires quieted. The brick road ended at a T intersection across the street from the university. Before Petey could make a turn, Angel pointed at the administration building. The gray stone tower in the center resembled a castle with a shorter battlement on each side.

"Up there?" she questioned.

Angel nodded, and Butch eased his grip. Marshal's head swiveled toward me, and his expression matched mine. I'd never heard the incorruptible Angel tell a lie. Did he guide us into the building because his father had an office there and hoped he'd find safety?

Petey guided the vehicle into the visitor's parking lot. "Get out," Marge ordered.

We obeyed, as she hid her gun in her waistband and pointed her finger at me. "And here's the way it's gonna be. We'll follow our talkative friend. So, stay together if you know what's good for you."

120

Angel led the teenagers as the adults followed. A few students and faculty passed in the halls but paid us no attention. We walked past Angel's father's office, but the light wasn't on. Angel pointed at a men's room. Marge sighed but nodded her approval.

I asked, "Me too?"

She agreed, but her frown displayed her disgust.

Once inside, I asked, "What's your plan?"

"Man, I don't know."

"You don't have a plan?"

Angel had a distressed expression."Nope."

"Great," I whispered.

"Got any ideas?" he asked.

"Not yet. Keep stalling. I'll try to think of something."

Without warning, Mack burst through the door. "What's taking you so long?"

"We're done."

"Well, hurry."

As we left the men's room, I leaned toward Angel. "Remember, stall them."

When we reached the main foyer, Angel stopped and turned a full circle. Marge grabbed him by the shoulder. "Well, which way?"

Angel pointed at the grand staircase, and we followed him up the century-old stairs. Years of footsteps on the gray-speckled marble wore the middle more than the edges. The students had abused the dark, oak banister leaving chips and nicks from top to bottom.

As we climbed, we met two campus police officers who were descending. They ignored my twisted facial expression as I tried to get their attention. Unoccupied classrooms were on the second level. Angel continued upward to the lecture halls on the third floor.

A professor explained a math problem which I could hear through the open door. Dozens of students in theater seats wrote in notebooks on their knees. Other lecture rooms buzzed with activity.

Marge stopped to rest. There was no central air-conditioning in the old building. Her face glowed red, and she huffed as she sat on a step. "You'd think they'd put in an elevator."

Petey lit a cigarette. I nodded toward the restroom with my knees together.

121

"Again?" Marge asked.

I nodded.

"Make it quick."

I slipped into the men's room as Angel and Marshal followed me. I pulled several cellophane-wrapped packages of firecrackers and waxed strings from my pockets and tossed them into a lavatory. Then I cut off a piece of the homemade fuse and tied it to the line on the first pack.

Marshal had firecrackers, too, so he and Angel prepared them. In a flash, we had eight packs ready.

"Are you going to leave them in the sink?" Marshal asked.

"No, someone might find them."

"How about the trash?" Marshal suggested.

"Good idea!"

I emptied a metal receptacle into another one. Marshal helped me light the waxed strings and toss them into the empty can.

"What if someone finds it?" Marshal asked.

He was right. I needed to hide it. So, I placed the basket on top of a toilet and closed the stall door. I crawled under and left it locked. Before exiting, I gave instructions. "Angel, Keep them busy on this floor."

"How, man?"

"I don't know; just do it."

Petey was finishing his cigarette as we exited the restroom. He squashed the butt in a brushed steel ashtray hanging on the wall.

Marge lifted her shirt to reveal the pistol. "This better not be a wild goose chase."

Angel gazed left and right. I figured he was familiar with the building since he'd accompanied his father to work sometimes.

Marge demanded, "Where is it?"

"Well, I uh, I uh, I uh…."

Marge said, "I'm waiting."

He said, "It's in a lecture hall."

"Which one?"

Angel pointed at a nearby room. She peeked into the classroom and appeared frustrated. "It's occupied, we'll wait."

Wooden benches lined the sides of the spacious hallway. Marshal, Angel, and I dropped next to Petey. Marge and the girls were on another seat beside us, while Einstein and Butch sat across the hallway next to Mack. The gangsters spied our every move. The only sounds were the professor and the clock with Roman numerals.

Tick, tock, tick, tock. Each second seemed like a minute. I pulled chewing gum from my pocket, removed a piece, and handed the pack to Marshal. After taking a stick, he gave it to Angel, who took the last one. My friend popped it in his mouth without noticing Petey's stare. Angel chomped on the fresh flavor, then glanced at Petey who glared like a cobra. Angel had a baffled expression. Petey blew smoke in his face. Angel coughed, and I swallowed a giggle.

A drop of sweat trailed from my hairline past my ear. Einstein bounced his leg, and Mack slapped his hand on the bouncing knee. "Stop it."

The clock displayed the time as twenty minutes until the hour. The red second-hand ticked in slow motion as I awaited the firecracker blasts.

Anxious, I raised my head and stared at the ceiling. Nothing much of interest, but Petey looked too. The turn-of-the-century building had exposed conduit and pipes on the ceilings and walls. The college added plumbing and electricity many years after the original construction. A steel pipe ran the length of the hall with sprinklers spaced fifteen or twenty feet apart. I got an idea.

First, I glanced left, then right, but I didn't see a fire alarm. I turned my head hard to the left and pretended to scratch my shoulder. Then I saw the red handle with the word FIRE printed in bold white letters.

The clock now read quarter till the hour. Only five minutes had passed since I last looked. Was time creeping as slowly for the students listening to the professor drone about math?

Bang, pop, boom, the firecrackers in the restroom exploded in rapid sequence.

I jumped to my feet and cupped my hands like a megaphone. "Gunfire! Gunfire!"

In a flash, panicking students and teachers fled from the lecture rooms. A din of shrieking and shoving people packed the hall in an instant.

"Shots fired! Run for it!" I shouted.

Marge leaped up and pulled the revolver from her waistband. She spun left then right while holding the pistol next to her ear as if looking for the gunman. I pointed at her.

"Gun!"

Marge, bewildered more than ever, shouted, "Where?" She thrust her pistol forward and took a policeman's stance. Shifting left then right, she looked ready to down the mad gunman.

The fleeing students and staff glanced back as they rushed for the stairs. During the commotion, I reached for the alarm but got knocked back. Bounced between escaping students, I touched it and got pushed away again. On my third try, swimming upstream atop a gaggle of coeds, I pulled the handle with my sweaty hand. A locomotive size horn wailed as girls screamed and boys shoved.

My friends followed me as Marge, and her crew looked perplexed. We melded pell-mell into the stampede and rushed down the traffic-worn staircase. The maelstrom enlarged as we passed the next floor. It was the single escape route. The herd suspended me with my toes touching only an occasional step. My friends rolled in the avalanche.

Every few seconds, I shouted, "Help! Gunfire, shots fired."

When I glanced back, I didn't see Marge or the men. The Miller girls bobbed along, squeezed between upperclassmen. When I exited the building, police cars arrived, and stopped traffic.

Fire truck sirens wailed louder as they approached. A hook-and-ladder rolled in with excited firemen. This would be their first use of the block-long vehicle since purchased five years prior. The city bought it to reach the tallest buildings in town. The fire marshal arrived in a red pickup truck and scanned the windows and roof for signs of smoke. He appeared disappointed when he removed his helmet and tossed it on the truck's seat.

I ran across the street and joined hundreds of on-lookers. Drivers stood beside their cars in halted traffic. Moments later, Sheriff Jones arrived. Clarence rushed to his side and scratched at his calamine covered neck.

Clarence said, "I'll charge in with force."

"Deputy, you stay with me." The sheriff motioned for an older officer. "Take two of patrolmen inside with you. Be careful and don't shoot unless they fire first."

The sheriff shouted instruction into a megaphone to other policemen who were pointing rifles toward the castle-shaped building. "Don't shoot. I'm sending men in to investigate."

While the officers searched the building, we sat on the curb. Deputy Clarence fidgeted and scratched under his collar. I noticed calamine lotion on his neck. Once, he bent over and clawed inside his socks.

I said, "He's got insect bites."

Clarence leaned back and rubbed his bottom against the door handle.

Butch said, "Looks like a bug found a hiding place."

"Man, that's the worst."

Clarence noticed me watching and glared back at me. Then I realized we'd infested his squad car with crawling critters the day of our capture. I guessed those aggravating biters had chewed on him for days.

I whispered, "If he hadn't arrested us, he wouldn't be itching."

A voice crackled from the sheriff's radio. "Nobody in here, but I see the remnants of firecrackers in a bathroom."

I snickered, and my buddies laughed. Clarence spun and glared. We swallowed our laughter and giggles. The deputy scratched and scowled at us. I covered my mouth to hide my smirk.

Clarence pointed a pair of fingers at his eyes. I read his lips as he said, "I'm watching you."

We slipped away from his suspicious view. Our kidnappers weren't in the crowd, so I guessed they'd escaped out the back. When we walked home, we kept an eye out for Marge's gang, but they didn't return.

Chapter 14

Hill's Jewelry Store

The following morning, we bicycled to Hill's Jewelry Store. Watches, rings, and bracelets adorned the display window, and a neon sign of yellow and green exclaimed, Gold Bought and Sold.

At the door, I read from a small sign. "The Copperhead, John Cooper, died here. John Jenkins, the proprietor, perished inside by a stray bullet."

A bell jingled as we entered. Mr. Hill was completing a sale, so we waited. His patron left, and he greeted us. Glasses sat atop his balding head, and a jeweler's loupe hung from a string around his neck. His face was round, which matched his midriff. Gray hair populated the circumference of his bald crown. The pinstripes on his black suit matched his scarlet tie. "How may I help you?" The shopkeeper had a soft and squeaky voice.

"Well, I'm not sure where to start," I said.

Marshal interrupted, "Is this really where John Jenkins died during the Charleston riot?"

He pulled his glasses down and measured my brother. "There's a question I don't get often. It was a long time ago."

"Almost a hundred years," Pippy interjected.

Mr. Hill said, "You are correct. This building was a dry-goods store then. John Jenkins was my wife's great-grandfather. They shot him dead where you're standing."

"Was he a Copperhead?" Butch asked.

"Heavens, no. Jenkins was a Republican. He was an innocent bystander who was minding his business. Eight or nine Copperheads lined up on the west side of the courthouse lawn and fired from over there."

Mr. Hill pointed across the street. "They opened fire without warning and killed six union soldiers and wounded others. When the fighting spread into the courthouse, they murdered a Union doctor. Then, Copperheads pulled rifles and pistols from a wagon on the east side of the square as they shouted, 'Hurrah for Jeff Davis.'"

Mr. Hill pointed eastward. "A local citizen on horseback rallied them. A soldier returned fire at a Copperhead, John Cooper, who was standing outside of this store."

We followed the jeweler to the storefront. "My wife's great-grandfather rushed to this spot to see the commotion. A shot intended for the rebel went through the glass and struck Mr. Jenkins."

"So, the same soldier killed Jenkins and Cooper?" Pippy asked.

"Yes, it's what the eyewitnesses claimed, but shots came from several directions. So stray bullets may have struck them, even from a Copperhead."

I asked, "Did they die here?"

"Cooper died on the spot. But they carried Jenkins a few doors down to the doctor's office where he perished.

Pippy commented, "We're standing at a place where a real Civil War battle occurred."

"Yes, young lady," Mr. Hill replied.

He pointed to his right. "After the shooting, the Copperheads ran east."

I asked, "Did they ever catch them?"

"Yes, word reached officers by telegraph in nearby Matton, and they dispatched Union soldiers by train. When they scoured the countryside, they rounded up a lot of the aggressors. But Sheriff O'Hare escaped to Canada."

"Did they hang the ones they caught?" Butch asked.

The jeweler replied, "No, they imprisoned them until the end of the war when President Lincoln pardoned them."

"It doesn't sound fair to just let them go," Cindy said.

"I suppose not, but Lincoln tried to heal the nation. He wanted everyone to forgive and forget."

"I wonder if the president knew any of the Copperheads?" Pippy asked.

The shopkeeper rubbed his chin and puckered his lips. "I never thought about it, but Lincoln lived in Charleston for a short while when his family moved from Kentucky. Later, he owned property south of town with his parents. Did you know he was an attorney and tried cases in the old courthouse?" The jeweler pointed across the street.

Pippy replied, "Yes, I did."

While I was very much enjoying Mr. Hills description of the riot, I remembered the reason for our visit. "Say, my grandfather was Tip...."

Marshal interrupted, "he owned Tip's Hardware Store."

The jeweler leaned back and examined me. "Now, I recognize you. You're the boys from the newspaper, Marshal and Patton."

We nodded.

I was hoping you'd come. The overweight businessman sauntered to a tall stool and sat behind the counter. "Your grandfather was a friend. Once I was in his store when the paperboy entered. As Tip paid, he made polite conversation. Tip asked, 'Will you be in Little League this summer, William?'"

Mr. Hill twisted on his stool. "The boy replied, 'No, sir. There won't be baseball this year.' Then Tip asked, 'No Little League?'"

Mr. Hill removed a handkerchief and wiped his neck. "The boy replied, 'The shoe factory closed. The ball diamond was on their land, and the bankruptcy court said we couldn't use it. The mayor is trying to figure something out, but they don't have money to build a new ball field'."

Mr. Hill said, "I overheard the conversation. Since I was a councilman, I confirmed the city's situation. There weren't funds for a new diamond."

"What happened next?" Butch asked.

"Well, Tip told me, if I could get the bankruptcy judge to sell the existing ballpark, he'd get the money."

"So, did the judge agree?" Pippy asked.

"He sure did. His son was the star pitcher for the first-place team." Mr. Hill burst into laughter.

"Did Tip's cousin donate the money?" Cindy asked.

"It's an interesting story. On the morning of the closing, the judge and I were in the bank waiting on your grandfather. Tip was a little late but showed up pulling a little red wagon."

"Like a kid's wagon?" I asked.

"Exactly. Tip pulled it into the office and closed the door. When he removed a blanket, there was a U.S. mint bag with the words One Cent printed on it. The judge remarked, 'It'll take a lot more than pennies to buy the land.'"

"What happened next," I asked.

"Tip slit the bag with a pocketknife. When Indian Head gold coins poured out, he grinned. I'd never seen one before, let alone a bag full. It took an hour to count and inspect those coins. When I calculated the value, there was enough to buy the land with money to spare. Tip said to use the extra for perpetual care."

"What's that?" Cindy asked.

"It means the city invested the money, and the interest pays for the upkeep on the ball field forever!"

Mr. Hill awaited our enthusiastic response. "Aren't you happy? Is something wrong?"

I swallowed my disappointment because Grandpa Tip had given away another bag of gold. I didn't speak for a moment but regained my composure. "*Uhm*, no, nothing. Everything is okay."

Mr. Hill continued, "When I saw the article in the newspaper, I suspected where he got the gold. His cousin was John Dillinger."

I didn't answer, but the jeweler studied my face. "Well, your face just answered my suspicion.".

I turned to leave, and my dejected friends followed.

"Wait, a minute."

We looked back, and Mr. Hill pointed his finger in the air. "I almost forgot. Your grandfather left you something."

He scurried into the back and returned with an envelope. "Not long before Tip died, he gave me this. He said he was preparing a treasure hunt for his grandsons. He instructed me to hold it until you showed up, looking for a clue."

Without opening it, we left. Once outside, I hurried to the Rexall drug store with my friends. We sat at a chrome-legged table and ordered root beers.

"Open it," Marshal said.

I slipped my finger under the flap and opened the envelope. When I removed a note with Grampa's handwriting, it said:

"Now   you've   learned   three   bags   are   gone.
The   final   clue   before   the   dawn.
Look   only   when   the   full   moon   shines
Amongst the dead, the grave confines.

129

"The   granite   spire   of   tallest   height.
Its   shadow   points   north   at   midnight.
An   iron   fence   impedes   the   goblins
Which whirl 'ore the grave of John Jenkins."

I said, "It sounds as if there's only one bag of gold left."

"It's still a lot of money," Butch said.

Cindy asked, "What do you make of this riddle?"

Pippy said, "Graves, it sounds like a cemetery to me."

Einstein spun toward her and wrung his hands. "Cemetery! I'm not going to a graveyard at midnight!"

Butch said, "Einstein's right. It says midnight during a full moon."

Einstein complained, "Goblins, midnight, full moon. Holy Geez Louise. Count me out."

Butch replied, "Before you wet your pants, let's just try to solve the rest of the riddle."

He leaned toward the note. "Which cemetery?"

I replied, "It says there's an iron fence. The Hilltop Cemetery on Madison Street has a wrought-iron rail around it."

Though I'd never entered, I was familiar with the graveyard because my grandmother lived nearby. The city aptly named it because the cemetery sat on the highest hill in town. During daylight hours, Marshal and I sometimes walked past on the aged, cracked, and uneven sidewalk. We stepped over the dilapidated concrete as we trekked up the incline by the tombstones. After dark, the most unholy time, we passed on the opposite side of the street. It was the perfect setting for a horror movie with scraggly trees; their unpruned, dead branches pointed skyward like a witch's fingers. Isolated from homes, without the streetlights, it was eerie. A stone wall kept the caskets from popping from the hillside. Just once did we climb the unlevel steps to the entrance, but we stopped at the wrought-iron arch — too afraid to enter. From there we could see tombstones leaning in all directions in the neglected graveyard. Each section of the spiked fence around the perimeter tilted back and forth. Most of the gravestones were limestone, and nature had almost erased the long-forgotten names, but a few were granite and still pristine.

"It's haunted!" Marshal protested.

Cindy flinched, and Einstein's face paled white.

"Haunted?" Pippy asked.

I said, "Grandma insisted she'd seen a Confederate soldier pacing amongst the graves under a full moon."

"A ghost?" Einstein asked. His voice quivered.

"Yep, he was roaming around the tombstones."

Marshal said, "He's back from the dead." He emphasized the word DEAD.

Cindy put her fingers in her ears. "Be quiet! I don't want to hear it."

Einstein's ever-sagging chin hung lower than usual, forming an open-mouth cavern.

"What'd your grandma do?"

"She said it frightened her at first, but she got accustomed to him over time."

Marshal continued, "She learned to ignore him. She said it was mutual respect."

"Your grandmother is a superstitious old woman," Butch replied.

"Geez, Louise, a ghost," Einstein moaned and wrung his hands.

"Man, did they bury your grandfather there?"

"No, the undertakers filled the graveyard years ago." I continued, "Grandma said there's a lot of Civil War dead buried there, including the Confederate."

"Why was a rebel soldier buried up north?" Pippy asked.

I answered, "He died on a train on the way to a Union prison camp, and they just dropped his body off at the station. The local undertaker said there was no shortage of gravediggers, though. So many men wanted a turn to put the gray-coat in the ground, they dug the deepest grave in town. The digging didn't stop until they hit water."

Marshal continued, "There's more. They threw his unwrapped body in with a splash, and everyone spat on the floating corpse. Then the townspeople took turns kicking dirt on him while Ole man Clark stomped it firmly."

I interrupted, "Farmer Clark lost two boys at the battle of Shiloh."

Marshall continued, "After he stomped on the grave, there wasn't enough soil left to make a mound."

"Is his grave marked?" Pippy inquired.

"I don't know," I answered.

Marshal added, "We never looked."

I said, "But, Grandma said he's buried next to Corley Appleston."

"The murderer?" Butch asked.

"Yep, the one the sheriff hung."

Cindy shivered and wrapped her arms around herself. She said, "This gives me chills."

Einstein said, "Please don't tell me, he shows himself when there's a full moon."

I shook my head. "Well, I never heard that version."

Marshal continued, "He arises whenever he wants."

Cindy shivered again and moaned.

Butch asked, "When's the next full moon?"

"You mean you plan to go?" Einstein asked.

"How else will we find the treasure?"

"Count me out, I'm not going into a cemetery at night." Einstein said.

Butch sneered at his cowardly brother. "I asked a question, and I'll ask it again. When is the next…?"

"Saturday," Pippy interrupted.

"How do you know?" Einstein asked.

"The drive-in movie theater is having a full-moon, double-feature, horror picture show on Saturday."

Einstein said, "That's where I'll be."

Butch responded, "Suit yourself, but I'll be at Hilltop Cemetery getting rich."

Pippy examined Cindy's face for assurance. She nodded her agreement, but Pippy spoke for them. "We'll be there."

Cindy added, "Probably…maybe."

I said, "We'll be on our grandmother's porch at the bottom of Cemetery Hill. Anyone with guts enough can meet there after dark."

Marshal added, "I want to be standing at John Jenkins tombstone at midnight, so don't be late."

I said, "Wear old clothes because we'll be digging for gold."

Chapter 15

Buried Treasure

On Saturday evening, we were at our grandmother's house. Our almost deaf Grandma went to bed when the streetlights came on, so adult supervision didn't restrain us. First, we found two shovels and a pickaxe in her shed. Then, we sat on the steps waiting for the others. The long shadows disappeared when the pumpkin-colored sky sank below Cemetery Hill. In a while, windows darkened as neighbors retired. After the bells in the Catholic church steeple chimed half-past eleven, five indiscernible silhouettes approached on bicycles. The front porch light exposed their faces.

"We had to wait on the girls," Butch complained.

"Well, we couldn't leave until our parents fell asleep," Pippy replied.

Butch rolled his eyes. Angel climbed off his bike.

"How d'you leave the house," Marshal inquired.

"Man, I crawled out of my bedroom window. I know I'll get caught."

"Stop worrying! Geez, I wish your window had stuck closed," Butch replied.

A black car puffing dark exhaust approached but didn't slow as it passed under a streetlight.

"Who was that?" I asked.

"I couldn't tell," Marshal answered.

"Butch, did anyone follow you?" I asked.

"I don't think so."

We waited awhile, but the car didn't return. The full moon offered a bright light between the broken clouds. I'd watched horror movies at the theater, and bad things happened on such a night. I figured no one wanted to leave the safety of the front stoop, but I stood and took a deep breath. "It's time."

"Let's go," Marshal added.

"Man-o-man, I hope we're not making a mistake."

Butch pointed to the Miller girls as he admonished his brother. "You're worse than the edgy girls."

Pippy and Cindy had their arms crossed as they shivered. Their matching expressions showed their mutual fear. "I've got goosebumps," Pippy whined.

"Me too," her sister said.

It seemed an excellent opportunity to hug Pippy. "Does that help?"

She nodded. Marshal rubbed Cindy's arms.

Butch asked, "Should we leave you lovebirds behind, or are you coming with us?"

I placed a shovel over my shoulder and took Pippy's hand. "Come on, Pippy, I'll protect you."

We walked at a rapid pace until we passed the last streetlight. As we slipped from the yellow-orange light, my feet seemed heavier. Pippy squeezed my fingers tighter, and everyone became quiet. The sidewalk inclined steeper as we climbed toward the cemetery.

Einstein stopped. "I'm not so sure about this."

"Don't be a pansy," Butch replied.

Einstein trailed behind the pack. It became more difficult to walk as the incline increased. Only by the light of the full moon did we avoid the uneven breaks in the concrete. Years of winter heaving and spring settling caused each section to tilt at odd angles. We avoided dinner-plate-size holes, now just pebbles and powder.

We were almost to the graveyard when a car approached, and we slipped into thick bushes. I was alone with Pippy in the darkness.

She asked, "Why are we hiding?"

I didn't want to admit my fear. "Just playing it safe."

She nodded. When she shivered again, I hugged her from the side. Pippy turned to me, so I put my arms around her waist. I enjoyed her willingness for my touch, but when the car passed, I turned my head. A light came from the window and scanned the bushes. The beam crossed our hiding place, so I held her close. When the passenger withdrew the flashlight, it lighted her face. It was Marge. I felt Pippy flinch when she saw our adversary.

"Her again," I whispered.

"How does she know to look here?"

"She always seems nearby," I replied.

"*Shh*, she'll hear you."

She laid her cheek on my chest as we waited. The driver punched the gas pedal, leaving a puff of noxious, oily fumes hanging in the summer air. Once gone, I eased my grip around Pippy's waist, but she didn't release me. Then, she relaxed her grasp and leaned back. Her once fearful face was different. She looked into my eyes and then at my lips.

I said, "What do we do now?

She said, "Follow your instincts."

She lowered her eyelids and puckered.

Butch pushed through the bushes. "Okay, you guys, don't start something you can't finish."

Embarrassed, we emerged from our hiding place and continued our late-night trek while holding hands. In the middle-of-the-night darkness, my reluctant teenage friends and I shuffled up the steep sidewalk until we reached the cemetery's wall.

The tilting stones struggled to restrain the hillside and the century-old caskets it held. The rock barrier was ten feet tall, but as we climbed, it became shorter. A pointed, wrought iron rail stood on top. Neglected, the sections tilted back and forth with occasional missing balusters. Honeysuckle vines twisted around the spikes and clung to the crumbling mortar. Had the trumpet-shaped flowers blared a warning, I may have fled.

We arrived at the first step and halted. I heard my heart pounding in my ears. I balanced greed and self-preservation in my juvenile brain.

Would the riddle really lead us to a hidden stash of John Dillinger's gold? Should I do this? Can I do this? Why am I doing this?

"This is it," Marshal, said, but he didn't move forward.

Two brick posts, one on each side, marked the entrance. A mason had carved a date into the cornerstone of one pillar.

"1827," I read aloud. I stared at the date for a long time. I was stalling.

Marshal said, "They set it one-hundred-forty years ago."

135

I pointed up the dozen, leaning limestone steps. "It's up there."

A distant train moaned while cicadas argued. The hair on my neck raised, and a chill quivered my body. Pippy slipped her hand from mine. "You go first."

Cindy joined her sister behind five hesitant boys. When Einstein tried to sneak to the back, the girls refused to allow his cowardice.

I forced my fifty-pound feet to climb each weather-worn step. I feigned bravery to impress Pippy. With an enormous effort, I reached the top and stood under the iron arch. A cloud passed, and the moonlight fell upon the cursive letters above us, which spelled Hilltop. The word Cemetery was missing but lay on the ground where it had fallen. I stepped over the Civil War-era sign into the graveyard for my first time.

Thunder groaned in the distance, and a breeze from an approaching storm raised goosebumps on my arms.

"Might rain," Marshal said.

Most of the shadowy tombstones were two or three feet tall, but in the back, stood a spire taller than the others. The gray stone glittered in the broken-clouded moonlight. A lightning bug perched on top, pulsated a warning like a lighthouse to a distressed ship.

I focused on the granite monument and hadn't seen a pair of prowling tomcats stalking one another. They'd tiptoed between the stones until both crouched before me. The feline confrontation erupted when eight legs launched, then met in a mid-air crash.

As extended claws swiped in a furious blur, I clenched my fingers and jerked my elbows back. I leaped airborne, hovered for a moment, then dropped in a crouch. As the cats tussled, Einstein won for first-out-of-the-gate. He knocked Cindy down as he made his retreat and never glanced over his shoulder as he streaked away. Now there were six of us—four boys and two girls.

The cat eruption subsided as fast as it had started—a draw with the two bleeding opponents alive to fight another day. I exhaled, stood, withdrew my fists from my armpits, and relaxed my fingers. Once everyone recovered, we continued our trek further into the funereal unknown. In a few dozen paces, we reached the eight-foot-tall spire, and the epitaph read:

John Jenkins

Beloved Husband and Father
Died September 28, 1864
43 yrs. 2 Months

"This is it," I said.

"John Jenkins' grave," Marshal added. I glanced over rows of tilting gravestones and waist-high pinnae plants. Planted years ago, the hardy perennials thrived without human care. A few of the fist-sized blooms lingered beyond their regular season. The deep-purple flowers appeared gray in the darkness, but their bold fragrance broadcasted their presence.

I closed my eyes and inhaled the calming scent. It was a short respite to gather the courage to continue. *We've come this far; I can't stop now.*

Trying to reassure myself as well as my friends, I said, "Mom grew up down the hill from this cemetery. She said, 'Don't fear the dead. It's the living ones who'll hurt you.'"

Pippy looked over both shoulders and said, "I'm afraid of both."

I squinted at my watch, which read one minute until midnight. An ash-white, full moon, crossing in the southern sky, peeped through an opening in the clouds. A shadow from the monument pointed downhill, and the apex ended on the door of a mausoleum.

"It's pointing toward the tomb," I said.

"North as Grampa Tip predicted," Marshal added.

Side-by-side we passed the drooping crown and slouching limbs of a weeping willow. As we neared the small limestone building, I could see it more clearly.

Atop the peak was a lightning rod attached to a thick copper wire snaking to the ground. The stone door hung on four iron hinges and carved in the white gable was the word, Postal. On each end of the inscription was an engraved angel blowing a trumpet. English ivy climbed the walls and covered most of the aging edifice.

Mounted on both sides of the entrance were two tarnished, brass plaques. Etched in the pitted plate on the top left, were the words, Julia - Died 1841. The sign below read, Ewan - Died 1833. The upper right panel was blank, but stamped in the one below was, Margaret - Infant Child.

"It's a family — mother, father, and baby," Marshal said.

"There are four chambers in the mausoleum, but only three contain bodies," I said.

Butch pushed me aside. "Out of the way, I'm going inside."

When he grabbed the tarnished doorknob, it turned in his hand. Butch stiffened. The handle slipped from Butch's grasp as the door swung open, and a shadowy apparition appeared. I saw the dark phantom... after Butch fainted. My friend had slumped onto his back as if he melted. His eyelids were half-open, but only the whites showed.

Angel fled. Three boys, one unconscious, and two girls remained on the hunt for the hidden treasure. The girls shrieked, but I couldn't hear them because I was screaming louder. I'd have run had my feet obeyed my panicking mind.

Pippy and Cindy had no problem running in place with arms flailing. Marshal froze like the wooden Indian at Grandpa Tip's store.

The shadowy ghost emerged before four wide-eyed teens. Now silent, with gaping mouths, we stared at the tall figure in the doorway. By the full moonlight, I saw his thin face and gray, bushy eyebrows.

His voice rumbled like a kettle drum. He said, "I've been expecting you."

We stood in stunned silence.

Crickets chirped,

       Chirped,

             Chirped.

An owl broke the human silence and shouted, "Who?" But by then, I knew who.

"I know you," I said.

Marshal added, "You're Sparky."

He nodded. The pencil-thin, six-footer stepped over the still unconscious Butch and tipped his wide-brimmed hat. The mysterious man wore a black, leather duster, a knee-length coat, smudged with white dust. I hadn't noticed it before, but he had squinty eyes.

"That's right. My nickname is Sparky."

"What're you doing here?" I asked.

"I live here. Well, I should say I sleep here most nights. Soon I'll sleep here every night."

He stepped to the side and pointed toward the open door. "It's a perfect place, quiet."

In the slanted light of the moon, I viewed an aisle. On the left side was a solid stone wall. Sparky tapped on the white partition.

"This side is full, two vaults, one on top of the other."

I asked, "Full of what?"

"Caskets."

I shivered. Sparky turned to the other side and pointed downward.

"There's only one occupied burial chamber on this side."

A quilt and pillow lay above the stone slab.

"Is this where you spend the nights?" I asked.

"Yep, right here."

Pippy gazed from a distance. "It's creepy."

"I guess so, but I'm glad because no one bothers me here."

"I know why," Pippy remarked.

"It's not so bad." He slipped his hands into the deep pockets of his oil-rubbed, cotton overcoat. Thunder rumbled in the distance as a storm approached. Sparky scanned the approaching clouds marching toward us.

A swooping bat from nowhere snapped a mosquito just inches from my nose. My friends were unaware of the dive bomber, so I shivered alone.

"This mausoleum is mine. These people are my family. Julia and Ewan are my grandparents, and baby Margaret is my aunt who died before I was born."

He stepped outside and pointed at tombstones to the east. "My great-grandparents are over there. I guess you could say it's our neighborhood. Someday, they'll bury me here too."

Butch woke and sat up. He studied his surroundings as if struggled to get his bearings.

"Where?" Pippy asked.

"Right where I sleep, on top of Margaret. I suppose I'm practicing for the long snooze. It's comfortable enough."

She asked, "Are your parents buried nearby?"

"No, they're in Lake Michigan. Lightning struck our sailboat."

"Were you with them?" Marshal asked.

"Yep, I was a boy then. A sudden storm approached, and Mom and Dad sent me below as they tried to lower the sail. The bolt split the mast and blasted them into the water. It was my first lightning strike."

"First?" Marshal asked.

"Yeah, it's hit me three times, so I'm a human lightning rod. People say I attract it." Sparky peered at the threatening sky, so I stepped back just in case.

"After my parents died, my grandparents raised me. When they died, I made it a practice to visit their graves every day. I could never leave them."

"Seems you were close," I said.

"Yes, and we still are. I come here to talk to them."

"Talk?" I asked.

"Grandpa is a good listener, and Grandma gives me advice. I need them."

I tilted my head forward and curled my eyebrows as I tried to decide if he was crazy.

"When they died, I inherited this mausoleum. One day I came to visit my grandparents, and the caregiver gave me a key."

"But, why do you sleep here; don't you have a home?" Pippy asked.

"Not anymore, they're tearing it down, so I've got nowhere else to go. Since I must move, I want to be close to my family. This way, Grandma can sing me to sleep at night. This is just right."

Whew, this guy IS crazy.

Even in the dim light, I could see my friends with tilted heads and squinting eyes appearing to reach the same conclusion.

"My grandma thinks you're a ghost," Marshal interjected.

Sparky smiled. "Not yet."

Butch rose and stared into the west. Occasional lightning flashes preceded the thunderclaps by several seconds. "Nasty weather is coming, should we leave?"

I examined the ominous clouds then turned back to Sparky. "You said you've been expecting us?"

Sparky said, "Oh, yes, Tip was a great guy and a friend to every hard-luck man in town. He often helped me, so I helped him bury a bag of pennies. He told me to show you where if you came looking."

We followed Sparky across the cemetery. He lifted his finger toward the crown of a hill. "It's up there at the Union Soldier section."

140

We climbed a gentle slope to the top. At the crest was a field of white gravestones placed flat with the grass. The hallowed plateau was about the size of a basketball court, but circular. In the center was a cannon with the stones radiating outward in descending rows.

"This is a memorial garden for men who served in the Union Army," Sparky said.

He removed his hat and held it over his heart. A gust of wind pushed his already disheveled hair behind his ears. Sparky looked toward the approaching storm and squinted his eyes. "The breeze means a front is coming. Cold fronts bring storms and lightning."

I ignored his weather forecast. "Did these men die during the war?"

He placed his hat back on his head. "Most did, and others died later. But everyone buried here served as an Illinois volunteer during the Civil War."

"There're a lot of graves," Pippy said.

"Seven of the dead were victims of the Charleston Riot," Sparky said.

He pointed to a marker below his feet. "Here's one. This is where they interred Major York. He was a surgeon in the medical corp. A Copperhead shot him in the back."

We were silent. Sparky's finger moved to adjacent graves. "Sallee, Goodrich, Near, Swim, and Hart. They all died in the riot—without weapons."

Lightning flashed in the distance followed by a rumble.

I said, "Storm's coming."

Sparky replied, "Don't stand on this hill when there's lightning. It's the highest point around here, and dangerous."

I asked, "So, where d'you bury the bag?"

Marshal said, "Yeah, let's get cracking."

Sparky looked at the threatening sky. "Don't say cracking, I don't want another crack of lightning."

"Follow me," he said.

He paused at the cannon. "This has been here since the Civil War. Colonel Mitchell of the Illinois Fifty-Fourth Infantry placed it here after the riot. Three Copperheads accosted Mitchel in the courthouse and wounded him. It was a miracle he survived. While he was fighting for his life, he saw Major York shot in the back and killed."

Sparky patted the cannon, then rubbed his hand up and down the barrel. "With so many Confederate sympathizers in the area, he feared there'd be another uprising, so he put this weapon on this high point. The Colonel pointed it toward a wooden bridge."

Sparky pointed in the direction where the soldiers aimed it. "You can't see it now, but in the daylight, it's visible about a mile away. The Colonel planned to blow the bridge if the Copperheads attacked."

"Can this cannon shoot that far?" Butch asked.

"Yep, and with amazing accuracy."

Butch questioned further, "Can a cannonball take out a bridge?"

"They fired not only iron balls during the Civil War. Sometimes, they packed shells with gunpowder and shrapnel, and those did a lot of damage."

"Why'd he put it in the cemetery?" Pippy asked.

"It was the high ground, where the army wants to be in a battle. Besides, the Colonel found it fitting since it was with his dead soldiers."

"Why is it still here?" I asked.

"The soldiers abandoned it after the war, so the City left it. They made it the centerpiece of the Union Memorial garden."

Butch seemed impatient with the long-winded Sparky, and he paced while waiting for him to finish. "That's interesting, but where d'you bury the pennies?"

"Right here. I'm standing on it," Sparky replied.

He stomped on a slab of white limestone and pointed between his shoes. "Three feet down, you'll find an army footlocker, and inside, wrapped in a green tarp, is your bag."

"Let's dig," Butch said.

A not-too-distant flash crackled in the charged air, causing Sparky to flinch. "I'm not staying on top of this hill."

He retreated to the safety of his shelter. As he ran down toward his mausoleum, he glanced back. "You boys and girls better go home and come back tomorrow."

I responded, "He may be right. Maybe we should leave."

When I turned around, Butch was already prying the stone slab with the pickaxe. He lifted it with little effort, and Marshal helped him move the grave marker to the side. They both pitched dirt with furious vigor.

Cindy gazed skyward when the thunder rolled nearer. A few miles away, flashes of lightning illuminated sheets of rain beating on cornfields.

She said, "The storm is getting closer."

Pippy added, "Let's come back tomorrow."

"Not me," Butch replied.

Marshal added, "We're too close now."

Marshal and Butch crumbed out the loose soil above the recently buried box. In a few minutes, a shovel hit something hard. They stopped digging and smiled at one another.

"We found it!" Butch cried.

Excitement rushed through me as my heart pounded. Rustling leaves, clinging to waving branches, warned of the approaching storm. The increased wind prevented my hearing a car or the four slamming doors. Flickering lights caught my attention after it was too late. I whirled around and saw Angel leading three bobbing flashlights. But Butch and Marshal dug at a breakneck pace still unaware of the impending danger.

As Angel approached, followed by Marge's gang, his dejected, hanging head expressed his sorrow.

"Man, I'm sorry."

Butch and Marshal still pitched dirt. Three beams of light illuminated the lid of the wooden box.

"Hold the light still," Butch said.

He dropped to his knees and pawed the soil away from the army footlocker. Marshal hunched beside him. "This is it!"

Marshal looked up and grinned, but his toothy smile soon sagged. Butch was still on his knees when Marshal tapped him on the shoulder.

"What?"

Marshal pointed upward with his jacked-up eyebrows. Butch looked puzzled but rose to his feet. His face sagged.

"Man-o-Man, I'm so sorry. They made me tell them."

Marshal and Butch stepped from the three-foot-deep hole as Marge waved a pistol.

"Move it!"

We teens huddled together.

"Lift it out of there," she ordered her male cohorts.

The men freed the box and pulled it out, then placed it on the ground at our feet. After they released the latches and opened the lid, Petey unfolded the oil-slick tarp and found a canvas bag.

"After all these years, we found it!" Marge exclaimed.

Petey replied, "There's only one, though."

Marge pointed her pistol at me. "Where's the rest?"

"Gone."

Marshal added, "Grandpa Tip gave it away. This is all that's left."

Marge gritted her teeth and made a devilish groan. Meanwhile, Petey and Mack lifted the box by the handles. They strained and started toward the car.

Marge waved her pistol with a menacing expression. "You keep your mouth shut about this. If you tell anyone, I'll come back here and fill you with lead."

I was too afraid to reply. As Marge pointed the gun at each of us, one at a time, we stared bug-eyed. She asked each teenager, "Understand?"

She waited until we nodded. I heard the car engine start. Before she left, she wrinkled her nose like a growling dog. Then, she sneered. "I suppose I shouldn't be so hard on you because you helped me find the gold. Tell you what, I'll share. I'll take the coins, and you can have the hole."

Only she found it funny. Her laugh sounded sinister as she sauntered away. We stood dejected beside the tarnished cannon while staring into the empty pit. Gone was the thrill of the hunt. Disappointment draped me like a wet blanket as my hopes departed with the despicable gang. It was hard to accept they had the gold.

"Do you suppose we should call the police?" Pippy asked.

I replied, "I think we should keep our mouths shut."

Marshal added, "We don't want her to come back and fill us full of lead."

A brief opening in the clouds allowed the moon to illuminate the serene cemetery. Tombstone shadows stretched across the grass. The wind stopped blowing, and the purple lilac blooms hung like bunches of grapes.

"The bad weather has passed," I said.

I mourned the loss of the gold, but at least I got a girlfriend. I slipped my hand into Pippy's. When I turned to look at her, I was shocked. Her hair stood straight up on the top and out on the sides.

"How d'you do that?" I asked.

"What?"

I pointed above her head. "How do you make your hair stand on end?"

Pippy slid her fingers through her fly-away strands. She looked puzzled, but her eyes bulged when she saw me. "Your hair is crazy too."

We leaned forward, studied each other, then looked at the others. She cried, "Everyone's hair is sticking out!"

Everyone was wide-eyed. Our hair defied gravity, so what caused it?

"Hey, you foolish kids!"

I turned, and Sparky was yelling and waving his arms. "Can't you see you're human lightning rods. Get to the lower ground! Hurry!"

In an instant, we scattered in different directions. I ran downhill then dropped behind a gravestone. Marshal and Butch hid beside John Jenkin's spire, and the girls were out of my sight. A few drops of rain splattered on my now relaxed hair. I saw Sparky slip back into the mausoleum.

He turned and shouted, "And don't hide under a tree." Then, he closed the door.

"Everyone okay?" I yelled.

"Yep."

"We're okay."

Was it safe to run for Grandma's house?

At that moment, everything illuminated like daylight. An intense flash with a clap of thunder shook my internal organs. Light surrounded the twelve-hundred-pound cannon. It jumped when struck by the lightning bolt.

The Civil War relic dropped from a six-inch hop. I smelled the odor of ozone from the electrified oxygen. Then, all was peaceful.

We raised from our hiding places and looked around. Then the cannon barrel trembled. The wheels quivered, and the ground vibrated. Until then, no one suspected the soldiers had left the abandoned weapon loaded.

The potential energy in the damp, packed powder was enormous. The twelve-pound shell erupted with a mighty roar chased by a five-foot flame. It seemed, for a hundred years, the ball had waited the dynamic release. Once airborne, the whistling projectile climbed and made an arc.

I felt the ear-shattering discharge vibrate my guts. It made my liver quiver. Citizens heard the cannon fire for miles. The blazing-hot missile made an arc and descended toward its intended target.

It landed where the Union soldiers had aimed it. The powder-loaded shell exploded on impact. The central portion of the old wooden bridge disintegrated, then the two ends folded. It collapsed before the oncoming getaway car.

Petey braked but couldn't stop as the bridge dropped before him. The airborne Ford Fairlane almost made it across the narrow, but deep ravine — but didn't.

It stood, grille down, in two feet of water when the police arrived. Three stunned gangsters crawled out of the missing windshield and slid down the angled hood. Marge lost her grip and fell. She sat in the waist-deep creek when the sheriff looked down at her. Petey yelled for help because he hung from the hood-ornament. Mack tried to crawl up the muddy bank without success.

In a while, firefighters extinguished the burning timbers as a few bystanders stared from the sides along with us.

Cindy whined, "Oh, we're in so much trouble."

I replied, "We did nothing wrong; it was lightning."

As the red and white fire engine lights faded in the morning light, a single fireman sprayed a hose on the smoldering timbers.

We watched the water run from the grill as the wrecker winched the damaged vehicle from the creek. When the operator lowered the rear-end of the twisted auto, the trunk popped open revealing the green, army-surplus box.

"It's mine." I pointed at Marge. "She stole it."

"He's lying," Marge replied. "It's ours."

Deputy Jones leaned over the trunk. Grandpa Tip's name was stenciled on the lid.

"It was my grandfather's," I said.

"I bought it from him," Marge replied.

The deputy looked at Marge and tilted his head. "If it's yours, what's in it?"

She didn't answer.

"Seems you'd know what was inside if you'd bought it," the deputy said.

The officer popped the latches and opened the lid. Then, he removed the canvas. He read aloud, "United States Mint. One Cent."

He turned to me with a quizzical expression. "One Cent? They stole pennies from you?"

Hushed silence was my response. I didn't want to reveal the real contents.

"Where did you get these?" he asked.

Once again, I remained silent as he stared at me.

"Someone better talk."

The sheriff approached. "What's going on here?"

The deputy pointed at the box. "The boy claims it's his, but she says it's hers."

He pointed to Marge. "The boy claims she stole it from him."

"She did," I proclaimed. My friends chimed in to bolster my claim.

The busy sheriff glanced at the bag. "It's just pennies."

The deputy said, "But, sir, it's evidence."

"Don't pettifog, Clarence."

"I'm not, Sheriff. This might be important."

The senior officer glanced into the trunk then back at the young deputy. He inhaled, then exhaled as he rubbed his chin and listened as Clarence insisted on his theory. The two wrangled for a while then the deputy pointed at Marge and her wily gang. "Sheriff, it would be stupid for them to steal pennies."

"No one said thieves are smart," the sheriff retorted. Sheriff Jones removed his hat and brushed his hair back as he examined us. He ran the edge of his hand through the fold in his Stratton felt hat then placed it back on his head. He pulled a stick of chewing gum from his shirt pocket and removed the wrapper. When he put it in his mouth, he chewed for what seemed forever. Unnerving tension wracked my body.

"Okay, open it," Sheriff Jones ordered.

The deputy smiled then removed a black knife from his cargo pants and flipped it open. The blade protruded six inches out with a scalloped, unsharpened side.

"Holy cow, what are you doing with such a weapon?" the sheriff said.

I grimaced as I awaited the exposure of our treasure. The deputy ignored his uncle's comment and slit the bag from top to bottom with one slash. Pennies spilled into the box. The deputy looked surprised, but not as much as me. My friends' mouths gaped too.

"It makes no sense...," said the deputy.

The exasperated sheriff raised his eyebrows and asked, "Well?"

The deputy shrugged his shoulders. "Clarence, give them their pennies," he ordered as he walked away.

Marge, Petey, and Mack stood speechless. So, did I.

Petey shoved his hand into the bag, but when he removed it, only pennies poured from his palm. "Pennies?" he asked.

"Pennies?" I echoed.

Disbelief turned to disappointment as we stared at the copper coins. The tow truck operator motioned for Clarence to sign his work order, so he walked away.

Butch moaned, "All this for a lousy bag of pennies."

"Dillinger must have stolen a real sack of pennies by mistake," I said.

Mister Miller parked and stepped out of his car. Pippy gave Cindy a we're-in-trouble look.

Cindy said, "We've gotta go."

Pippy nodded her head then rushed to the car. Her father held the door open without a word to the girls. As he walked to the driver's side, he gave me an icy stare. I knew I'd need to keep my distance from the Miller's house for a while. Butch walked away too.

"Won't you help us carry the box?" I asked.

"Nope. You can have it," Butch said.

I turned to Marshal and said, "It looks like it's just you and me."

Petey's shocked face changed. A red flush crept up his neck and he gritted his teeth. Then, he grabbed me by the neck. "Where's the gold?"

Stunned, I didn't answer.

"Where is it?" Marge asked.

"I don't know. Gone, I guess."

Mack clasped Marshal's arm like a vice. "Answer her, where's the gold?"

"That hurts," Marshal said.

Petey clenched the hair on the back of my head and pulled me to him. His breath smelled of cigarettes. He jerked my head back. "If you don't talk, I'll break your neck."

I uttered, "Uh, uh, uh."

Then he tilted my head forward, and my forehead smashed into his chest. Beneath his Vee-neck shirt hung a gold medallion nestled on his chest hair. I pulled back, and he leaned forward. The medallion spun. It was Grandpa Tip's pendant.

I grabbed the St. Christopher medal and snapped it from the chain. I took a clump of hair with it. Petey yelped and loosened his grasp. As he danced and rubbed his aching skin, I escaped.

Petey's howling distracted Marge and Mack for a moment. I rushed to Deputy Jones and thrust the medallion in his face.

"What?" he asked.

"This was Grandpa Tip's medal. He kept it in his office."

"So?" The deputy followed my finger as I pointed to Petey.

"He had it, so he stole it," I said.

Deputy Jones squinted his eyes as he peered at the man rubbing his chest. He folded his notebook and slipped it into his hip pocket as he stared at the trio. Marge seemed to notice the deputy's gaze.

"They were there; they must have killed Grandpa Tip!" I cried.

Marge flinched. She glanced left and right. Deputy Jones unbuttoned his holster as he approached the trio.

Still holding Marshal's, Mack pulled a hidden revolver, and held it to Marshal's head. "Come any closer, and I'll shoot the boy."

Marshal stopped wiggling as Deputy Jones drew his pistol and aimed. Sheriff Jones noticed the commotion, reached inside his car, and grabbed a shotgun. "Take it easy. Let the boy go and put down your gun."

"Get back," Mack demanded.

Marge pulled a weapon from behind her back and pointed it at the deputy. "You heard him. Get back!" Marge yelled.

Deputy Jones didn't budge, but I ran behind the car with the sheriff.

The sheriff shouted, "I've got a bead on you, Marge, don't move!"

Bystanders fled for safety.

"Put down your gun, or he gets it!" Mack yelled.

Deputy Jones lowered his weapon and placed it on the ground.

Mack said, "Now back up if you want to enjoy good health."

Deputy Jones backed away until he stood beside the sheriff. I felt safe behind the squad car but worried for my wide-eyed brother. Mack removed the pistol barrel from Marshal's head and aimed it at the sheriff. "We're taking this boy, and we're getting in the tow truck. If you follow my instructions, no one will get hurt."

Marshal's expression showed he had a different plan. He stomped on Mack's foot and shoved him. The awkward gangster flipped backward and slid down the muddy embankment.

Marshal bolted for his escape. The scoundrel Marge pointed her pistol toward the sheriff and pulled the trigger, but nothing happened. Water dripped from the barrel.

A quick-thinking fireman turned the firehose on Marge and Petey, and t hey fell backwards down the muddy slope. The sheriff and his deputy rushed to the edge. The gangsters flailed in the murky stream. I ran to look at the wet and muddy crooks too.

"Nice work," the sheriff said to the fireman.

He nodded and smiled while dousing the smoldering bridge timbers. Sheriff Jones let Marge's gang flail for a while before throwing them a rope. He wouldn't let Clarence arrest them until the fireman had rinsed off the mud. Clarence appeared excited to make the arrest. As the deputy's car departed, the sheriff put his hand on my shoulder. "Come on, boys, I'll give you a ride home."

Chapter 16

The Stranger

Marshal rolled pennies at Grandpa Tip's desk, as I watched. He folded the ends of a penny roll. "Fifty dollars."

I surveyed our accomplishment. "A hundred rolls," I added.

My brother separated the coin tubes into two piles. We didn't wrap one odd-looking penny but used one from my pocket to fill the wrapper. "Fifty rolls for you and the same for me."

"What do you plan to do with your twenty-five bucks?" I asked.

"Buy a new bike, how about you?"

I said, "Don't know, I'll save it for now."

Dad interrupted, "Stop counting your riches, we've still got work to do."

I shook my head. "We thought we'd found a bag of gold coins".

"But they're only copper pennies," Marshal said.

Dad replied, "Don't be discouraged. You solved a murder, an amazing accomplishment for two teenagers."

"Yeah, we found Grandpa Tip's medallion too," Marshal said.

When he turned to admire the St. Christopher medal hanging around the eagle's neck, someone knocked on the door. Marshal ran to unlock the door. A muffled conversation followed, and Marshal reappeared followed by the fisherman we met at the lake.

"This is Mr. Herbert," Marshal said.

My father stood and shook his hand, and I did too.

"John Herbert, you can call me John."

"I'm Abe...."

John interrupted my father. "I know who you are."

Dad appeared puzzled. "The store is no longer in business, so I'm not buying."

The man replied, "I'm not a salesman. I read about your father's death in the newspaper, and it saddened me. He was a friend."

Dad wrinkled his brow. "I never heard him mention you."

"Ours was a low-key friendship. I enjoyed my privacy, and Tip respected it."

"Oh, I see," Dad replied.

"When your boys solved the case, it impressed me." Mr. Herbert rubbed my head. "Good job. Tippy would have been proud of you."

Dad still looked perplexed. "So, tell me about your relations with my father."

"We met as boys in Indiana. We joined the Navy together."

Dad offered Mr. Herbert a seat with an extended arm and open palm.

"I washed out. Navy life wasn't for me."

"My father served three years," Dad said

"So, did I, but my time was in prison," said Mr. Herbert.

"I'm sorry."

"Me too. In fact, I served several sentences and didn't see Tip again until I moved to Greencastle."

"That was long ago."

"Yep. Tippy wanted me to hire him, but he drank too much back then."

"Oh, what was your business?"

Mr. Herbert smiled. "Bank security is the best description. They improved their defenses because of me."

"Well, there were a lot of robbers back then," Dad said.

"Yes, George Nelson, Bonnie and Clyde, and Ma Barker, to name a few."

Marshal added, "John Dillinger too."

I said, "We're related."

The older man replied, "Is that so?"

"He was my grandpa Tip's cousin," Marshal said.

"Once, my father met him," I inserted.

Dad smiled and said, "When I was just a little boy."

Mr. Herbert removed a pack of cigarettes from his shirt pocket, he offered one to my father. Dad accepted it. My father moved an ashtray so they could share.

"I can tell you a lot about John Dillinger," Mr. Herbert said.

"Really," I asked.

"Yep. I studied all the bank robbers. I even kept a scrapbook. It's why I'm here. Tip and I worked for years writing a book about the criminals of the thirties."

"I didn't know about the project," Dad replied.

Mr. Herbert exhaled a column of smoke. "That's too bad. Tip had our only copy, and I was hoping you'd found it."

Dad scanned the room before he answered. "I don't think it's here. We've looked everywhere except the safe, and we don't know the combination to it. But, if it's there, I'll let you know."

Mr. Herbert nodded. "Thanks, it's an amazing manuscript with never-before-told information—revelations, in fact. I met a few notorious criminals while in prison. It's in the book, and a lot more."

"Very interesting," Dad replied.

"I predict it'll be a best-seller."

"Is that so?" Dad asked. "Why?"

"The man the FBI gunned down outside of the Biograph Theater in Chicago wasn't John Dillinger."

Dad had a curious but suspicious expression. "That's a bold claim."

"That's why I said it's a revelation," Mr. Herbert responded.

"I've heard the conspiracy theory, but they can't prove it. Do you have proof?"

"Incontrovertible. John Dillinger is still alive."

Dad had a bug-eyed expression. "No!"

"Yes, your father's cousin is alive."

"But Dillinger's father identified his body," Dad said.

Mr. Herbert snuffed his cigarette. "Not at first. The senior Dillinger first claimed the body wasn't his son."

Dad stood. "Do you mean he changed his story so his son could escape?"

Mr. Herbert nodded. "Yep, so he could start a new life."

"Holy Cow, did my father know?"

"Yes, he did."

Dad placed his hand on his cheek. "Wow."

"Look at this." Mr. Herbert handed Dad a coin.

"It's an Indian-head," Dad said.

Mr. Herbert said, "Saint Gauden's, you may recognize it from the newspaper."

While Dad fidgeted with the gold piece, Marshal and I eased closer.

Dad asked, "Is this the exact same coin as in the picture?"

Mr. Herbert nodded. "Dillinger wants you to have it."

Dad asked, "So, you know where Dillinger is at these days?"

Mr. Herbert nodded. "Dillinger spent the last thirty-five years as a quiet citizen with few friends. He regretted his criminal life. Tip helped him make amends over the years, but he couldn't right all the wrongs."

Dad said, "I suppose not."

Mr. Herbert looked at my father with pensiveness. "Call me if you locate my manuscript. It needs finishing touches, then off to the publisher who's already waiting for it."

Mr. Herbert rested his hands on his knees. "I'll share the proceeds with you since you're his nearest relative. It's only fair."

Dad asked, "How will I reach you?"

"You won't; I'll find you. I'm a bit of a recluse and don't have a telephone."

Dad nodded. Mr. Herbert brushed back his salt-and-pepper hair, he looked healthier than most men his age. Though snow was on the roof, he wasn't white-headed like Grandpa Tip had been.

Mr. Herbert scanned the store and pointed to a neon sign hanging inside the plate-glass window. "Tell you what, if you want to talk to me, turn on the sign. If it's on, I'll stop."

Dad nodded. "I work during the week, so I can only meet you on the weekend. So, if you see the light on, I'll be here the next Saturday morning."

Mr. Herbert nodded then leaned forward in his seat and glanced at the pennies on the desk. "What are these?"

I said, "Dillinger stole four bags of gold from the Greencastle bank, but one sack was only pennies. We're gonna convert them to dollars."

He said, "Hmm. You don't say." Mr. Herbert put his finger on a silver penny and pulled it closer. After putting on reading glasses, he examined it. "This one

154

is steel, so take it to a coin dealer and have him appraise it. Also, ask him to give you the history behind it."

Mr. Herbert pitched the one-cent-piece back on the desk, stood, and shook my father's hand. On his way out, he pointed to the statuette. "Another thing. I suggest you remove the paint from your eagle. I once had one, and when I scratched it, the metal was beautiful."

We turned toward the statue. Dad responded, "I was thinking of scrapping it…."

When we looked back, he had left. .

Chapter 17

The Steel Penny

The next morning, we went to Pappy's house. When he greeted us, I pulled the steel penny from my pocket and handed it to him. "How much is this worth?"

Pappy examined the coin. "It's worth a dollar, more or less."

Marshal said, "That's great, do you want to buy it?"

"Sure, they're not very rare, but I don't have one in my collection."

After Pappy removed a dollar from his billfold, he put the bill back. He reached into his pocket and sorted through his change and handed Marshal two quarters. "You won't have to break a dollar this way."

"Thanks, Pappy," Marshal said.

Pappy found five dimes for me.

"Thanks, oh yeah, can you tell me about the steel penny?"

"Sure, it's made of steel rather than copper."

"Why?" Marshal asked.

Pappy opened his hand to show us the coin. "During World War II, there was a shortage of copper, so the mint coined pennies from steel. The government minted them for just one year, so these might become rare someday."

"Wait, a minute. If they made this penny during the War...?"

I leaned closer to examine the coin. "Oh my gosh, the date is 1943."

Marshal asked, "Why's 1943 important?"

"They minted this coin nine years after John Dillinger died!"

Marshal's chin dropped.

I continued, "There's no way John Dillinger stole this penny."

Marshal said, "The bag is a fake"
I turned toward Pappy. "Thanks again and so long."
We rushed from his porch and jumped on our bikes.
"There might be a bag of gold somewhere, Patton."
"Yep, the treasure hunt isn't over."

#

The next day was Saturday, and Marshal and I were alone at Grandpa Tip's store. We were there to clean, but we were too excited because of the gold. My pile of dust was tiny, and Marshal hadn't collected much either.

"We're talking too much. We'll never get done unless we work faster," I said.

While Marshal cleaned the office floor, I swept the aisles. Someone had tracked a white powder across the floor and into the office. After sweeping, I mopped the spots and let them dry. Then, I polished the wood floor with a floppy wool applicator the way Grandpa Tip had showed me. Dad planned to sell the building, and he wanted it to look perfect. Now, it appeared to have a thick layer of glass on top of the wood planks.

I lay on the counter and waited for the fresh wax to dry. While dust bunnies floated in the sunbeams, I hoped they'd stay airborne and not settle on the drying floor. My eyelids felt heavy, and I fell asleep. I awoke when I landed on the floor. "Ouch."

It took me a few seconds to realize I'd fallen from the counter. With my hands spread out, I felt the wax with my palm, and it wasn't sticky. As I lay on my stomach, I saw a dull spot in front of me. I raised up to my hands and knees. There was a shoe print. I touched it but it was below the surface. I looked around, and other spots were visible too. Someone had tracked from the entrance to the office.

Marshal shouted from the other room. "Do you see what I see?"
"Footprints?" I asked
Marshal walked from the office. "It leads from the front door," he said.
I followed him into the office where there were more spots.
"We waxed over footprints," Marshal said.
"What would leave prints like these?" I asked.
Marshal shook his head. "Dad won't like this."

Dejected, I sat at the desk. We gazed at the footprints. They seemed to be everywhere, but there were more around the safe.

"Shoot, I can even read the stamp there. It says, Brown Shoe Company."

I said, "It looks like a boot."

We stared at the footprints for a while.

Marshal said, "Oh, well. There's nothing we can do about it now."

I sighed. "All I can think of are the missing coins, anyway." I said.

"Where can they be?" Marshal asked.

"Who knows? The possibilities are limitless."

"Let's make two lists," Marshal said. "First, people who might have it, and second, where Grandpa might have hidden it."

I removed a sheet of paper from the desk drawer, and I searched for a pencil. The only writing instrument I found was a fountain pen. After I unscrewed the cap, I examined the dry tip. When I took it apart, there was plenty of ink, so I touched the pen to my tongue. When I scratched on the paper, the ink began to flow. I was careful because fountain pens could be messy.

"Do I have to wait all day?" Marshal asked.

I ignored his sarcasm and said, "Who could have stolen it? Maybe Marge and her boys did."

He said, "They had the St. Christopher medal."

I nodded. "Okay, write their names. But remember, how taken back Marge was when we only had one bag and again when it was just pennies?"

I spun the pen between my lips. "You're right, how about Mr. Hill? Grandpa Tip left a note for us with him. Did he read it before we got there?"

He said, "You're stretching. Even if Mr. Hill solved the riddle, he wouldn't have found the gold. The riddle would have just led him to Sparky."

"Uh-huh. Mr. Hill didn't have access to the gold, so I'll strike his name."

Then, I leaned back in the chair and concentrated. "But Sparky is someone we should consider."

Marshal hiked-up an eyebrow. "Put a star beside his name."

"Anyone else?" I asked.

"How about the priest? He was friends with Grandpa Tip. He may know more than he's telling."

I tilted my head and closed one eye. "Not likely."

Marshal agreed with a head nod, but I wrote the father's name, anyway.

Marshal said, "I don't know who would have the gold."

"Okay," I said, "let's work on the second list. If nobody stole it, where would Grandpa Tip have hidden it?"

"Not in the cellar, we cleaned there already."

I added, "I would have hidden it in the tunnel, but he didn't. All we found was a clue inside of a bag."

Marshal said, "I wish our friends would help. We need more ideas."

"Fat chance," I replied. "They said they'd had enough."

I didn't say it, but I missed Pippy.

Marshal added, "Well, they don't know about the steel penny, and they might get excited again."

"Not likely. Let's just consider where it might be. We'll find it without help." I replied.

Marshal stretched as he turned to look around the room. "Do you suppose Grandpa Tip hid the gold in his office?"

"If he did, why'd he send us on a wild goose chase across the city?"

Marshal replied, "Good question. If he hid it here, where?"

"The safe is the most logical place," I replied.

"Ole Linclas?"

"Yep."

Marshal strolled toward the safe and squatted. Then he fiddled with the dial. "We can't unlock the safe without the combination."

The word combination rattled my subconscious—a yet unrealized idea.

Marshal turned the dial left and right with his ear on the thick, steel door.

"Are you a safecracker?" I asked sarcastically.

"Worth a try, but I don't hear or feel anything."

"Was Grandpa Tip planning to tell us the combination the last time we spoke to him?" I asked.

After Marshal rose from his squatting position, he rubbed his chin. "Now that you mention it, he wanted us to solve a riddle."

I said, "What was Grandpa Tip saying before we left for the movie?"

"He was telling us why he nicknamed his safe Linclas. Don't you think it's a dumb name?"

I said, "Yes, it's the way his mind worked. Even the nickname was a riddle."

I smiled, remembering Grandpa Tip's riddles. From our earliest youth, Grandpa Tip taught us to solve his puzzles. Easter Egg hunts involved problem-solving excursions for chocolate bunnies, birthdays required hours of deduction to find our presents, and my grade school graduation was the worst. It took a week to locate my new underwater wristwatch. Marshal jerked me from my recollecting when he pointed to the pencil sketch. He said, "'It's the combination to remember' is how Grandpa Tip described this etching."

An unsettled feeling bounced inside my skull. Grandpa Tip had taught us to pay special attention to out-of-place words in his riddles. I concentrated on the word combination.

Grandpa Tip once said, "Words that don't fit are the most important hints. They're like broken branches that skilled trackers notice."

Marshal continued, "It's the combination to remember. What a weird way to describe a drawing."

I said, "It is strange. Is the sketch a riddle?"

Marshal held up a finger. "Oh…, Oh, you may be right."

He rushed closer to the historical print. Abraham Lincoln, pointing upward, was speaking before an enormous crowd at the fourth senatorial debate. Douglas sat ahead of a gaggle of newspaper stenographers. They recorded every word of the speeches then printed them in newspapers with editorial comments.

Lincoln later had the transcripts from the seven debates published in a book. The book's popularity required several reprints catapulting Lincoln to the presidency.

I tapped my finger on my cheek. "Combination, combination, combination."

The word rolled around the inside of my skull as I tried to form an idea.

Marshal repeated, "Combination, combination…."

His voice trailed to a whisper. When I searched the sizeable artwork for a clue, Marshal did too.

I said, "Linclas is the names Lincoln and Douglas combined, but it doesn't tell us anything. Any ideas?"

"Not yet, the safe combination is numbers. Could they be in the drawing?"

The artist, in calligraphy, had written "Lincoln Douglas Debate." Cursive letters loomed taller than the date below, which was September 18, 1858.

"Maybe that's it," I said.

Marshal squatted cross-legged before the safe. First, he spun the dial, then turned right to the number eighteen. Next, he dialed past eighteen then stopped on the second rotation. When he reversed the dial and stayed on the number fifty-eight, the handle didn't budge. "What next?"

"Try 9-18-58," I said.

Marshal tried twice without success. He even tried reversing the normal right-left-right but still couldn't unlock it. "Dang it," he said.

Frustrated, I studied the print while Marshal continued his futile efforts. After scanning every inch of the old sketch, I noticed the artist's signature on the bottom right corner. When I squinted and chewed on my outstretched tongue, I made out the faded letters. Though I read Clyde Miller, his name didn't ring a bell. I leaned closer until I was looking cross-eyed just beyond the tip of my nose. I turned my head left and then right and read the date below his signature. 15-17-64.

Wait a minute, that's not a date."

I slapped my palm on my forehead. "I found it."

Marshal jumped up and ran to my side. Then I pointed to the date below the artist's name and tapped on the glass. I shouted, "Grandpa Tip wrote the combination below the signature. He wrote it where he would always find it."

Marshal rushed to the safe. While I spouted the numbers, Marshal tried them.

He said, "I can feel a click at each one."

After the third and final number, he pushed on the handle and grinned. He pulled, and the door swung open. I rushed to look over his shoulder. On his hands and knees like an anxious dog, he peeked. He removed papers and handed them to me.

"No coins, just papers," he said.

I placed the documents on the desk without looking at them.

He said, "We'll find it, yet."

Then, Dad entered carrying three bottles of cola.

I joked, "You brought us pop, Pop."

He said, "Yep, oh, wow, you got the safe open."

"There's nothing of value," I said.

Dad flipped through the pages on the desk. He held the loose leaves by one end and shook them, but nothing fell out. "Strange, there's no deposit."

"What?" I asked.

Dad said, "At the close of business, Grandpa Tip always prepared a bank deposit for the next day. But he didn't make one on the day he died, so I expected to find it in the safe."

"What can it mean?" I asked.

Dad shook his head and dropped into a chair with a pensive look. "It's not the missing money that concerns me, but I'm puzzled why he broke from his routine. He walked to the bank every day, rain or snow. The missing deposit makes no sense."

Marshal said, "Petey must have made Grandpa Tip open the safe. He is in jail for stealing Grandpa Tip's pendant."

Dad shook the stationary again and replied, "It's possible that Petey stole it." Dad tapped on the papers stacked on the desk. Something caught his attention and he leaned forward. He read the first page. "Manuscript."

When he turned the page, he read the title and subtitle.

"'*Twenty-Four Bank Robberies. An Autobiography by John Herbert Dillinger.*'"

Dad repeated, "John Herbert Dillinger."

I said, "It says autobiography. Mr. Herbert must be John Herbert Dillinger. He's alive!"

Dad said, "Mr. Herbert must be my father's cousin." Dad turned to the next page and read aloud: "'Following is the autobiography of the bank robber John Dillinger. Someone died in the hot alley beside a Chicago theater those many years ago, but it wasn't me.'"

I said, "He got right to the point."

Dad read, "'I was a gangster who could sense danger. Near the end of the movie, the hair on the back of my head raised, so I slipped out the rear door of the Biograph Theater. An unlucky man beside the lady-in-red was mistaken for me, and the nervous FBI agents killed him.

"'When I heard the gunshots, I ran like a jackrabbit down the alley and disappeared. The shooting was the lucky break I needed to leave my life of crime. Join me as I tell my life story.'"

Dad closed the manuscript. "That's enough for now. We need to get home for dinner."

Dad picked up the manuscript as he left. After our evening meal, Dad read the entire book to our family.

Dillinger described his life from juvenile delinquency to his supposed death at the hands of agent Melvin Purvis. Included in his stories of robbing the twenty-four banks and four police stations was never-before-published information. He wrote of jailbreaks, car thefts, and shootouts. Dillinger had killed a man, but the court ruled it self-defense. But his ruthless gang members murdered people, so his guilt was by association. The director of the Federal Bureau of Investigation, J. Edgar Hoover, wanted Dillinger captured or killed.

Dillinger explained, many people resented banks during the depression, so the general populace didn't hate him. Strange, many even admired the gangster. But Dillinger admitted his thievery was wrong, and he regretted that people were killed.

It disappointed me that his account of the last thirty-five years was missing. Nor did he tell of the Greencastle gold. When Dad finished reading, he packed the pages into a satchel. After he put the salesman's case in the back of his closet, Dad made us swear to secrecy.

#

The next day Dad plugged in the sign to signal Mr. Herbert, or should I say, John Dillinger. We sat at Grandpa Tip's favorite table, and I looked at the shiny floor.

I pointed at the footprints below the wax. I showed dad the dust in the dustpan from the day we cleaned. "This is what we swept."

Dad ran his finger through the grit, then rolled it between his thumb and forefinger.

"What is it?" I asked.

He said, "Mortar, someone with dust on their shoes tracked it in here."

"He wore boots," I said. I pointed to the clear footprint now preserved under the wax.

"So, he did."

Dad didn't seem too concerned about the floor.

He said, "I keep thinking of the missing bank deposit."

Marshal said, "We've looked everywhere."

163

Dad replied, "I'm going to the sheriff's office to tell him about the missing cash. It might be important."

He left, and we were alone again. My mind drifted toward the missing gold. "Let's talk to Petey," I said.

Marshal replied, "But he's in jail."

"If they let us talk to him, we might get a clue where the gold could be."

Marshal replied, "I guess so."

#

We rode our bikes to the jail, just a few blocks from the town square. Though the desk sergeant was reluctant to let us see the prisoner, he yielded once Petey agreed. Petey entered the visitor's area wearing a striped jail uniform and a suspicious look on his face.

"What do you want?" was his blunt greeting.

I said, "We want to know what happened in Tip's Hardware Store and how you came to have his medallion."

Petey said, "Like I told the sheriff. Mack and I visited the store looking for information on the gold. We hoped the owner might know where Dillinger stashed it. We entered, but we didn't see anyone. We shouted, but no one answered. I heard a noise in the office so I investigated. The monkey shrieked, and I almost jumped out of my skin. Then I saw him sitting beside the old man."

"Grandpa Tip was already dead?"

"You got it. Dead when we got there."

Marshal asked, "Was the safe open or closed?"

"Closed."

Marshal asked, "If what you say is true, why d'you take the medallion?"

Petey shook his head, "I didn't take it on purpose. When we realized Tip was dead, Mack went through the drawers, and I searched for a clue. I saw the medallion and picked the thing up, but I didn't mean to steal it."

Marshal asked, "How did you and Mack get the cuts and bruises on your heads?"

"It was that darn monkey. I picked up a little league baseball plaque on the old man's desk and read the inscription aloud. It said, 'Batter up.' Holy smokes, that primate grabbed a miniature baseball bat and beat Mack and me on the head. We ran, and I carried the medallion out with me. I didn't even

164

know I had it until we got outside on the sidewalk. I pushed it into my pocket as we hurried away."

Marshal said, "Sound's farfetched to me."

"Well, it's the truth. Mack will tell you the same thing."

We thanked him and left. Outside, we ran into the sheriff who was removing the wrapper from a stick of gum. He said, "Petey hadn't changed his story since his arrest."

I said, "It seems far-fetched, but the monkey does have a mean swing."

The Sheriff poked the gum into his mouth, then shook his head. "If we don't get more evidence, the district attorney won't take the case to trial. Unless we get something to tie him to the crime, I'll have to release him."

"What of the missing deposit," Marshal asked.

"It's suspicious, but we can't connect it to Petey and Mack. They may have stolen it, but we can't prove it."

We wished the sheriff a good day and Marshal and I pedaled. A week later, I read in the paper Marge, Petey, and Mack made bail. The prosecutor dropped the murder charges but scheduled a trial for theft of the medallion. They weren't to leave the county while awaiting trial. We needed to find evidence if we were to prove they murdered Grandpa Tip.

Chapter 18

John Herbert Dillinger

The neon sign glowed at Grandpa Tip's store for a few weeks as a signal for Mr. Herbert. Dad sat in the office on several Saturday mornings, but Mr. Herbert never showed himself.

On this day, before the sun woke, Dad entered our bedroom.

"Boys."

I sat up in bed. "Yeah."

He said, "My boss called, and they need me at the factory today. So, I won't be available to wait at the hardware store for Mr. Herbert. Can you handle it?"

Marshal sat up. "Sure."

Marshal and I pedaled our yellow, banana-seat bikes past trousers dancing on clotheslines, as we headed toward town. My canvas, newspaper bag hung from the tall handlebars. Mr. Gower's dog chased us for a block until I tossed him a dog biscuit.

In twenty minutes, Marshal unlocked the hardware store. I turned on the fans, and we sat at the desk. After opening a deck of playing cards, I shuffled.

"I'll keep score," I said. I pulled a pad from a drawer and grabbed the fountain pen. As I shuffled, Sparky strolled in with Babe running alongside.

"Well hello," I said.

Sparky unhooked the leash from Babe's collar. I hope you don't mind if I let him run free."

"Nope, it's okay."

The monkey made a beeline for me and hopped in my lap.

"He's glad to see you," Sparky said.

Babe crawled up and bounced from shoulder to shoulder. Then, the primate leaped down and ran to Marshal. He bounded onto Marshal with excitement. Sparky dropped into a chair and scanned the cards. "What are you playing?"

Marshal replied, "Nothing, yet. What are you and Babe doing today?"

"We're going to sit on a bench at the courthouse."

"Makes for a long day," I said.

"Where else have I got to go?"

I nodded. Babe dropped from Marshal and ran to Sparky. He crossed his legs, and Babe jumped into his lap. While watching the monkey pick fleas from his fur, I saw Sparky's boot. On the sole was a Brown Shoe Company imprint.

I leaned forward for a closer examination and saw white mortar embedded in the tread. Sparky's other foot was next to a footprint. They appeared to be the same size.

I glanced at Marshal and raised one eyebrow. He followed my eyes to the print on the glossy hardwood, and he sat up straight. From his expression, I knew he got my message.

I wanted more definite evidence, and I had an idea. I removed the cap from the fountain pen and scribbled. "This is empty," I said.

While Marshal and Sparky gabbed, I opened the bottle of ink and took the pen apart. I dipped the tip into the ink and pulled a lever to suck it into the cartridge. Since no one was watching, it was easy to fake an accident. With a simple fumble, the bottle fell to the floor, spilling in front of Sparky.

Babe leaped away as Sparky jumped to his feet. How odd, but when a person tries to avoid a spill, they step in it. Sparky stood with both boots in the puddle.

"Now what?" he asked.

"Don't worry," I said.

I scattered bright-white typewriter paper on the floor.

"Step on this," I instructed.

Sparky took a cautious step onto a piece of paper with his left foot. He did the same with his right. I spread more. "Keep stepping on these until your boots are dry."

By the time Sparky and Babe departed, I had several perfect prints. I snickered as I examined them. I laid one beside the waxed-over footprint, and they were a match.

I said, "These marks on the floor weren't here when we went to the movie. So, Sparky was at the hardware store the day Grandpa Tip died."

Marshal agreed with a nod.

He said, "But on the day Grandpa Tip died, Sparky was here when we got here. The Sheriff said Sparky found Grandpa Tip dead."

Just then, Mr. Herbert entered. "Hello, boys. The sign is on, so I hope you have the book."

"Yes, sir, we brought it." Marshal replied.

Marshal walked to the desk, opened a drawer, and removed the manuscript. He handed the pages to Mr. Herbert.

"Wonderful." The old man rubbed the title sheet like a genie's lamp. After he sat, he examined the first page before flipping through it. "It's all here," he said.

Marshal and I smiled. No one spoke while he looked through the pages. We just grinned and nodded.

Marshal interrupted his inspection of the pages. "The book says you're John Herbert Dillinger."

He shrugged his shoulders and sighed. "Looks like you caught me. Now that you got me, what are you gonna do with me?"

Marshal blurted, "Nothing."

I added, "I suppose you're family. I mean you were Grandpa Tip's cousin. It doesn't make much sense to turn you into the cops."

The corners of Mr. Herbert's lips curled upward, and he extended his hand. "I'm John Dillinger. It's nice to know you."

I shook his hand with a grin as wide as a country mile. Marshal did too.

"So, when do you plan to release your book?" I asked.

Mr. Dillinger rubbed the manuscript and smiled. "I have a few finishing touches, but soon."

He slipped the manuscript into a brown, leather satchel. "Well, boys, I guess I'll go now."

"Wait."

I held up an outstretched hand like a traffic cop. "We'd appreciate your help."

Marshal nodded. "If the bag of pennies wasn't from the Greencastle bank robbery, where are the gold coins? Are you sure you stole four sacks?"

John eased back in his chair and pulled a pack of cigarettes from his pocket. We watched as he lit one and dragged an ashtray closer. He smoked non-filtered ones and spit a tobacco seed. He held the package out and offered me one.

"No, I'm only thirteen."

He said, "What's your point. I started when I was ten."

"Thanks, anyway."

Dillinger shrugged and put the cigarette pack in his pocket. "You asked if there were four bags. Yes, I'm sure of it. We opened them all. Tip acted as my proxy to give the gold away. We donated all but the last bag. I agreed to allow Tip to give it to you boys if you could solve the riddle. Tip earned the bag of coins for helping me all these years. He wanted you boys to have it."

I said, "But someone stole it because we found pennies."

We reviewed our entire hunt, which made sense to Dillinger until the ending when the box didn't contain the Saint-Gaudens pieces.

Dillinger explained, "Tip arranged with Sparky to bury the coins at the cemetery. Sparky is your obvious culprit. I never trusted him. A crook can always recognize another."

"We thought he might be the thief," Marshal said.

I continued, "Sparky must have switched it."

Marshal interrupted, "And we know where it might be."

Dillinger snuffed his cigarette in the ashtray and stood. "Let's go."

"You mean you'll help us?" I questioned.

"Got nothing better to do. Is this place far?"

Marshal replied, "Nope, Hilltop Cemetery."

The former outlaw wrinkled his brow. "Cemetery?"

"It's where Sparky sleeps," Marshal said.

Dillinger said, "Since when? I suspected he hid at the Jameson boarding house when I stayed there. I heard he moved in after Miss Jameson died."

"Not any longer," I answered.

"Oh well, he must have moved because they're demolishing the Jameson building."

I replied, "Sparky said he'd just moved into his family's mausoleum."

Dillinger said, "Sounds creepy. Oh, well, let's check it out. But first, lock this manuscript in the safe, and I'll get it later. Jump in the pickup truck, and I'll take you there."

After I locked the door, Mr. Dillinger invited us into his truck with a hand gesture. The old vehicle had a blanket draped over the seats. The gearshift was a stick, and the pad was missing from the clutch pedal. Empty, squashed cigarette packages littered the dash.

John Dillinger slipped into the driver's seat and pressed a button under the steering column. The engine struggled to start but fired with a puff of black smoke. The keys were dangling from the ignition.

"Why do you leave the keys inside the truck?" I asked.

"Who'd want to steal this pile of rusted metal?"

The jalopy jumped as he let out the clutch and left the curb. The manual transmission chattered at each shift.

He glanced at me and smirked. "I've worn the teeth on the gears badly."

We turned at the town square then headed north. At the highway, we turned toward Hilltop graveyard. He slowed at a railroad crossing and each track jolted me.

Mr. Dillinger smiled as he sped up again. "Shocks gave out a couple years ago."

I flinched when a spring poked me. John Dillinger chuckled. Up ahead, a Sheriff's car sat diagonally across the road. Clarence stopped traffic with an extended hand.

Marshal said, "Is that a roadblock…"

I continued, "To catch you?"

Dillinger chuckled then pressed with both feet on the brake. Somehow, he stopped before bumping the new Mustang convertible ahead of us.

"They're not looking for me. I quit worrying years ago. The cops are stopping traffic, so they can back the crane up to the Jameson Hotel."

"Crane?" I asked.

"Hotel?" Marshal questioned.

"Yep, the city's gonna tear down the old hotel. They took the building for taxes ten years ago when the owner died. She had no relatives. I heard the city had so many complaints of vagrants and varmints they're demolishing it."

Two flagmen helped the operator back up the crane. I'd never seen such a large machine. Dillinger shuffled through empty packages on the dash. "No crane big enough around here. Appears the demolition company had to bring one in from out of town."

While taking advantage of the wait, he lit a cigarette. I leaned forward and looked through the top of the windshield. The workmen lowered the hydraulic levelers onto railroad ties then shut off the engine.

Demo work had already begun. A block and tackle protruded from a missing window. Workmen were lowering a steam radiator while workers below waited to place it on a flatbed trailer.

"Look, they're removing the scrap metal," Dillinger said as he flicked ashes onto the street.

The tallest ladder I'd ever seen leaned against a round turret on the corner of the building. Two men held on while a man on top reached upward with bolt cutters. He couldn't reach the lightning rod which sat at the point of the round roof. So, he snipped the ground wire above his head, leaving several feet dangling from the still affixed metal pole.

Dillinger pointed at the building. "I lived on the fourth floor. I'd sit in the round room and watch the sun drop over the horizon. At 9:00 each evening the Nickel Plate steam engine stopped at the depot and took on water.

"Before the train left the station, hobos appeared at Miss Jameson's kitchen door. Men running the rails jumped off in Charleston wanting a meal."

Marshal said, "My Grandma said vagrants arrived at her backdoor before Grampa Rardin even got home."

I added, "She fed them if she had leftovers. If not, she'd give them potatoes and fresh vegetables from her garden. The drifters camped together and made mulligan stew with the handouts."

Dillinger said, "Three or four showed up at Miss Jameson's every evening. She served them on the back porch. Here's the strange part. After a while, I noticed one less person was leaving than had arrived. I decided Sparky hadn't left."

Marshal asked, "Where was he?"

"I suspected he was in the boarding house. There were lots of places he could have hidden."

171

Once the equipment was off the street, I could see the Sheriff stopping traffic from the opposite direction. The two officers moved their vehicles and allowed the cars to pass. Dillinger tossed the cigarette out of the window and ground gears until he found one that worked. The truck hopped as he released the clutch. As we eased past the five-story building, I gawked at it.

Though I'd passed the mansion many times, I'd never noticed its height. I got a better look at the turret on the corner. There was a round room on each floor—stacked the entire five stories and continued up past the roof. The pointed peak had a lightning rod on top. A wrap-around, front porch sagged in places and had collapsed on one end. Paint curled on the siding.

Workers were removing an ornate oak door with sidelights on both sides and a transom across the top. Six men struggled to lift the unit.

Dillinger said, "It's a real shame. The Jameson Hotel was nice once. It sat on a twenty-acre estate in its heyday before the town grew. The old lady sold off much of the property when times were hard. Back then, the proprietor did a good business since the railroad station was nearby."

I asked, "Do you remember when it was open."

"Not as a hotel, but I lived there after Miss Jameson converted it to a boarding house."

"Was the place spooky looking back then?" Marshal asked.

"It was on the decline for certain. At night the building creaked. Once during a storm, I thought the building might collapse."

A girl in the front seat of the convertible ahead of us turned her head toward the motel. It was Pippy. I look closer. Sly was driving and Griff sat in the backseat. My heart dropped.

She was laughing when the police allowed the traffic to flow. The Mustang sped away as Mr. Dillinger worked at the gearshift. Dillinger waved as he passed the officers and resumed speed. "Those are nice policemen," Dillinger glanced in the rearview mirror.

I said, "I figured you hated cops."

Dillinger looked shocked. "Why?"

I said, "Because you had gunfights with lawmen, and they shot up your gang."

"Boys, they were just doing their jobs. I was young and dumb, and I was lucky they didn't kill me. What I did wasn't right. Times were different, and it didn't seem so wrong, but it was."

I felt uncomfortable with my remarks, so I changed the discussion back to the old hotel. "Why d'you live in the rickety boarding house?"

"I was on the lam."

"Lam?" I asked.

Marshal said, "What's that mean?"

"I was hiding from the police, so I kept a low profile. Bank robbers get caught when they live too high and fancy."

"Anyway, I liked the lady who operated it. She was a character, but she sure could cook. Her biscuits melted in my mouth."

I asked, "Character, how so?"

Dillinger showed his teeth as he smiled. He drove past the cemetery steps and turned into a drive on the far side. The truck stalled once on the way up the hill and rolled backward as Dillinger started it again. Once over the crest, he parked in the grass. Mr. Dillinger stepped from the truck, and we followed him. Outside the gate, he slid down a tree trunk, so I dropped in the shade. Rows of tombstones adorned the rolling hills.

Dillinger began his tale. "Old lady Jameson was a character for sure. She took a liking to me and told me things she told just a few others. She explained the creaking at night wasn't just the building resisting the wind. The spinster seldom slept and hustled about most of the night through hidden staircases, halls, and rooms."

I said, "Hidden?"

Marshal asked, "Why?"

"She told me her grandfather built them for servants. He built the hotel, so the guests had minimal contact with the maids and cooks. The employees worked, slept, and ate out of sight of the customers. When her grandfather died, her father took over the operation."

"Lots of private rooms and passages," I commented.

"But there's more," Dillinger continued. "She believed the ghost of Abraham Lincoln roamed the halls at night. Miss Jameson said Lincoln stayed at the hotel the night after the Lincoln-Douglas debate. The 'ole girl figured he was reviewing his life as he lay dying and got stuck at her hotel."

173

"Reviewing his life?" I asked.

Dillinger said, "People say, a person's life flashes before them as they die."

"Like a movie?" Marshal asked.

"Yes. Miss Jameson figured Lincoln died when the moving picture stopped at her hotel. She said it was like the film broke before the end."

Dillinger chuckled, and so did we.

I said, "Seems, farfetched."

"Well, that describes her. She was a unique person. She hoped to catch him, so she could gently send him on his way."

"Sounds to me like she was a nut," Marshal said.

I nodded.

Dillinger said, "She believed Lincoln's ghost hurt her business. The place got a reputation for being haunted, and she wanted to get rid of her phantom."

"So, people saw Lincoln sometimes?" Marshal asked.

"Guests claimed to see a tall man in a top hat dart here and there in the darkness."

"I don't believe in ghosts," I said, trying to convince myself.

Dillinger said, "There's more. She never electrified the building."

"Why?" I asked.

"She didn't want workmen running wires in the walls and attic. She believed it would drive Lincoln's ghost deeper into the hidden crevices. We used kerosene lamps for light."

I added, "You don't suppose that hurt business, do you?"

Dillinger laughed and said, "I told you she was a character."

Marshal asked, "Why d'you stay there…"

"For so long?" I added.

Dillinger said, "I'm not afraid of a ghost. I've been close to death several times. Once a bullet clipped my ear and stung like Satan spit on me. Anyway, the boarding house was a good hideout. No one bothered me."

I asked, "Do you think Sparky was the ghost, Miss Jameson tried to catch?"

Marshal continued, "Do you think she thought he was Abraham Lincoln?"

Dillinger raised his palms. "I often wondered, but I don't know for sure."

I said, "If a guest saw him sneaking in the dark, they couldn't tell for sure. Sparky is tall and thin."

Marshal added, "Not too many people would take too good a look at a ghost, anyway."

Dillinger chuckled, "Yeah, I guess you're right. It's hard to examine someone when you're running away. One lady claimed she saw him, but she couldn't describe him. She passed out and woke up in a puddle of her own making."

I smiled. "Maybe you stayed because you had a thing for Miss Jameson."

Dillinger tilted his head back and looked down his nose. "Son, to call that woman plain would be a compliment. She was tall with no shape. When God gave out hips, she heard lips, so she asked for two helpings. She'd smother a man if she ever got one to kiss her."

We laughed as the former gangster rose. "But what a cook. Now, show me where you think they hid my gold."

Marshal pointed to the back entrance. The crow-black gate was off the hinges and leaning against the stone wall. We passed through, and it looked different in the daylight, not as frightening. The only ominous sign was a leafless, skeletal tree. The sole sentry was dead.

We crested the hill where the cannon rested several feet from its original position. It had jumped after the lightning-strike. John Dillinger said he'd heard the cannon fire from his home, so I figured he must live within a mile or two. Marshal directed our attention toward the Postal mausoleum. "Sparky sleeps in there."

"Kind of creepy," Dillinger commented.

We descended the hill past the ground-sweeping branches of the sorrowful, weeping willow tree. At the crypt, I knocked, but no one answered. When I pushed the door open, daylight poured in, and the musty odor seeped out. A spider had created an artistic web across the opening.

"Sparky's not been in here for a while," I said.

The pillow and blanket lay where we'd last seen them.

Marshal pointed. "He sleeps above the baby's grave."

I added, "But not lately from the looks of the spider webs."

Once I brushed the spider's silky strands aside, I noticed white grit on the floor like at the hardware store. I pointed toward it. "Mortar dust."

Dillinger asked, "Why's that important?"

"Someone tracked the same stuff into Grandpa Tip's store It appears to have come from here. We saw mortar embedded in the soles of Sparky's boots too."

Dillinger nodded as he studied the pallet. He pulled back the quilt, and he found a crowbar and a wooden stake. With the blanket removed, we could see the mortar joint, which once sealed the lid.

Dillinger picked at the loose mortar. "He chiseled out the mortar. The crypt is open."

"Let's look in there," Marshal said.

I shivered at what we might find. "The marker says there's a baby in there."

Dillinger pushed the crowbar below the lid. "Just one way to know." He pried until we could get our fingers into the crack. Marshal and I lifted and tilted the slab. After Dillinger braced the lid open with the wood, I pulled back a canvas tarp. On one end sat a small wooden box.

"I bet there's a casket inside of the box," I moaned.

"It looks old. I think you're right. Let's not disturb it," Dillinger replied.

When I pulled the canvas from the crypt, we saw Sparky's belongings. There were a winter coat and hat, a candle, a hammer, and a cold chisel.

Dillinger picked up the tools. "This is what he used to chisel the mortar."

Marshal removed the coat, and underneath, he found a bag. When he held it to the light, I could see printing.

"U.S. Mint-One Cent," I shouted. "I'd say this contained the pennies he swapped for the gold."

Marshal nodded as he slipped his hand into the bag. He rummaged around then pulled out a leather bank bag. I grabbed it and moved closer to the light of the open door. When I unzipped it, I found a bank-deposit form.

I said, "It's Grandpa Tip's. He prepared a deposit, but there's no money in here."

Marshal added, "So that's were Sparky got the cash to buy the pennies."

Dillinger and I nodded.

Marshal said, "So, Sparky killed Grandpa Tip."

Dillinger said, "It's not solid proof, but incriminating. For certain, he robbed him. But he could claim Tip was already dead when he stole it."

I said, "So, we know Sparky robbed Grandpa Tip on the day he died. Also, Sparky was at the hardware store before Petey and Mack."

Marshal asked, "How do you know?"

"Had Petey and Mack seen the bank bag, they'd have mentioned it. It would have proved they didn't intend to rob Grandpa Tip. I can almost hear Petey say, 'If we wanted to rob him, why'd we leave the cash?' Someone had already stolen the bag when they arrived, and I suspect it was Sparky."

Marshal said, "Grandpa Tip always left the money bag on his desk. So, Petey and Mack would have seen it."

I added, "And Sparky was Grandpa Tip's friend, so he knew where Grandpa Tip kept it."

I nodded.

Dillinger said, "It's interesting and important, but it doesn't tell us where he hid the gold. Let's look for other clues."

Dillinger rummaged through the crypt and held up a kerosene railroader's lantern, a worn leather belt, and a glass ball. He held it in the light, and it refracted like a prism. Blue, yellow, and red colors flittered on the walls. He walked outside and examined the cut glass in the daylight. We followed him.

"What is it?" I asked.

Dillinger rolled the thing in his palm.

"It's a doorknob, a glass doorknob."

He handed it to me, and I saw a metal bracket on the bottom to attach to the door.

"Is this a clue?" Marshal asked.

"I think so," Dillinger replied. "It's unique. I've only seen doorknobs like this at one other place — the Jameson Hotel."

I handed the knob to Dillinger, and he tossed it up and caught it when it dropped.

"Looks to me, Sparky hasn't completely moved from the old hotel. From the looks of the spider webs, he hasn't been here for at least a few days. So, I suspect the gold might be there."

I said, "If he were the Jameson ghost, he'd know good hiding places."

Marshal said, "But they're tearing down the place next week?"

Dillinger said, "Yep. That means he'll be moving the loot."

The former gangster smiled as he walked toward the mausoleum.

"After we put everything back, we're going to the Jameson to get my gold."

Chapter 19

The Jameson Hotel

By the time we rolled up behind the Jameson, the workman had left for the day. Mr. Dillinger parked off the alley between a dump truck and a pile of old carpet. Clouds in the distance looked ominous and rumbling thunder rattled the windows in the five-story building. Dillinger led the way toward the abandoned hotel.

A screen door hung by one hinge, and wire milk-crates sat on a loading dock. We entered through an unlocked door and entered the basement. Several commercial washing machines and dryers sat rusting.

"I thought there was no electricity," I said.

Dillinger replied, "Only in the basement. It runs the laundry, dumbwaiter, and the elevator."

A mound of bedsheets taller than me lay on the concrete below a sheet-metal tube.

"Laundry chute," Dillinger answered before I asked. "It goes to every floor, including the attic."

Marshal said, "It's weird the dirty sheets are still here."

Dillinger replied, "Just as they left them the day she died."

A large motor was on the other end of the basement. When I pointed, Dillinger said, "For the elevator."

A smaller motor sat beside a phone booth sized cabinet without a door. "Dumbwaiter?" I asked.

Dillinger nodded. We climbed the stairs to the kitchen. Workman had pulled a commercial-size, cookstove from the wall, ready for removal. Flypaper dangled from the cracked and peeling ceiling. A freestanding sink stood with a pie-safe next to it.

Dillinger opened the pantry then closed it. I followed as he pushed through a swinging door. The dining room tables were big enough to seat six people each.

We moved toward the front of the building, and a massive fireplace decorated the lounge. Though workman had stacked most of the wingback chairs on the lawn, a few were still in a circle for workman's coffee breaks, I figured. Men had rolled the carpet for disposal.

An ornate staircase led upstairs, and tufts of fabric remained around tacks on oak treads. Next to the stairs was a counter for a clerk, and I wrote my initials in the dust. When I opened a door behind the clerk's station, I discovered a small room with an old telephone operator's desk. "Hey, look at this."

Though the outdated device amused Marshal, it didn't faze Dillinger. I figured they'd been common when he was younger. Marshal plugged and unplugged the phone lines.

"Hello, Jameson Hotel. How may I direct your call?"

I chuckled. Behind me was a curtain, so I pulled it aside. A narrow, steep staircase led upstairs.

"For the employees," Dillinger said. "It leads to the servants' quarters."

"Cool," Marshal said.

He pushed past me and climbed, so I followed him. When I was on the third step, a noise came from upstairs, and everyone stopped.

Dillinger warned, "Be careful."

Once upstairs, we were in a hallway with a window on both ends. Fist sized chunks of plaster were missing from the walls in several places, and wallpaper dangled from the ceiling. The staircase continued up, but we didn't climb choosing to explore the second floor, instead. Shelves lined one side of the hall with moth-eaten linens still stacked in piles. There was no carpet on the plank floor, and brooms, mops, and buckets were sitting where maids had left them.

Doors on the left led to the servant's plain bedrooms. Two twin beds and dressers were the furnishings except for a nightstand. A single window provided natural light, and the faded, water-stained curtains hung over cracked panes of glass. Something moved in the featherbed mattress, so I backed out not wishing to investigate further.

A passage down the hall led to a guest hallway with frayed, red and gold carpet. I entered a guestroom with the number 201 on the door. It was roomier than I expected, and no furniture remained except the musty, maroon drapery.

Dillinger said, "The rooms are the same, but the suites have round rooms in the corner."

We walked back into the hall. I investigated each doorway on the left side, and Marshal opened each one on the right. As Dillinger had said, the guestrooms were similar, but one still had old furniture. A fourposter bed with only three posts, a dresser with a missing drawer, and a small table with a cracked mirror remained. We continued exploring.

When he opened the last door on the right, Dillinger led us into a suite. First, we entered a bedroom the same as the others we'd seen. Then we passed into a circular room in the turret. It wasn't large. There was space for two chairs, and four curved windows offered an abundant view of the grounds. The old glass was thicker at the bottom which distorted it somewhat. Dillinger explained the glass was a liquid and settled over a century.

"This is like my room, but mine was on the fourth floor."

"Oh," I said as Marshal nodded.

Boom!

"What was that?" Marshal asked as he looked at the ceiling.

"It came from upstairs," I said.

I cocked my head, heard a shuffle, and then it was quiet. Dillinger had questioning eyes. "Too loud for an animal," he said. Dillinger pulled a pistol from his jacket. He pointed it upwards, beside his ear, as he stared at the ceiling.

He must have realized my fear when he saw my half-dollar size eyes staring at the revolver. Marshal had stepped back too.

Dillinger whispered, "Don't be afraid. I know how to use it."

Whatever or whoever was upstairs will deal with a man brandishing a gun. Marshal and I followed Dillinger back to the hallway in a caterpillar walk. Three pairs of feet marched in lockstep. When he stopped, Marshal bumped into him, then I ran into my brother.

"Not so close," he whispered.

The first step of the stairs creaked as we tried to climb quietly. We entered the second-floor, guest hall and paused. I relaxed when Dillinger put his pistol away.

He said, "When I lived here, I heard noises that I couldn't explain. Miss Jameson said it was Lincoln's ghost."

He noticed my wrinkled brow and smiled. "Don't worry, she was a nut. Old buildings make noises."

His words calmed me. I mustered the courage to check out a room with an open door. It was empty except for the wide drapes across the window. I eased through the darkness and grabbed the fabric with both hands. I thrust the curtains apart. A man dangled from a rope around his neck. I screamed, "Eek!"

I staggered backward and tripped on the wrinkled carpet. It may have been the thud from my fall or my screams, which brought the others. At a run, I passed them in the hall.

I ran for a dozen yards before I glanced back. Dillinger and Marshal weren't following me. Was that laughter I heard? I crept back and leaned my head around the door frame. They were poking the dead man.

"Practical jokers," Dillinger said.

It was a dummy wearing a construction hardhat. Embroidered on the pocket of the worn-out shirt was, "Edwards Demolition."

I entered the room. "Hilarious," I said.

Marshal snickered as he turned, but he stopped and looked up at the ceiling. It sounded as if someone was dragging something on the floor above us. Dillinger put his finger on his lips. He pulled his revolver from his jacket again and pointed it at the ceiling.

"Too loud for a ghost," Marshal whispered.

"Sparky?" I asked.

Then, someone slammed a car door, so we rushed to the window. Marge's crew waited for a passing automobile then hurried across the road. Once on the sidewalk, she paused and pointed our direction but above us.

"Is that Marge?" Dillinger asked.

I said, "Yep, she must have followed us."

"She sees something upstairs," Dillinger whispered as he looked up at the ceiling.

Marshal looked up and asked, "Is someone upstairs?"

I looked at Dillinger, "Be careful, she carries a gun."

Dillinger responded, "That's a valuable piece of information."

As Marge's gang stepped onto the porch, Dillinger led us to the third floor. This story was similar to the others. After checking the guest's rooms, we entered the employee hallway again.

I opened a cabinet on the wall and poked in my head. It was the laundry chute. When I looked below, I saw the pile of sheets in the basement. But when I looked up, someone was staring at me. When I pulled back, I must have looked terrified.

"What's wrong?" Dillinger asked.

"I saw someone."

"Sparky?" Marshall asked.

"I don't know," I replied.

Dillinger shoved his head into the opening and looked. "I don't see anyone."

I said nothing.

"You look as if you saw a ghost," Marshal said.

When my diaphragm unlocked, I said, "I might have."

Dillinger said, "Pshaw."

I said, "I know what I saw… maybe." Then, I began to doubt my own eyes.

Dillinger opened a cabinet next to the laundry chute and said, "It's a dumbwaiter."

"Does it work?" Marshal asked.

I was still trying to decide if I'd seen someone, and if so, who?

Dillinger pressed the button, and the platform lowered. It startled me back to reality.

"The electricity is still on," he said.

Though hesitant, I followed Dillinger as he searched the third floor. When we entered the corner suite, I mirrored his footsteps.

"Now what?" He mumbled as he looked out the window.

Deputy Jones was sneaking across the lawn and darting between the trees.

"Clarence Jones," I answered. "He must have followed Marge and her men here. They're out on bail."

"Should we expect anyone else?"

Just then, Sheriff Jones parked his car a block away. He didn't get out but watched with his arm hanging out of the window. He held a cigarette between his fingers.

"The Sheriff couldn't quit," I remarked.

Marshal added, "Clarence drove him back to smoking, I bet."

Deputy Clarence eased past a fishpond. In the center, atop an aging fountain, a concrete fish pointed upwards with an open mouth. It was clear, water had once shot into the air from the statue.

The deputy walked near the pond, and one shoe sunk into the muck. I snickered as Clarence pulled on his foot. He freed himself, then shook his leg. Several globs of mud flung from his shoe.

Dillinger shook his head and said, "Not the city's finest."

I replied, "Nope."

Dillinger said, "Let's hurry to the fourth floor."

The windows of the old mansion rattled as storm clouds darkened the sky. *Was it thunder, was someone walking above us?*

Dillinger exit into the hallway, but opened a closet door, instead. He climbed a ladder, and we followed him.

Upstairs, he said, "This was my room."

"Why the ladder?" I asked.

"I don't know. The crazy proprietor had secret passages throughout the place."

We looked out of the curved windows from the fourth floor. Clarence was crouching and duck-walking toward the hotel while carrying a revolver.

Marshal said, "He claims he's watching us, but I'm watching him now."

I added, "He's got a gun."

"Think it's loaded?" Dillinger asked.

I shrugged my shoulders. When Clarence sneaked onto the porch, we watched him through the missing roof. His clean shoe fell through the rotten boards to the knee. He dropped his revolver, and it fired. It bounced end-over-end from the porch and into the bushes. The bullet grazed the mailbox, tinged off a bird feeder, and went through a shiny ball on top of a concrete stand before flying through the windshield of the deputy's car.

"I guess he loaded it," Dillinger said.

Sheriff Jones placed his hand on his forehead and slid it to his chin.

Dillinger said, "He doesn't appear too pleased with his deputy."

I said, "It's his nephew."

Dillinger nodded. "Ahh, that explains it."

The junior officer pulled and twisted until he removed his leg but without his shoe. His uncle shook his head and appeared to shove the base of his palm into his eye socket. I'd seen my mother do it when she had a migraine. Undeterred, Clarence clip-clopped inside minus a shoe and pistol.

Dillinger walked away from the window and led us upstairs. We looked throughout the fourth floor but didn't find the gold. We approached the staircase, and I heard a scream.

"Was that a woman?" Dillinger asked.

"It sounded like Babe," Marshal said.

"Who's she?" Dillinger asked.

"He's a rhesus monkey."

"What?"

Marshal said, "Babe is Grandpa Tip's, uh, I mean Sparky's."

I asked, "What if it was the ghost of Lincoln? I saw someone in the laundry chute, and I don't think it was Sparky."

Marge and her boys must have heard the scream too because I heard rapid footsteps downstairs. It wouldn't be long before they came looking, so we rushed up the stairs into a ballroom. The dance floor was oak, and a grand piano sat beside a small stage with a music stand.

"She had nice dances here, but only in the cooler months," Dillinger said.

I'd felt the temperature increasing as we climbed higher. There weren't servant quarters on this floor.

I saw an elevator. "There weren't elevator doors on the guest floor, why?

"The elevator was for the ballroom. Miss Jameson gave up space in the servant's quarters on each level when she installed it."

"But why not serve the guest levels?" I asked.

Dillinger replied, "Hoping to take advantage of the dancing craze of the roaring twenties, she converted the fifth floor from storage to a dance hall."

"So, this room was once used for storing stuff?" I asked.

"Yes, she moved everything to the attic. She had the carpenters extend the elevator shaft since there's no stairway to get up there.

"There's an attic?" I asked.

"Yes, we'll go there next," Dillinger said.

"You don't suppose the elevator works, do you?" asked Marshal.

Dillinger said, "Let's see. Maybe the demolition crew has been using it."

As we walked across the ballroom, I said, "It's big enough to play basketball."

"High ceiling, too," Marshal added.

I'd never seen an elevator such as this one. It had two double doors that swung out. When I stepped inside, I felt it move. Dillinger saw my questioning expression.

"It's ancient."

He pulled the doors closed and pushed the up button. The elevator lurched then crawled upwards. As we rose, I peered through the little window in the door and saw someone move across the room. "Stop! I saw someone."

Dillinger pressed the down button and opened the door as he pulled his pistol. While stepping forward, he scanned the room while aiming down the barrel of his revolver. We stood behind him, and my knees shook.

"No one here now," Dillinger said.

"I know I saw someone. He was tall and had a beard."

"No one here now," Dillinger replied. He put his gun away.

Spooky.

We backed into the elevator while still looking across the empty ballroom. After I closed the doors, Dillinger pressed the up button, and we lifted again. As I peeked through the elevator window, I saw someone sitting at the piano. But when I blinked, he'd gone. Dillinger released his touch when the floors aligned. I didn't say anything.

After we exited, we glanced left and right. Triple windows in each gable provided the only light. Spider-web draperies covered the top panes. The opened, lower sashes allowed a cool breeze to pass through the room.

I said, "A storm is coming."

The attic was the same size as the ballroom below, but the floor was pine and not varnished. There wasn't a ceiling, just exposed rafters. The underside of the roof deck were spaced a few inches apart..

I pointed. "Why are there spaces between the decking?"

Dillinger replied, "This building has wood shingles. When built, they spaced the decking for shakes."

186

"Wood shingles?" I asked.

"But isn't it a fire hazard?" Marshal asked.

"Well, yes. But it was the way they did it then. Over the years, coal dust from the smokestacks settled between the shingles and made them even more volatile."

I lowered my gaze. Miss Jameson's staff had crammed the attic full of trunks and furniture. A stack of mattresses almost reached the rafters, and musty, feather pillows formed a mound.

"Maybe Sparky's hiding up here," Dillinger said.

I added, "Or Lincoln's ghost."

I had a feeling someone was watching me. I wondered if it was Sparky or Lincoln. The falling temperature may have been from the approaching storm, but I wondered if it was a result of the supernatural.

Marshal said, "Let's get busy while we still have daylight."

We spent the next hour looking through crates and trunks as the thunder grew louder. Marshal played with a billy club with a leather strap. "A cop must have left it," he commented as he practiced swinging and catching it.

I found a Union Civil War uniform in an old chest. Though it smelled of mothballs, I put on the jacket. A single row of brass buttons adorned the front, and each sleeve had three. The silk lining was black with a scarlet red border at the bottom.

Dillinger said, "Miss Jameson's grandfather was a lieutenant in the Illinois Twenty-First. He mustered in Mattoon and served under Colonel Ulysses S. Grant."

I buttoned it. "Oh, yeah."

He said, "She repeated the story a dozen times in the three years I lived here."

I pulled a sword from the scabbard and examined it. The steel blade had a brass handle and a black leather grip. "This might be worth a lot of money," I said.

I swung it, then thrust the point into an imaginary enemy soldier. "Do you suppose he used it in battle?" When I wrapped the belt around my waist and over my shoulder, the tip of the sheath dragged on the floor.

Marshal rummaged through a trunk of women's clothing. He found a black boa which he wrapped over his shoulders, and laughed as he placed a hat with white feathers on his head. He adjusted it with his left hand while swinging the boa with his right.

"You resemble Miss Jameson," Dillinger quipped. "Except you're better looking."

I added, "If he only cooked."

Dillinger grinned.

Chapter 20

Deputy Clarence Jones on the Chase

Meanwhile, on the first floor, Deputy Clarence crept from the lounge to the dining room. Movers had stacked kerosene lamps, silverware, and china pieces on the round mahogany tables. They'd packed much into wooden boxes for shipment. The shipping label said it would ship to Shelley & Shawn's Antiques in O'Fallon, Illinois.

He was admiring a teapot when something banged behind him. He turned, and the door was still swinging. Clarence reached into his cargo pants and removed his knife. He eased forward, then pushed on the door. There was no one was on the other side.

When Clarence entered the lobby, a cold breeze met him. With the front door removed, the wind from the approaching storm caused the draperies to wave. The noisy slapping of the fabric against the walls and glass made it difficult for him to hear Marge and her gang moving upstairs.

But when Clarence heard a metallic crashing sound coming from the upstairs hall, he climbed the main stairs to investigate. When the bumbling deputy stepped onto the landing, he was looking upward when he should have been watching his step. A workman had left a piano dolly there.

When Clarence lost his footing on the rolling sled, he dropped on his bottom and grabbed both sides of the cart. His chin bounced on his chest as the wheels dropped on each step. He hung on when others may have failed. He gained momentum as he shot through the missing front door and launched from the porch. In his flight, what he lacked in style, he made up for in distance. He broke the city record for the ski jump and may have exceeded the state measurement if it hadn't been for the tree. The front wheels climbed the trunk flipping the deputy on his back.

Deputy Clarence looked up at the leaves of the tall maple tree. He lay sprawled on the ground. In the squad car, Sheriff Jones shook his head.

Undeterred, the deputy stood and brushed off his clothes. Then, he rushed back inside and picked up his knife. Clarence hurried up the steps and down the hall. He ducked in a doorway when he saw Petey untangled himself from a knight's armor. The clanging metal arms and legs separated in opposing directions as Petey tried to stand.

"Are you trying to wake up the dead?" Marge asked.

Petey tried to stand but slipped and fell. "Sorry, why's a tin man here, anyway?"

Mack shook his head as he watched Petey flail. Mack grabbed Petey by the collar and lifted him on to his feet.

"Knock it off, and watch where you're going," Marge demanded. "How can we sneak up on those kids with you making so much noise?"

Clarence followed as Marge's gang climbed to the third floor. While Marge checked the servant's quarters, the men inspected guestrooms. Clarence crept upstairs and stepped into a guestroom where he could watch the gang. Through a cracked door, the deputy saw an animal shoot across the hallway ahead of Petey.

"Was that a cat?" Petey asked.

Mack turned. "Where?"

"This way." Petey hurried down the hall and darted into the room where he'd seen the bushy tail enter.

"Just leave it alone. It's wild!" Mack yelled.

Petey glanced back. "But what if the poor thing is lost or hungry?"

Mack followed his shorter friend into the room, and Clarence followed. When Clarence peeked inside, he saw Petey's feet protruding from under the bed.

Petey said, "She's a long-hair cat."

Mack said, "It'll bite you."

Petey's legs kicked from under the bed. "Here, kitty, kitty, kitty. I touched it, but it's hiding. I've almost…."

"Leave it alone!" Mack interrupted. "Why do you want another kitten?"

190

"Got it." Petey squirmed and wiggled backward while pulling his reluctant new pet from beneath the bed. Once on his knees, Petey held his black-and-white catch and looked into its eyes. "It's cute; I'll keep it."

Mack recoiled when he saw the white stripe running down its black back. Before he could yell, "skunk," the angry mammal raised its tail and ejected an odorous stream. The yellow musk oil splattered on Mack's chest, causing him to stumble backward. Then the polecat clamped onto Petey's nose with its needle-sharp teeth.

Petey squealed, "Ow, ow, help me!"

But Mack wasn't there. He'd bolted from the spewing varmint, passed Clarence, and bounded down the stairs. The deputy hovered over the banister, watching the screaming man descend. Then through the window, Clarence saw Mack shoot from the porch and run full out across the lawn. Mack stopped to peel off his shirt then bent over and vomited. After pitching his smelly shirt, he ran again.

Bare-chested, he dove into the fishpond. After he skimmed across the top, he sank into the shallow water. Mack rolled and dipped then sniffed his arms each time he surfaced. The sheriff watched with a quizzical expression. Then, the deputy rushed down the hall and peered into the room where Petey was still screaming.

Marge was already there, and Petey was spinning with a skunk attached to his face. The yelping Petey stared into the eyes of his new pet.

"Get it off!" he shouted.

Even from the hallway, Clarence could barely stand the skunk stench. Marge gagged. She held the critter by its hind legs as Petey pried its jaws apart. After a flurry of thrashing claws, it released its grip, spun, and dropped. The skunk escaped leaving Petey with a bloody nose and Marge checking her arms for scratches.

Petey pinched his nostrils and tilted his head back.

"So," Marge asked, "Are you okay?"

He responded, "No, I'm not okay! I'll probably need a rabies shot. I'm leaving."

"But the gold," Marge said.

He said, "I don't care."

"Don't go."

Petey pointed to his injured nose. "See, I've had enough. I'm bleeding, the cops arrested me for a murder I didn't commit, and I even got clubbed by a monkey. I'm done!"

"Don't give up now. We're so close."

"Close!" he shouted. "Close?" he screamed louder. "What makes you think we're close? I don't even believe there's gold anymore. How did I let you talk me into this wild goose chase?"

"Don't leave."

Petey pulled a handkerchief from his pocket and pressed it against his nose. "I'm gettin' out of here while I'm still alive, are you coming?"

Marge shook her head then Petey stomped away. The deputy stepped from the shadowy doorway and looked over the banister as Petey descended. Then, he rushed to the window.

Mack dunked his head and washed his hair as the sheriff watched. He lit another cigarette. He was now a two-pack a day smoker.

Petey exploded from the entrance and stormed down the steps. Clarence watched the two conversing while Mack was still sitting in the pond. Petey offered Mack a hand. Mack stood and Petey stepped back.

"Stinks, don't he?" Clarence whispered.

With Petey several paces behind, the men stomped away down the sidewalk. Sheriff Jones flicked the butt out of the car as the two departed. Something or someone seemed to catch the sheriff's attention several floors above Clarence.

The deputy looked up and listened but heard nothing. When he went back to the guestroom and peeked inside, Marge wasn't there. Gazing up the staircase, he saw her ascending to the fourth level. He tiptoed on the steps, and when he got upstairs, he saw her dart into a room.

Clarence crept forward but paused at the door. After listening for a moment, he peeked inside, but Marge wasn't there. He turned left and right, then he looked in the closet. He removed his hat and scratched his head.

He was leaving when a clanging sound came from the fireplace. A pistol landed on the hearth. He poked his head inside and looked up. He saw Marg's backside as shee was climbing.

He crawled into the fireplace and saw ladder rungs mounted in the mortar joints. He stood inside and saw Marge hurrying away.

Clarence yelled, "Hey, you're on bail. You're not allowed to have a gun."

192

Marge glanced back, then she climbed faster. At the fourth floor, Marge tried to open a metal door, but it wouldn't budge. When she saw Clarence climbing behind her, she continued upward.

As ashes fell on him, he chased Marge. Clarence leaned back and saw someone above Marge. The climbing figure exited and slammed the metal door closed.

Marge reached the same door, and she tried it, but it wouldn't open. She looked up at the daylight above her, then climbed.

Clarence looked up and she was gone. He reached the top and grabbed the bricks. Then, the steel step pulled from the chimney wall. He banged his chin but caught himself. The metal bar clanged against the masonry as it fell. He clung on while his feet searched for a toe hold.

"Help!" He begged. "I'm falling!"

Marge darted to the wide-eyed deputy and grabbed him around the neck. She pulled on the bug-eyed cop as he struggled and kicked. Though she was strangling him, he made it up and out. Once on his back, he gasped for air.

As Clarence recovered, Marge peered into the chimney. "The top rung fell. We can't go back this way."

Clarence rubbed his neck and looked around. They were on a flat section of the roof. The roof was too steep to climb. He stood and looked over the edge. The ground was seventy feet below him.

The sheriff was standing beside his car. Clarence waved, and Sheriff Jones waved back. The sheriff lit a cigarette from the butt of the one he'd finished then picked up his microphone.

Deputy Clarence said, "It looks like he's calling for help. It'll take the hook and ladder truck to reach up here."

Marge sat on the roof and leaned against the chimney awaiting their rescue.

Chapter 21

We Find the Gold

In the attic, I moved toward the corner. I was unaware Sparky had crawled through the ash door and was hiding not far from me. An accordion wall partitioned the turret from the main room. On it, hung a sign which read, "Danger-Mechanical Room." The folding door crossed the corner, and a padlock hung from the hasp. Dillinger and Marshal joined me as I examined the lock.

"It's locked," I said.

Dillinger said, "It doesn't look too secure, we can break it."

Each of us tried different ways to pry the hasp from the door without success. When thunder clapped nearby, I jumped, and the room grew darker as the clouds swallowed the sunlight.

"Try the sword," Marshal suggested.

I said, "No way, it might break."

Dillinger said, "With the thunder, the neighbors won't notice gunfire. Stand back."

When he aimed his revolver and fired, the lock fell on the floor in pieces. Dillinger slid the door open, revealing a round room with curved walls. The walls and ceiling lacked plaster, and the exposed rafters resembled an upside-down ice cream cone. I recognized this as the inside of the conical roof peak above the suites.

A suitcase sat on top of a three-foot-tall metal box. Stenciled on the green cabinet were the words, Ellis Elevator Company. Cables in conduit ran from the mechanical box toward the elevator. Babe sat on top, tied by a leash. When I released him, he jumped into my arms then climbed to my shoulder.

Dillinger rushed to the valise. "Let's hope it's the coins."

The latches flipped open with a flick of his thumbs. When he raised the lid, a smile crossed his face. Marshal and I hurried to his side. The luggage was full of gold coins. Dillinger handed us each a gold-piece. "Look at these, they're beautiful."

They were the same as the ones Pappy had shown us.

"Miss Liberty is smiling," I joked.

"Hello, Hettie," Marshal added.

I felt a tug on my belt and looked back. Sparky had pulled the Union sword from the scabbard.

"Not so fast," Sparky said. "Those coins are mine."

Dillinger reached for his pistol, but Sparky poked the tip of the sword into my back. He said, "You pull a gun, and I'll run this through the boy."

Dillinger removed his hand from his jacket and held both palms out.

Sparky said to Marshal, "Boy, get his pistol — real slow. One false move and your brother gets it."

Marshal reached into Dillinger's jacket and pulled out the gun.

Sparky said, "Now put it on the floor."

Marshal obeyed.

"Okay, kick it over here."

Marshal kicked the revolver, and Sparky picked it up. He pointed it at us, then pushed me toward the others. He motioned for us to move. While keeping a watchful eye, Sparky eased over to the suitcase and closed the lid.

I said, "So, you swapped Grandpa Tip's gold for the pennies."

Marshal added, "And killed him too."

Sparky said, "It was the only way."

"But he was your friend," Marshal said.

Sparky snapped, "No one was my friend. I was nothing to them. Everyone else had the money, the nice homes, and the power. When I saw the gold, I knew it was my turn."

Dillinger said, "You've got what you want, so go."

Sparky shook his head. "Nope, no can do. You'd have me arrested."

Thunder rolled overhead.

Dillinger said, "It doesn't have to be this way. Let the boys leave."

Sparky banged the handgun on the grounded metal box and shouted, "Shut up, I'm in charge, now."

The electron-charged clouds rumbled as if responding to Sparky's rant. While holding the sword, he thrust his right arm straight up while the revolver in his left touched the metal cabinet.

Sparky's hair began to rise. He resembled Albert Einstein as the charged air smelled of ozone. It smelled like Grandpa Tip's electrical panel. Sparky's swung the sword in a circle motion over his head. It was close to a copper wire which was drooping from the lightning rod.

"Be careful!" I yelled.

Sparky snarled. "Shut up. I'm in charge."

Louder now, thunder rumbled overhead. Sparkles of flickering light danced on the cable above Sparky, and there was a buzzing like a nest of bees.

"But...," I said.

Sparky, out of control with anger, yelled, "Nobody listens to me. Well, that'll change. From now on, I'm the one people will hear.. I'm the one people will respect. Now, the power is mine... all mine"

He raised the sword and touched the cable. It may have been irony or the inevitable, but Sparky was too tempting a target for the built-up electrons in the sky. An angry cloud released its abundant charge into the lightning rod on the round peak of the Jameson Hotel. Since the workman had cut the ground wire, the voltage blasted down Sparky's vertical sword. The murderer conducted the electricity exceptionally well. The power passed through Sparky and the revolver into the grounded mechanical cabinet.

With the circuit complete, Sparky once again earned his nickname. Cats have nine lives, but Sparky only had four. When he dropped to the floor, the glowing pistol remained welded to the metal box.

"That was shocking," Dillinger said.

He stepped over Sparky and examined the smoldering gun. "Too bad. It was my favorite revolver."

I asked, "What about Sparky?"

Dillinger glanced down at Sparky. "I wasn't so fond of him."

Sparky lay face-up with his eyes closed and eyebrows missing. The singed tips of his spiked hair smoldered. Though dead, he had a doesn't-he-look-natural smile on his charbroiled face.

Marshal stood over him. "He looks content."

"More like well done," I replied.

Dillinger said, "Well, he wanted the power. I'd say he got the whole load, then some."

The gun was smoking, but so was the roof. Around the hole, wooden shingles glowed orange, then burst into flames.

"We'd better get out of here!" I shouted.

Marshal added, "… while we still can."

Dillinger grabbed the suitcase, and we ran to the elevator, but it didn't work. Dillinger said, "The lightning knocked out the power."

Babe bolted for the window and jumped for a tree, but the branch was too small for us even if we made the jump. The ground looked a long way down from my location. Flames raced across the rafters, and smoke swirled above us.

"Dumbwaiter," I yelled. I spun around, but there wasn't one. The dumbwaiter didn't go up to the attic. I pointed. "Laundry chute."

The three of us took turns looking down at the pile of linen in the basement.

"What do you think?" Marshal asked.

Dillinger replied as he gazed below, "What a drop."

As the flames spread, time was running out. After I peered into the chute, I said, "I bet if we spread our elbows and feet, we can slow the fall." I said, "I'll go first."

I sat on the ledge and took a deep breath.

Marshal said, "Don't look down."

"Here goes," I said.

I pushed myself off the ledge. I slowed my descent with my elbows, but soon they burned from the friction. I dragged my heels and slowed my drop. I landed on the laundry, and it wasn't too jarring. On my back, I looked at Marshal six stories above me.

"You okay?" He shouted.

"Yes," I replied.

He dangled the suitcase above me. "Here come the coins."

I rolled away, and it landed. I looked up and shouted up. "Use your heels to brake."

"Here I come!" Marshal shouted.

When he hit, he rolled from the mound and sat upright on the concrete. He looked over his limbs as if amazed he broke nothing. He said, "I made it."

I crawled back up the pile of laundry and saw Dillinger looking down at me. I shouted, "It's your turn."

There was a long pause. "Sorry, boys. I'm too old to fall that far. I'll find another way. Good luck."

Marshal said, "Let's get out of here."

I stared up and waited, but Dillinger never reappeared.

Marshal said, "Remember, the building is on fire. Let's go!"

I hung back, then followed. As we rushed from the basement, we saw Marge and deputy Clarence climbing down the ladder on the tall fire truck. Once on the ground, Marge was handcuffed and placed in the squad car.

We crossed the street, and I laid the suitcase on the curb. I sat on it. Marshal sat beside me as a crowd gathered. The fire chief called for every truck in town, and off-duty firemen reported for duty. It seemed no one wanted to miss the fire of the decade. While the firefighters on the hook and ladder sprayed the engulfed attic, others hosed the fourth floor. It was as high as their hoses reached.

The mayor arrived to witness the inaugural use of the specialized equipment. Robert, the reporter we'd met earlier, took pictures of the momentous event for the newspaper. As he passed, he noticed me. "Well, hello, what are you doing here?"

"Just watching."

He replied, "Yeah, exciting, isn't it?

"Yes, sir."

He said, "Something like this doesn't happen around here very often."

I just nodded. After Robert left, I noticed a man in the crowd ten yards away who was tall and thin. He wore a black jacket and a stove-pipe hat. When he turned, I saw his short beard and black hair. I spun to Marshal and tugged at his shirt. "Hey, look at that guy. He looks like Abe Lincoln."

"Where?"

When I turned back, I didn't see him.

"He was there a minute ago."

I stood on my tiptoes and looked about but didn't find him. I wondered if Miss Jameson was right about the assassinated president's ghost. With the building ablaze, did he move onto to the everlasting?

Marshal said, "It was probably one of those Lincoln imitators."

Attracted by the spiraling black smoke, Angel, Einstein, and Butch approached on their bicycles. They parked beside us as we watched the arching columns of water disappear into the orange inferno. Unfazed, the flames swallowed the river as if the firemen were just spitting on it. Even from the street, I felt the heat.

"Long time, no see," I said to my pals.

"Hi," they responded in unison without taking their eyes from the fire.

"Been up to much?" Marshal asked.

Einstein replied, "Naw."

In silence, we watched the spectacle as the roof collapsed into the attic. When the bullets in the inferno popped, Marshal and I looked at each other without speaking, but he nodded when I raised my eyebrows.

By the time the attic collapsed into the ballroom, I felt guilty for excluding my friends from the treasure hunt. Though they'd abandoned us, my conscious was bothering me, so I threw out an offer.

"Hey Butch, I found another clue for Dillinger's gold. Do you want to help us look for it?"

While staring mesmerized at the flames, he said, "No thanks, we're camping on the Embarrass River tomorrow."

Einstein chimed in, "We're going fishing with trotlines."

I placed both hands on the suitcase beneath me. "Are you sure?" I'd hate for you to miss out on a fortune. I mean, it could be close, real close."

The three looked at each other. Butch rolled his eyes, and Einstein snickered.

Angel said, "Don't worry about us; we're fine."

I asked, "What about the Miller girls?"

"Forget them," Butch responded. "Pippy's father punished her for sneaking out to go to the cemetery. There's no way she'd get involved in another treasure hunt."

I glanced at Marshal, and he shrugged his shoulders. I said, "Don't say we didn't ask."

199

Though six hoses sprayed the fourth floor, they didn't slow the blaze's destruction. A tanker truck arrived from a nearby town with volunteer firefighters aboard as the third story burned. After the flames consumed the second level, Butch, Einstein, and Angel got bored and left.

Marshal said, "I don't see how Dillinger could have escaped."

I sighed. "Probably not."

When the ballroom collapsed, the orange glow illuminated everything for a block. I saw Pippy and Cindy. They smiled as they approached.

Cindy asked, "Patton, why are you wearing a Union soldier's jacket?"

"I found it; do you like it?"

She nodded as she slid next to Marshal and held his hand. Pippy snuggled close, and I put my arm around her. Someone poked me in the back. It was Sly and his bodyguard, Griff. "Hey Punk, what are you doing with my girl?"

"Your girl?" Pippy said, "I'm not your girl."

Sly grabbed Pippy by the wrist. "We'll settle this later. You're coming with me."

She writhed to get loose. "Stop, you're hurting me."

He pulled, but Pippy resisted. I marched up to him. "Let go of her."

Sly laughed. "Oh, so you're a tough guy, now. You think you can take me?"

I gulped, then I closed my fist. I feigned bravery. Babe chattered as he clung to my collar. I said, "I told you to let go of her."

Sly let loose of Pippy. Then, he reached down and picked up a limb. He broke it over his knee and swung it side-to-side.

I pulled the nightstick from Marshal's belt and held it above my head. "Now, it's an even fight."

Sly raised the branch and turned sideways. He took a baseball batter's stance. "I'll send your head over the center field fence." He took a couple of practice swings. He said, "Batter up."

Before Sly could swing again, Babe pulled the nightstick from my raised hand. In a blur, he ran up Sly's leg and onto his shoulder. Sly dropped the club and reached for the monkey, but he was too slow. Babe's first whack slammed Sly's head forward. The second swing caused his knees to buckle. Sly weaved back and forth but stayed on his feet.

200

Still on his shoulder, Babe swung the club and hit Griff above the ear. The big brute dropped forward like a felled tree. Sly flopped across him. In a flash, Babe was back on my shoulder.

Pippy rushed to me and took my hands in hers. We stared at each other.

I asked, "What do we do now?"

"Trust your instincts," she replied.

I kissed her. She kissed me back.

She said, "I'm sorry about deserting you."

I said, "A wise man once told me, the past doesn't have to dictate our future."

As the first story burned, flames spread to the trash in the rear yard and consumed Mr. Dillinger's rust-bucket truck. After another hour, the firemen successfully doused the last smoldering embers in the basement. Soon after, we walked the girls to their home with Babe following us.

The next day, I read in the newspaper, arson investigators found only the remains of one body in the ashes. Though we never heard from John Dillinger again, we hoped he'd survived and returned to his self-imposed exile.

Pappy was amazed when we told him our story. But we had to tell him, so we could secretly sell the gold. We planned to donate a portion to the city to remodel the swimming pool, so we asked Pappy to help.

Pappy stacked the piles of coins. "Why give some away?" he asked. "It's so much."

I said, "The money was Dillinger's. He was trying to make restitution for his life of crime. I think he'd like this."

Pappy said, "Well, it wasn't really Dillinger's."

My gaze dropped to the floor. "I know, but whose?"

"The bank?" Pappy asked.

I said, "No. Dillinger said it didn't belong to the bank. It belonged to some crooks, but he never said who."

Pappy said, "Well, okay, then. I suppose it's a good thing you're doing."

I stood, 'We only have one string attached to the donation."

Pappy removed his glasses. I looked at Marshal, and he nodded. The city must name it the "John Herbert Public Pool."

Pappy asked, "John Herbert?"

I smiled, "It's short for John Herbert Dillinger."

201

Pappy raised his eyebrows and nodded. "I think the City will agree to that." I said, "No one needs to know who he was. It will be a riddle."

Made in the USA
Columbia, SC
24 September 2020